SCENES FROM DEATH AND LIFE

Scenes From Death and Life

William Cooper

Smaller Sky

First published in Great Britain by
Smaller Sky Books, 217 Woodstock Road,
Oxford OX2 7AD, England

www.smallerskybooks.co.uk

ISBN 1 903100 00 3

Produced in Great Britain by

Axxent Ltd,
The Short Run Book Company,
St Stephen's House, Arthur Road,
Windsor, Berkshire SL4 1RY

Epigraph:

'I know that losing a child is different from losing a husband/wife – you have lost your life with your wife, and your past – with the death of the young, it's the future.'

(Unedited private correspondence.)

Chapter I

Too Old at 67

Henry and I were walking down the corridor after his monthly Board Meeting. Outside the door of his office he paused and said:

'Can you spare a moment to come in, Joe?'

Henry was my Chairman. I said:

'Yes, of course.'

"Of course" not dictated by sycophancy or docility – I doubted if Henry could find anywhere a greater admirer than me. I admired him physically: he was tall and slim and handsome, with high shoulders surprisingly sharpened by his tailor, and a firm narrow waist held in by a corset he was forced to wear as a consequence of injuring himself when he jumped out of an aeroplane during the War. He had dark wavy hair bryl-creemed after the fashion of his youthful days: his complexion was pale and his large light eyes had heavy rings round them, caused, I presumed, by the pills he had to take constantly to ease the pain of the afore-mentioned injury. He was so handsome that he couldn't help knowing it – he took the knowledge in his elegant stride.

And I admired him temperamentally: he was highly intelligent in a suave and flexible way. The formerly dashing element in his nature had grown into a sort of ruthlessness – which was highly necessary in the new Chairman of an organisation which was in a serious financial mess that he had been brought in to put right. He was well into the process of doing just that. His past experience in banking was a help: so was his natural eye for an organisation that would work, in contrast with the one he was presented with – which wouldn't. We were a governmental organisation and his rank was that of Permanent Secretary. We could be denominated truthfully if slightingly as a Quango – the Q stood for 'quasi', which in my estimation stood only one notch higher than 'pseudo'. However there was nothing 'quasi' about Henry. *I* thought he was a very good man, a 100% genuine as you might say.

We went into Henry's office, which also was handsome. Spacious and white-painted with a row of tall windows looking out on the tops of trees and beyond them the Thames. There was a huge desk with a collection of telephones, and a long designer-built sofa upholstered in black leather. Whenever I entered the room my eye was caught by one of the pictures, a drawing of Henry's wife. I thought it was pretty creditable. And who was the artist? Henry, of course! On an earlier occasion I had signified to Henry himself what I thought of it. With a slightly rueful yet not entirely displeased smile, he said:

'Lucian Freud did a better job.'

He was referring to a portrait of his wife by Lucian Freud that hung in his flat. I had admired it when he invited me in to lunch with him. We discovered that for each of us Lucian Freud was a first choice among contemporary English artists. It seemed that Henry and I were pre-destined to get on with each other.

This was an April morning, and the room was filled with light. '*Whan that Aprille with his showres swoote ...*' The tree-tops were just visible in the windows but the Thames was not, as Aprille was in the act of dashing one of his showres swoote against the window-panes.

Henry motioned me to sit down at one end of the long designer-built sofa and sat down at the other end himself.

'Shall I get Victoria to give us a glass of sherry?' (Victoria was his personal assistant.)

I was going to say No; but then, reminded of what was in the wind, I thought I had better say Yes.

What was in the wind was the termination of my membership of his Board. My two-year contract was up. I said:

'Yes, thank you.'

Henry went and pressed a buzzer on his desk, gave the instruction, then glanced at a couple of papers lying in front of him. I cogitated.

Victoria was a beautiful upper-class girl. How Henry had come by her through the elaborate posting-arrangements of the

Government Service I didn't know. In the privately enterprising world of publishing it seemed to be *de rigeur* for any successful publisher to take on as his secretary a beautiful upper-class girl – if not a beautiful aristocratic girl. It argued that there was a fair supply of upper-class and aristocratic girls looking for jobs which did not entail entry by going through the Civil Service system of hoops first of all. Or perhaps it was the defunct idea, still echoing on, that publishing was a career for gentlemen. Ho, ho, ho! Career for accountants, more like!

It just strikes me now, having written the above passage displaying familiarity, perhaps unusual in a government official, quasi or otherwise, with publishing, that I ought to inform a reader of this novel who doesn't know already, that I was a lifelong writer of novels in my non-official hours – nothing quasi about that. Also 100% genuine, as you might say. (That was how I saw it, anyway.) My getting on with Henry was all the more firmly pre-destined by his having already read some of my novels and claiming to have enjoyed them. In the ears of an artist, praise is music...actually it was not praise unalloyed. One day, when we had got to know each other better, he had confided to me that there was a passage in one of my novels which had offended him.

Instinctively I knew what it was.

It was a passage in which I had expressed my detestation of what I had seen fit to call the 'spying classes'. In my regard, I had written it in capital letters at that: ALL SPIES ARE SNEAKS. Whichever side they are on.

It had offended Henry because he had once been in MI5.

He had got out, of course. 'I saw the light,' he said to me, as we were composing the differences in our views on the subject.

Moved to idiotic response I said; 'I'm not exactly proud of everything I've done in my life.'

Henry gave me a smooth sardonic glance for my pains. 'I don't believe it.'

Nevertheless the situation was tided over. We smiled at each other.

My cogitation was ended by the appearance of Victoria with a bottle of sherry and two glasses on a tray. I couldn't resist giving her a look indicating my appreciation of her beauty and her class.

Henry noticed it as he came back to sit at the other end of the sofa. Henry didn't miss anything. (I've been given to understand that spies don't miss anything, that even policemen don't.)

Henry poured our glasses of sherry; and we politely sipped to each other's health.

'I expect,' he said, 'you know what I've asked you to come in and talk about?'

'The expiry of my contract as a Member of your Board,' I said easily – I was not out to make things more difficult for him.

'Yes, indeed.' There was a faintly melancholy tone in his voice. 'I'm going to lose both you and Alice at the same time. I don't wish to. I should like to keep the same team.'

In private we referred to Alice Hargreaves as the Statutory Woman on the Board. She was an active, bright, left-wing'ish sort of person with whom I tended to form an alliance against the more right-wing'ish Members, one or two of whom were a shade less than bright.

I must explain. One held one's Membership of the Board through personal appointment by a Minister.

Now in Government Ministers come and go. The Minister who appointed Alice and me had gone.

'I should have liked,' Henry said, 'to have had your contract renewed for another two years.'

So should I, come to that. I wondered why he hadn't brought to bear his universally acknowledged skills in manoeuvre and manipulation – and got what he would have liked.

Deeply as I loved and revered Henry, I was unable to give myself an entirely satisfactory answer to the question. Could it be?.. Could it?..

'I made my case,' he said. 'But various points were made against it.' He turned the gaze of his large grey eyes upon me. Then went on.

'I was reminded of your age. You are sixty-seven.' Ironically – 'I don't need to tell you.'

On my side I was reminded of the fact that retirement was expected of a Civil Servant, (which, technically, I was not,) at the age of sixty, at the very latest sixty-five. I had spun it out to sixty-seven. Not bad, I thought. I said:

'Actually I was already sixty-five when I was appointed. I was born in 1910.'

'I know, I know...' He paused. 'Your age doesn't worry me. But it appears to worry others. I was told that questions are being asked.'

He was speaking in code, which I promptly broke. 'You mean by Staff Side?'

The Trades Unions were generally in favour of the elderly being eliminated to make way for the young – they knew where future membership subscriptions were going to come from.

Henry nodded his head, then sipped some more of his sherry. The rain continued to dash itself against the window-panes. The thoughts of both of us were moving, not surprisingly, along the same lines. My income was going to drop.

'Of course you have your writing,' he said.

'Everyone,' I said, 'over-estimates my income from writing.' He knew that as a consequence of my having been an 'irregular' Government Servant, first temporary and then part-time, during periods when neither was pensionable I had ended up without a government pension. His lips were tightened in a wry expression. He remained silent.

'It's a bore,' I said.

He looked at me. 'If your books are made into a television serial, all that will be changed.'

I laughed. 'The nature and aims of television will have to be changed first.'

There was nothing for him to say to that, so he drank a little more sherry.

My thoughts turned elsewhere. I said:

'Do you know who's going to do my job?'

Henry hesitated thoughtfully. In my job I was styled a personnel consultant, generally keeping an eye on the quality and movements of the staff. After his pause, Henry said:

'I'm not sure that I shall ask for another person. In your two years you have straightened things out for us so well that I think I may be able to manage it myself in the future.'

The silence after that remark seemed long, very long. I finished my sherry. My tenure in the government service was finished. It was clear that this seance with Henry was over. I put down my glass.

'There'll be an occasion later,' he said, 'when I shall have the opportunity to thank you, Joe, in public. In private I should like to say to you that your presence has been a comfort and consolation to me.'

'Thank you, Henry.'

I hadn't heard anything I hadn't expected to hear.

I didn't ask who the new Minister was to be, since I knew in my bones that Henry was not going to exert his powers of persuasion upon him. Henry was not going to ask for somebody else to do my job – since he meant to do it himself! I had to admit he would jolly well. And by so doing increase the firmness of his grasp on the organisation. Did I say there was an element of ruthlessness in Henry's admirable nature?

So that was that. I stood up to go. My fate was decided, no more grounds for hope. I was OUT.

We shook hands. I left Henry's office and went to my own.

It remained for me now to go home and break the news to Elspeth.

Elspeth and I had been happily married for nearly thirty years. She was fifteen years younger than me. At the age of 40 I'd had no intention of marrying a woman of my own age. I'd fallen in love with Elspeth in her youthfulness. That was that... (Also it was nice occasionally to think there was someone to look after me in my old age.) Happily married: does it make sense to say we were closely married? We were both affectionate and demonstrative – for instance, we often kissed each other when we happened to pass in the corridor of the flat.

I broke my news when I got home. She put her arms round me.

'Never mind. We shall be all right.'

'I suppose we shall.'

'I'll go on working.' She had a part-time job with a housing association. 'I don't bring in very much.' She smiled at me.

Thinking of my literary earnings, now shorn of their bonus from the government service, I said:

'Neither shall I.'

We went in to supper. She had cooked an escalope of veal in marsala; and there was a bottle of claret already opened on the table – she had obviously guessed I might be coming home in low spirits. Nothing affects low spirits so favourably as a delectable dinner. So the atmosphere was not unrelievedly gloomy.

In due course it was time to go to bed. I lay down beside her. We chatted a little. She took her usual firm, affectionate hold of me. I did not say anything.

'What are you thinking, darling?' she asked.

'Too old at 67,' I muttered. After a pause. 'What are you thinking?'

She took her time to answer, conveying what she meant with a squeeze –

'Not too old for me.'

Chapter II

Changes in Direction

'Are you going to be in for dinner on Thursday night?' Elspeth asked. 'Your diary doesn't say you're going to be out.'

'Then I'm going to be in... One's diary is something one has to stick to like the Ten Commandments. Why do you ask?'

'The girls want to come in and talk to you.'

'Both of them at once?'

'Yes.' She gave me a secretive look.

'That's Two Commandments. Do you know what they want to say?'

'Yes. But I promised not to tell you. They want to break it to you themselves.'

I thought of eggs being broken on the edge of a basin. 'Sounds interesting,' I said.

Elspeth smiled to herself: 'It is.'

Of our two daughters the elder was called Viola, and she was aged twenty-four; the younger Virginia, aged twenty-two. I had always adored both of them, and tried to pass it off with a quip – 'Everything Dr Freud says about fathers and daughters is true.' I'd occasionally wondered if Elspeth took the quip as easily as I made it.

Viola was working for a tycoon in the City. She had been to one of the superior colleges in London which teaches a girl so-called secretarial, managerial and social skills. Actually they didn't teach them how to curtsey to Royalty, but I pretended that was the only fault I could find. The particular skills were not skills that Viola particularly wanted to acquire, but she was not prepared to go to University. She was one of those unhappy creatures who are paralysed by examinations. (I say that with feeling, since I didn't recall having sat down for any of my Finals with my breakfast inside me.) We promised Viola that after GCE we would never expect her to take another examination, ever. She was now earning an adequate salary, with a tycoon who came from somewhere in the Near East, rich and ambitious, glamorous, slick if not frankly unscrupulous, Ruler of a Business Empire. He was called Ali and he clearly meant to become Sir Ali: I took to referring to him as Ali Baba until Viola, being a bit of a stickler, reminded me that Ali Baba was not one of the Forty Thieves. Viola got some fun out of watching from a distance his performance, but it was very equivocal fun and she was far from happy.

Virginia had gone to University and graduated in Science. (I was a graduate in Physics, myself.) And then she had decided she wanted to go to Art School. To Art School she went after a certain amount of argument in the family circle. Of our two daughters she was the one with whom I'd had regular collisions throughout her adolescence, over a spectrum of subjects beginning early – from the way to hold a knife and fork to the way to discourage wolf-whistles from men on building sites. (Her elder sister's resistance to my interfering usually simmered in quiet – till a point of furious explosion.)

All this had happened years ago, we were now in 1977. Just recently Elspeth had reported to me Virginia's saying: 'You know those things I used to have rows with Daddy about?.. Well, he was right.'

What father would not find that irresistible?

In the meantime I had learnt the great lesson of parenthood, brought to the point of formulation in language by reading about the struggles of Trollope's Duke of Omnium, when his offspring proposed to marry persons he didn't want them to marry – *You can't do anything about your children.*

The Duke's children got their way: and *he* was a leading Duke in England, wealthy, powerful and a former Prime Minister. What hope was there for me, far from Dukedom? Actually the Duke throughout was becoming more understanding and human – and steadily more desirous of peace-and-quiet. Both Elspeth and I were happier with peace-and-quiet. (Some people, it seems, need rows to bring them to life.) Both Elspeth and I loved the girls.

By now the girls were attractive young women. Virginia was taller than Viola, and they both had long straight legs like their mother. (And like me, for that matter.) They had inherited Elspeth's fairish hair and nordic eyes – Viola's dark blue, Virginia's grey splashed with hazel – Elspeth's delicate complexion, Elspeth's alluring mouth curling up at the corners, and alas! Elspeth's not very shapely nose. I thought they were beautiful.

By a merciful turn of Fate they were getting on well with each other nowadays. One of the mainstays of feature journalism in the daily newspapers was Sibling Rivalry – one gets a bit sick of it. Our siblings were not at each other's throats; in fact they spent hours gossiping on the telephone and went on shopping (for clothes) expeditions together.

Viola came straight from the office: she was wearing her sleekly-cut couturier navy skirt and an expensive-looking flowery blouse actually from Wallis; small dangly earrings that were a birthday present from Virginia. A bushy sort of haircut, slightly boyish, which suited her small features.

Virginia came straight from her School of Art, which was in the country, some distance outside London. Appropriately, not to say conventionally dressed in scruffy black trousers with paint stains on them; and a black woollen jumper, shapeless but nevertheless not so shapeless as to conceal her shape. Large dangly earrings. Glistening fair hair with unusually fairer streaks in it.

Beautiful girls. We all sat down to dinner. Silence.

'Well,' I said helpfully, 'What's all this about?'

The girls exchanged a glance.

Viola said to Virginia, 'You say!..'

I looked at Virginia.

I realised it was a serious occasion. I waited.

'It's like this,' said Virginia. 'We want to change our careers.'

Surprise for me. 'Both of you?' I said. I looked at them. 'Have you been getting together?'

'Yes, Daddy. Wasn't that a sensible thing to do?' Virginia.

'It didn't occur to us to do anything else.' Viola.

I glanced at Elspeth. She was listening attentively, although she knew what they were going to say.

As Virginia had gone first I looked at Viola.

She said: 'There's a rumour going round the office that Ali is being investigated by Scotland Yard.'

That meant investigated for fraud. I can't say it was really any surprise to me.

'We don't know much about it,' Viola went on. 'But we are being called upon to turn up all sorts of papers, documents, contracts...'

I waited.

'And there are quite a lot that can't be found...' She paused.

'I see.'

'The office is in a state.'

'Does it involve you?'

'No more than any of the others. We are all in a tiz-woz – and pretty fed-up.'

'I take it that you are very fed-up.'

'Have been for months.'

(Viola had previously been employed by a firm that went bust altogether – the Official Receiver came in and everybody was declared redundant. Not an encouraging start to a girl's career.)

'Are you telling me now that you want to get out?' I asked.

'That's right.' Viola paused. 'I've had enough of the City.'

Viola had a strong moral sense: both girls had a strong moral sense. Not from explicit teaching by Elspeth and me, but, I supposed, induced by family atmosphere. Both girls had what we playfully called Nonconformist consciences. Was that surprising when Elspeth's father was a Methodist clergyman, and my mother's family, Wesleyan to a man (or woman) abounded with local preachers. Playfully we might have been speaking of Nonconformist consciences, but that is not to say we didn't see that this particular form of moral sense went to the roots of our family atmosphere. And a good thing too!

Viola was fed-up with the City. So it was no use my suggesting she should look for a job in the empire of another tycoon. I sympathised with her. (After these events Mrs Thatcher spent many years constantly preaching to the nation about "Creating Wealth". I cannot rid myself of a lurking belief that tycoons,

17

creating wealth on a large scale, are probably pinching it on a large scale as well.) Ali was not the first to be investigated by Scotland Yard – and would not be the last.

Our little family dinner was a special treat prepared by Elspeth. We were beginning with smoked salmon: both girls loved it. But the present turn in the conversation had reduced some of the enjoyment.

There was a pause. I looked at Virginia.

'And you want to change, too?'

'I'm afraid so.' Virginia was not smiling. 'I know I made a hell of a fuss to go to Art School when you and Mummy thought I ought to make use of my degree in science.' She looked down at her plate. 'I appreciate your forbearance now...'

Elspeth and I had nothing to say to that. We could always be sure Virginia would end up honest with herself. (Viola was always honest with herself from the start, too honest for her comfort, though she never divulged this.)

Virginia had chosen this particular School of Art because it was fashionable at the time, reported to be "advanced". I'd had to keep quiet about that, because Virginia knew I didn't believe that Art advanced. There's no such thing as Progress in the Arts was my belief. Science and Technology advanced: anybody could see that. Art changed. Does anybody see an advance from Leonardo to Picasso? What anybody can see is a change, a difference – a hell of a difference!

Pupils from Virginia's School of Art won current competitions.

'And are you fed-up, too?' I said to her.

'I am!' There was a sharp edge in her tone of voice. It resembled the tone which came into Viola's voice when her simmering resistance finally exploded.

'What's wrong with the place?'

'They don't teach us to draw!' Virginia turned on me. 'I want to learn to draw. As an artist I want to be a portraitist one day. How can you be a portraitist if you haven't learnt to draw?'

'I don't know.' I ate some of my smoked salmon. (Viola and Elspeth were tucking in to theirs in spite of the drama of the occasion.)

'We are expected to join the exodus into Conceptual Art. "It's the idea that matters, not the execution." What's the use of that to me?'

'I don't know.' I looked at her. 'Have you pointed that out to your teachers?'

'Yes, of course.' She drew in a breath. 'And I'm not the only one. There are several of us who are dissatisfied.'

'Sounds like a rebellion.'

'An unsuccessful rebellion. They've made it clear they're not going to change. Actually they can't change. They've come up through the schools in the Sixties and Seventies – the "Slap it on! Screw it in!" schools. They can't help us because they can't draw themselves!' She paused for another breath. 'I don't make an impression doing the things they want me to do. I can see that. But how can my talent for drawing – and I don't know if I have one... How can my talent for drawing be tested if I'm never seriously required to draw?'

If I knew enough about it to give her a fair answer – which I didn't – it seemed to me, that at the present juncture a fair answer would be unlikely to turn away her wrath.

I thought she would have to leave the School. To pay a School fees for not teaching you what you want to learn is scarcely good business practice.

There was a long pause, during which Virginia became aware of the slice of smoked salmon on the plate in front of her. She was 10 years too old for me to say 'Get on with your dinner!' In any case the occasion was too serious. However she promptly started to eat again –

'This is very good,' she said, not lost to reason. She drank some wine.

Elspeth and Viola and I had finished our smoked salmon. Elspeth went out to get the next course. I looked at the girls in turn.

'So you both want to do something different?'

They nodded their heads in vigorous assent.

'We need a change,' said Viola. 'A change in direction...'

'And what's the new direction you've both settled on?' I asked.

They looked at each other. Virginia finished her smoked salmon. Viola spoke up –

'We thought the medical profession.'

They looked at each other again, as if to gain encouragement thereby. I sympathised with that.

'That's right,' said Virginia.

I had nothing to say, feeling somewhat stunned.

Elspeth came back carrying a casserole holding boeuf bourguignonne – a delicious smell came out of it.

'Well,' she said to me; 'Have you got over the hump in the argument while I've been out.'

'We're just on the pinnacle of it.'

Elspeth sat down and served us with the beef and some vegetables. I poured out some more wine.

Then I said:

'The medical profession... What does that mean?'

Virginia said promptly: 'I want to become a doctor.'

I looked at Viola – who replied with a shade less enthusiasm:

'I'm thinking about training as a nurse.' She glanced at her sister.

They had been getting together. Which of them had played the leading role? I imagined the project was more plausible for Virginia than for Viola.

'The idea is to do something useful,' said Virginia.

It was on the tip of my tongue to say I'd never seen Conceptual Art as the slightest use to anybody other than Directors of galleries and dealers. But this was not the moment for quips. I said:

'I approve of that.'

Everyone round the table was in the grip of a Nonconformist conscience – who was I to question that? And having had in my time a fair share of hospital experience – the most recent instalment being the successful replacement of an arthritic hip – my esteem for doctors and nurses could not have been firmer. Viola said:

'We wanted to know what you and Mummy think of it before we do anything definite. I think Mummy approves.' The girls were expert at handling Elspeth.

Virginia as a doctor, Viola as a nurse... I could see Virginia as a doctor. Viola as a nurse was more difficult. I should have thought she might be too sensitive and physically fastidious. But she must have thought about it at length. Maybe I was wrong. (In the end it turned out that I was wrong.)

The serious conversation of the evening was launched. How long would it take Virginia to qualify? Five years? Possibly less if her degree in Science counted in her favour.

'And I think I may be able to get a grant,' she said with an encouraging smile. I was paying for her at the School of Art. 'So I shall be off your hands.'

I smiled at her. *Au fond* I didn't believe I should ever feel either of them was entirely off my hands. At the moment I doubted if Virginia would get a grant that would pay for her completely.

'That's good,' I said, as thoughts of being "too old at 67" crossed my mind.

'And you?' I said to Viola.

'Two or three years, depending on how far I want to specialise. I want to work with children.' She had always been good at getting on with little children – put to good service when young friends of ours brought tiny offspring to our parties.

'It will mean taking exams again,' I said.

Viola looked down at her plate, and a faint rosy colour appeared on her neck and spread up to her face.

'Yes,' she said simply.

You can imagine the discussion went on in some detail and at considerable length.

'It would be nice if we could both train at St. Anne's,' said Virginia.

'It's a teaching hospital.' Viola.

'I know that.' St. Anne's was a hospital in our locality, a University Hospital with a very high reputation. (It was where I'd had my arthritic hip replaced successfully.)

There was no doubt about the upshot. For the time being Virginia was going to launch herself into becoming a doctor, Viola a nurse. To my mind it was a pretty vertiginous change of direction; but if they had settled it, Elspeth and I were acceptant –

You can't do anything etc...

Expecting that the discussion was going to be difficult, Elspeth had prepared to end our dinner with a pavlova containing raspberries from the deep-freeze, raspberries being our favourite fruit. Elspeth, that wisest of all beautiful wives, was a believer in awkward family discussions being smoothed by attractive food. By the end of this occasion we had eaten all that was put before us – and were on most harmonious terms with each other.

So... It's all very well to make decisions about the future; but the future has to be lived. That remained ahead for all four of us. It's arguable, from our example, that the future should keep its mystery.

Chapter III

A Chance Meeting

We first met at a party. Some time in the early 1980s.Typical Brownian Movement in a huge room full of people brought us momentarily face to face.

He was about my height – smallish medium – so his face was on the same level as mine: I took to it straight away. It was a long face, worn and lined; yet the erect carriage of his head gave him a sprightly look. Probably in his early fifties. I thought he looked to be fun – it was a face I'd like to talk to.

We were clutching our glasses of wine.

'Hello,' I said as an opening.

'Hi,' he replied.

Somehow we were both amused by the exchange.

As I was the senior I said;

'Who are you?'

'I'm James Yavner. A.k.a. Jim Yavner.' He spoke with an American accent: 'I'm Head of the English Department at Avalon University in the States.'

'Good Gracious!' I exclaimed. The party was being held in the Vice-Chancellor's lodge of Prince Consort College, a college of London University founded by Prince Albert on the lines of a *Technische Hochschule* for the purpose of educating students in various branches of technology. An admirable fellow, Prince Albert.

'Then what are you doing here?' I went on. 'This place is a hide-out for scientists and engineers.'

'We Americans get around.' His eyes were sparkling. 'I met Lord Bantock at a dinner-party and he invited me.'

'What a good idea! George Bantock's a very good chap.' (He was the Vice-Chancellor.)

'And you,' he said. 'Who are you?'

I told him my name and said I was a novelist.

'I guess I've heard of you.'

'That's the first step towards reading me.' I was getting too old to indulge in woffling with strangers.

He was looking at me shrewdly. 'I'll certainly do that.'

I raised my glass to him.

He returned the compliment. I said:

'Throughout the early 1970s I used to have short spells in the USA at least two or three times a year – reversing the so-called Brain Drain to North America of our best young scientists and engineers. But I didn't travel around campuses. So I've never been to Avalon.'

'It's a large private university.' Adding somewhat coolly, 'I would call it second rank Ivy League.'

The University was on no account to be confused, he explained, with a long-established small Liberal Arts college also at Avalon. The University, recently established and very handsomely endowed, had rapidly acquired some alumni who were very rich indeed. It was now unquestionably in full-bloom.

'It has a high reputation for its Science and Engineering Faculties,' he said. 'And a flourishing Medical School.'

'Nothing second-rank about that,' I said teasingly.

'Actually I'm a Yaley.'

We were looking each other in the eye.

'Actually I was at Oxford.'

We laughed at each other.

There was a pause. Then he returned my enquiry –

'And what are you doing here?'

I explained that George Bantock was an old friend of mine and invented for me, when my job under Henry came to an end, a minor teaching job at Prince Consort –

'He wrote me a letter saying his Council and the Senate were worried by the illiteracy of their students, and he thought that I – having been educated as a physicist and then having spent the whole of my official career working among scientists and engineers – would be a likely person to encourage them to read works of literature and learn therefrom. George is a distinguished geologist – I may say he's done more than well out of advising the oil industry. He's also a cultivated man, has a passion for Henry James. Calls himself a Jacobite!'

Yavner gave a quizzical sort of grin. 'Sounds like you wouldn't call yourself a Jacobite.'

I didn't comment.

'I admire Henry James a lot,' he said. 'But I wouldn't call myself a Jacobite either.'

'He has a notable way with language, but he does go on so... One keeps wanting to say "Oh, Henry, please!"'

He laughed. 'You have a point there.'

We paused for a moment, assimilating a slight difference in view.

Then he said, shifting the conversation back:

'So you're here to encourage science students to read works of literature.' He paused. 'I guess that means novels, Mr Lunn.'

'How did you guess that, Professor Yavner?'

He gave a little glance off-stage. 'You know?..'

'Do you enjoy it?' he went on.

'It's quite fun. I've been doing it for some months now. The students come to my class, it you could call it that, voluntarily; in their own time, at their own expense... They're not unaware of their so-called illiteracy, and they're anxious to remedy it. A lot of them realise that up to now they've been missing something. More important than that, it dawned on them that they're going to spend a lot of time writing technical papers... It's by their papers they shall be judged. So it's well if they can make themselves readable.' I paused. 'It's a small class so far, but they're beginning to get the hang of it. I've got them reading works of literature, reading novels; and talking about them... Talking, for instance about what makes the novels readable. They may have no literary education to speak of, but they're not fools.'

'This is interesting.' (He pronounced it "in-ter-est-ing".)

I drank some wine.

We were being buffeted by people around us but we stuck together.

'And what are you doing in England?' I asked.

He explained that Avalon, like several American universities, ran a centre, a sort of subsidiary campus, in London; to it undergraduates came for a semester to take courses which counted as part of their degree studies.

'I'm teaching here for a year,' he said.

'You like it?'

'Love it. I love London.' He looked at me. 'Some of my colleagues, when they come for a semester to the Centre, look on it as a sabbatical. Ve-ry re-pre-hen-sible... You know? But my wife, Rosalind, is looking forward to getting back home: she misses the children.'

'How many children have you?'

'Four. How many do you have?'

'Two. I should like it to have been four.' I smiled. 'I should have been willing to go on having children indefinitely. I like them. I like having them around me.' I paused. 'Somehow I see one's children as one's future. When my time is up, they will go on....Not an original thought!'

'I agree.' He smiled reminiscently. 'When we had four Rosalind decided she'd call it a day.'

'I said, 'We had no choice. Elspeth had such difficulties over our second she was advised not to have any more.'

'Too bad.'

'Yes.' I was struck by a mood of sadness. 'And that's not the end of the story. It appears that our elder daughter, Viola, is going to be unable to have any children at all. Something wrong with the genes, we're told. We don't talk about it very much. *She* doesn't talk about it. But Elspeth and I wonder if it's going to deter her from getting married.'

'There's no reason why it should.'

'You don't know Viola.'

It suddenly struck me how confiding the conversation had become in a few minutes. After all, we had only just met.

The same thing must have struck Jim Yavner.

He looked at me speculatively. 'So you bestride the Two Cultures?' He meant Prince Consort, my engineers and their literary studies.

He was making fun of me.

'I shouldn't put it like that – lest it sound as if I might be liable to do the splits at any moment.'

'Don't you feel torn in two directions?'

'Not really. Though I enjoy the literary culture, live in it – writing novels means more to me than anything else I do in life – I don't in the end think as much of the literary culture as I do of the scientific culture. It's technology that's of crucial importance to the well-being of the country – there doesn't seem to me any way of getting round that. And the scientific culture is really of central importance in my inner life – its principles govern the way I think one should look at things. You may think the feeling comes of my being rooted in the scientific culture as a start.' I watched the expression on his face as I came out with the honest truth –

'Though I'm a devoted practitioner of the literary culture I'm *au fond* a paid-up member of the scientific culture.'

'This is really interesting.'

Sincerity had apparently not ruined my reputation in his eyes. Hooray!

'I'd like to know about your teaching,' he said. It sounded sincere on his part. 'Have you taught before?'

'Schoolmaster before the War. Teaching physics to grammar-school boys.' I grinned. 'Invaluable experience of how to keep a class in order without actually hitting them over their heads...' I became serious. 'My Prince Consort undergraduates are the reverse of obstreperous. They're sacrificing their spare time to come and listen to me.'

'I'd like to see that happening in Avalon.' He smiled sarcastically. 'They've established their right not to come and listen to me if they have something more interesting to do.'

He must be referring to relics of the so-called 'Student Revolution' of 1968. I said:

'Ah... It's their Mommies and Daddies who are paying for them.'

'Yeah... Their Mommies and Daddies want their pound of flesh. They expect their kids to be awarded degrees. If their kids flunk out they write to the Chancellor demanding a re-run.'

'Good God!'

'We Americans are on the ball. You know?'

I liked his irony. 'Tell me more!' I laughed – feeling brotherly sympathy for him.

At that moment we were interrupted. The masses around us parted like the Red Sea for none other than the Vice-Chancellor of Prince Consort College to join us.

'Professor Yavner! Joe, Dear Boy!' George shook hands. He was always addressing me as Dear Boy though I was ten years older than him. I didn't demur – nowadays I was always addressed by barrow-boys in street-markets as Young Man.

'So pleased to see you both.' George was saying. 'Thank you so much for coming.' He looked at our glasses which were half-full. 'Let me get you some more wine!'

'I'm OK, thank you,' said Yavner. 'So am I,' said I.

George looked from one to the other of us with lively pleasure shining from his face. Like Yavner and me, he too was smallish medium in height, quick in his movements. His face was usually shining, and its most distinguishing feature was a sharp nose, which he normally bore pointing up in the air – so reminding me of some small animal. (I realised we must be looking like three small animals, chattering together.)

I had often claimed, when we were much younger, that George was going about with his nose pointing upwards sensing for jobs. He was now – in descending order of importance in public estimation – Television's celebrated Professor of Earth Sciences (sic), Vice-Chancellor of Prince Consort College in the University of London, Peer of the Realm, and Fellow of the Royal Society. (If you are inferring that for your narrator the list is in ascending, not descending, order; you are correct. Rare scientific distinction at the top of the list instead of the bottom. All the same the public in its ignorance could not be grossly blamed – George was a very skilful, one might almost have said gifted television performer.) Thus George was rewarded with jobs, amply rewarded – some people thought more than amply.

George exchanged a few cordial words with Yavner and then turned to me.

'I was terribly sorry to hear of Robert's death.' Robert was an even older, and closer, friend of mine than of George. Very distinguished and also rewarded with a Life-Peerage. 'It was very sudden,' George said. 'A terrible shock to you, Dear Boy.'

'It was a massive heart-attack.' This was not the moment to discuss it, especially as I could not hide from myself the fact that I was going to gain from it financially. Robert had made a lot of money and with some of it had set up a Discretionary Trust of which I was one of the beneficiaries. (The importance of this at the present juncture of my career will not be lost on you.)

George was facing me with a sincerely condoling expression aimed past the sides of his nose. Then swiftly he reverted to his social duties towards Jim Yavner.

'I hope,' he said to Jim, 'that you and Joe are hitting it off. I'm honoured to have him on the staff of this institution.'

Yavner gave me a glance conveying his appreciation of George's blarney. Really, I thought, Jim Yavner is a good chap.

A waiter came through the crowd with a bottle. We held out our glasses.

Yavner signalled to someone in the crowd –

'My wife, Rosalind.'

His wife broke her way through to us. I wondered where Elspeth was.

'I must go and shake hands with more of my guests,' George said busily. 'If I see Elspeth I'll send her to you.'

According to my observation, George showed signs of a *tendresse* towards Elspeth – I suspected that Lady Bantock's observation tallied with mine. He shook hands in parting from Jim Yavner, then left us.

Rosalind Yavner joined us. Introductions and small talk, interrupted by the appearance of Elspeth –

'George says you want me.'

I said facetiously, 'I always want you. But I didn't send for you. That must have been George's own contribution.'

'He kissed me on both cheeks.'

Smiles were exchanged between all four of us as I introduced Elspeth. We chatted for a few minutes during which the crowd seemed to become even denser, and conversation even more difficult.

'I hate to break up the conversation,' said Yavner. He looked at me. 'I guess we have plenty to say to each other.'

'I should have thought so.' I wanted to meet him again.

'We've rented an apartment in the Little Boltons,' he said. 'There's a raft of Italian restaurants in the next street.' He glanced at his wife. 'We'd love to have you join us for supper at one of them. We can take a cab.'

I glanced at Elspeth, who was clearly agreeable. I said:
'Let's go!'

We were borne away by taxi to the Little Boltons, thence round the corner into a street where Yavner directed the driver to one among a covey of Italian restaurants.

We installed ourselves, now able to look at each other more closely – and favourably, I may say.

Rosalind Yavner was slightly taller than her husband, her fair hair greying – one of the few middle-aged American women I'd ever seen who hadn't had the colour of her hair tinkered with. An attractive woman, her good looks enhanced by a remarkably leisurely manner – it was difficult to imagine Rosalind Yavner getting heated over anything, while it was nevertheless apparent that she was far from lacking in character. I could see that Elspeth liked her. (In contrast with such super-leisureliness Elspeth was much quicker on the lead.)

I should have been happy to take Jim Yavner back to my club, (which didn't admit ladies,) where we could have had a table to ourselves and talked about literature without let or hindrance all night. On some future occasion, I resolved.

We settled down at the table and agreed on an ordinary Italian meal: Jim was taking charge. Parma ham and melon, then *osso bucco*: a bottle of Chianti. I was in high spirits.

Elspeth was keeping an eye on me. It conveyed the imperative to be on my best behaviour – she had more commonsense than me, and less sympathy with my favourite party-trick of masquerading as the oldest *enfant terrible* in the business.

Nobody was making an effort to impress. While we were waiting for the food the Americans drank dry Martinis, Elspeth a Noilly Prat and soda, I a whisky. The drink was not socially necessary – the evening was already off to a good start.

Jim explained to Rosalind the reason for my presence at George Bantock's party –

'Joe is saving the souls of engineers and scientists at Prince Consort University by encouraging them to read books.'

'The idea is that they're somewhat low in literacy,' I said, 'and in due course they will have to write scientific papers and the like.'

'Joe is a scientist himself, as well as author of – how many novels?'

'Sixteen or seventeen... I can never remember exactly how many.'

Rosalind smiled at me, leisurely... 'I've read you.'

My heart was won and so, I could see, was Elspeth's. On how little support may one depend in this unrewarding world!

Jim said: 'I want to hear about your course and how you teach it. I guess we've got Arts students at Avalon who are hardly more literate than your students in technology.'

'That's for you to say, Jim – but I take your word for it.'

Jim was chewing a piece of Parma ham. I decided to do the same. (Likely to keep us both out of the conversation for a little while.)

Elspeth said to Rosalind, 'Are you a great novel-reader?'

'In my fashion...' She smiled. 'Does having read your husband qualify me for the title?'

'Of course!' Elspeth laughed.

They were enjoying themselves.

'I know I ought to have read many many more novels than I have.' Rosalind glanced across the table at her husband. 'But I'm not going to let it bother me. Life's too short.'

Elspeth said, 'That's right. That's how I feel.' (On the sidelines I was thinking about the relative lengths of life Elspeth and I had still available for reading. Elspeth fifteen years more than I.)

Jim had disposed of the Parma ham – the man with the sharpest teeth gets through the Parma ham quickest.

'I'm waiting to hear, Joe, which novels you ask your students of technology to read.'

'The best ones, of course,' I said teasingly. 'I'm interested in the realistic novel – pretty exclusively, I suppose. It's what I write myself. So I'm really focussed on the nineteenth century classics. In my opinion they wrote better novels then than we do now.'

'Jane Austen, George Eliot, Anthony Trollope,' he began, as it were prompting me.

'Exactly.' I smiled. 'They were the best...'

'I agree they were marvellous, the Victorians...' Then he said, 'But not solely the best!' He had other candidates up his sleeve.

I laughed instead of commenting. But then I said:

'Whom do you favour, Jim?'

'Oh, I teach the standard American course... Conrad, Lawrence, Joyce and Woolf...'

'Help!' With mock unobtrusiveness I crossed myself four times.

One can't cross oneself unobtrusively, mock or otherwise, when the other person is sitting a couple of feet away.

Yavner grinned. 'Feel safer now?' He'd taken my difference of taste with *sang froid.* What a relief!

'Do you know,' I said, grinning back. 'I think I do... I always cross myself when anyone mentions James Joyce. It's so necessary, *Finnegan's Wake* led literature up a cul-de-sac don't-you-know.'

'Oh really?' He was laughing. 'Sounds like you don't favour the Moderns?'

'I just favour the pre-Moderns still more. You know?' I had invented the term "pre-Moderns" on the spur of the moment.

There was a pause. Instead of shutting up, I plodded on.

'But my main quarrel is with Joyce because he has had the greatest influence. His two main assumptions seem to me to be fallacious. First of all that Time passes in discontinuous discrete moments; when we can all see that it is flowing continuously all the while. Second that what you experience in your discrete moments can be expressed in words. How often, my dear Jim, have you, yourself, said of something you're feeling, "I can't put it into words"?'

He said mildly: 'Modernism has its roots much earlier than those writers.'

'Of course it has. In my limited view the rot was already showing in Henry James, with his crucial question about a literary work – "Is it written?" My own crucial question is – and always has been – "What is it saying?" I paused. "Is it written?" focuses on style, on technique, on the beauty of the language. If you want to put it that way – on literary surface... My own question focuses on content, on the deeper meaning – which I tend to judge against observable reality as true or false, good or pernicious... Now you see why I feel the way I do about Modernism, where everything tends to be reduced to Aesthetics! Aesthetics!..'

'This sure is in-ter-est-ing. I want to hear your case some time.'

'Then dine with me at my club one evening.'

'Sounds fascinating... I'll hold you to that, Joe.'

Elspeth had been eyeing me.

All appeared to be well for the time being.

The *osso bucco* was put before us. The chianti was poured into our glasses.

Chapter IV

A Letter Out Of The Blue

My friendship with Jim Yavner prospered during his last weeks in London. We met several times in different locales – meals in pubs and restaurants. Elspeth took some time off from her job to go on shopping trips with Rosalind in classy stores, Harrods and Harvey Nichols and the like: they indulged in window-shopping at the couturier places down Sloane Street, which was just as well for the pockets of Jim and me.

'You know,' Rosalind said after one of these excursions, 'in Harrods we saw some of Jim's students from the London Centre.'

'They can't be short of money,' I said, thinking of "second-rank Ivy league".'

'That's right,' said Rosalind easily acquiescent.

'They could buy Rosalind and me any day of the week,' said Jim, with feeling.

Rosalind said restrainingly, 'Jim says some of them do have difficulty in...'

'Making ends meet?' said Elspeth.

'Exactly.' Rosalind smiled at her.

Elspeth looked pleased.

'We don't have a Harrods back in Avalon,' said Jim.

Rosalind looked at Elspeth. 'How about if we go just once more before Jim and I leave London?' – spoken in her usual unconcerned tone of voice.

Jim and I exchanged glances but not speech.

Elspeth, without looking at me, said:

'Of course.'

Before Jim left London I took him to my club, ensconcing him at the long table, among the shining faces of my fellow members. (Jim and I had just come up from the bar too, so I can't claim that our faces were not shining.) By the time the meal was over it was clear that he was a great success with my fellow members. 'Bring him again!' they said.

After dinner we went up on the roof-garden to which the dining-room opened out. We had ordered another bottle of wine. It was a perfect summer evening, the air warm, the evening sky glowing; the flowering-plants in their tubs freshly-watered, exhaling their scent and a smell of damp earth. It was just the evening for the leisurely drinking of a bottle of wine. Neither of us smoked.

Suddenly Jim said, 'I have to make you an apology, Joe.'

I couldn't imagine what for.

He went on. 'I've just finished reading your sequence of three novels in paper-back.'

Actually there were four but I didn't say so.

'I apologise for only just having got around to them.' He looked at me. 'You've got something, Joe.'

I said playfully, 'Have I got what it takes to make a post-war literary landmark?'

'I see why Burgess hailed the first.'

I drank a little of my wine, silently savouring the smell of the summer air and the light of the evening sky...

There was a long pause. Finally I said to Jim:

'Do you know what this' – I waved my hand towards the quiet surroundings, the half-empty bottle on the table, the stillness of the flowering plants – 'do you know what this suddenly made me think of? You know? The poems of Li Po... Composed in a boat while floating idly down the Yang-Tse – idly and drunkenly.'

'In the Arthur Waley translation?'

'Correct.'

He grinned. 'So drunk he fell overboard.'

'I'm not that drunk.'

'Me neither. Nether of us is drunk.'

I thought about it. 'You could say neither of us is a poet, either.'

'Ah... That explains a lot.'

I felt we were trembling on the edge of a literary discussion.

'Explains all,' I said finally.

He nodded his head, accepting finality – and unclouded amity.

A few days later he and Rosalind left the country, to go back to Avalon.

'They didn't want to go,' Elspeth told me.

'I'm not surprised.'

'Rosalind was practically in tears when she said Goodbye. In fact she was in tears... I think she really felt free from the constraints of American academic society – which are getting worse.'

I said, 'She has such a leisurely manner I shouldn't have thought she was seriously worried by... whatever you call them.. the constraints of American academic society.'

'I think the leisurely manner is her way of telling herself she's not bothered by them.'

I thought it over. 'She's an interesting woman."

Elspeth smiled to herself.

I said, 'Her husband's an interesting man.'

Elspeth went on smiling, now at me. 'You really fell for him.'

'That's true. And I was right to do so. He's generous-minded, tolerant, humorous – and clever. '

'And' – she gave me an amused look – 'he really likes your books.'

'That, of course, is my idea of the qualification for entering Paradise... You know St. Peter asks the final question when you arrive at the Golden Gates – "What do you think of the novels of Joe Lunn?"'

'Does he really call you Joe, not Joseph?'

'Of course. Heaven is Americanised just like Earth – God calls him Peter but all the Apostles call him Pete.'

Elspeth was laughing. She said; 'Rosalind invites us to go and see them in Avalon.'

'Visit with them, you mean... It would be nice. Anyway, they'll soon be over here again, I don't doubt.'

A few days earlier Viola had telephoned to say that she had been accepted by Queen Anne's University Hospital to begin her training as a nurse with support from the International Red Cross. She sounded in high spirits – she usually did. (The surprising alternative was when something really upsetting happened at the office – then it was a burst of tears.) It was a while since we had news of Virginia, who was waiting for replies to her applications for support in training to be a doctor. (The girls were temporarily sharing a flat with some of their friends – Elspeth and I never ascertained how many friends.)

The change of direction was under weigh.

Six weeks passed by and a change of direction presented itself to me. Out of the blue a letter headed Avalon University London Centre, from its Dean who signed himself Will Gower. It said –

This letter is to say I am looking for an English teacher to fill a post which has fallen vacant on the staff of the London Centre, as a result of a prospective appointee accepting at a moment's notice another post elsewhere. I have discussed the emergency with Professor James Yavner, Head of the Avalon Department of English Literature, who I believe is known to you, and he has suggested that I approach you. Actually I approach you with utmost diffidence, in view of your distinguished reputation, and with sincere apology for the haste with which I beg you to let me know if you are interested. I should appreciate most of all your coming here to discuss the matter personally, and in any case, as soon as you can find it possible. May I say that we should feel greatly honoured if you were to come and join us, and feel convinced that, in the event of your being willing to consider the appointment, we could arrive at mutually satisfactory terms. I look forward to hearing from you.

Elspeth and I read the letter together.

'Well,' I said, 'Jim Yavner's doing his best for me.'

Elspeth touched my hand. 'What do you think about it?'

'I shall certainly go and see this man.'

'It sounds –'

'A better job than my present one at Prince Consort – that's if they will let me do what I want.'

'It sounds as if Will Gower is out to please.'

'He's in a jam, anyway.' I paused. 'I wonder...'

'What?'

'I think Jim Yavner didn't think much of my irregular status at Prince Consort. He once asked me if I oughtn't to be doing something better...'

'What did you say?'

'Beggars can't be choosers.'

'You're not a beggar, darling.'

'I know. But you know what I mean. Old George Bantock was doing his best for me. We mustn't forget to give him credit for that.'

'Now it's Jim Yavner. That's nice. It ought to cheer you up.'

'Don't count your chickens! I haven't heard yet what the job is – what they want me to do and what they're prepared to pay me for it.'

'Jim must think it's OK.'

'It sounds as if they're in a jam – haven't got another candidate.'

'Haven't got a better candidate.'

'Lays it open to me to exert a little levverage.' (I pronounced "leverage" *a l'Americaine*.)

At that I was prepared to let the conversation drop. Elspeth took the letter from me.

'Will Gower,' she said. 'I wonder if he's Welsh.'

'It would be Gwilym.'

'Perhaps it really is?'

'Or Gwyn, or Gwelfor... or Gwendolen.'

We were both amused. Then we did let the conversation drop.

At the bottom of his letter the Dean gave the dates of the next semester, at the top his telephone number. I rang him straight away and arranged to see him at the Centre immediately after lunch on the following day.

The Centre was elegantly situated in an extensive low building, with a colonnade, on the outer edge of a park. I was shown up to the Dean's office which was smaller than I'd expected, though it probably seemed smaller because it was so crammed with books, shelves, filing cabinets, telephone, personal computer, folders, papers, etc. In the wall facing him was a gap on the other side of which was his secretary.

The building had obviously not been designed for offices originally – perhaps that was why it had an unusually comely look. There was a beautiful view from the window, tree-tops all green, a blue sky, and Georgian mansions in the distance. Bosses always have rooms on the first floor – the *piano nobile*... I though of Henry's office, that huge room looking over the Embankment; but then Henry was nothing if not *nobile*, very *nobile*. (I wondered about Mr Will Gower...)

The Dean stood up, smiling, to shake hands with me. An active, rotund fellow with apple-cheeks and curly brown hair; deep-set brown eyes glintingly shrewdly. His complexion retained a permanent sun-tan, giving him an open-air look. Momentarily I caught what I thought was a cunning glance – all my observations immediately coalesced into a single impression. A Welsh farmer!

'So glad you've come, Mr Lunn,' he said. He gave me a humorous grin – the glint in his deep-set brown eyes changed to a twinkle. 'Glad, Mr Lunn. I think I ought to say relieved!..' He paused. 'Please sit down!'

I sat down on the sole chair – there was a sofa but it was laden with newspapers and periodicals. One could say there was a limited empty space on top of his desk immediately in front of him: otherwise papers were piled high on each side of that. He was in his shirt-sleeves and wearing bright green braces. The telephone rang – through the gap in the wall he told his secretary not to put the call through. Then he pulled a shutter across the gap.

'So...' He paused. 'First of all I must say how much I enjoy your books. I enjoy them very much indeed.'

He couldn't have made a better start than that. I tried to hide my craven appreciation of flattery under a brusque manner.

'That's what they're meant for. Art is meant to give pleasure. Or damn' well should be.'

'Provided certain members of the English Faculty at Avalon University are not listening to us, I'll agree with you.'

'Jim Yavner would agree, and he's Head of –'

'Jim's a good guy.' This man didn't waste time. 'If you come to teach for us, Jim Yavner will be your boss.'

It looked as if I'd been right in seeing a cunning glance... I said mildly –

'I thought he was due to retire in a year or so.'

I recalled an occasion in our amicable sparrings when Jim had shown signs of being bitten by "the literary-theory bug", a bite which led to an attack of the Derrida-Foucault mania that he admitted was catching on in the American Universities. He could not yet be said to be showing serious signs of it; but what about his successor as my boss, were I to take the job and want to stay in it?

There was a pause.

'I was interested by your letter,' I said, feeling I had to say something.

'You'll have gathered from it that I'm in straits,' he said. 'We run a course here on the English novel. I re-engaged the guy to teach it who taught it last year. At a moment's notice he's asked permission to withdraw – in favour of a senior appointment at a university in the Gulf.'

I laughed. 'He couldn't say NO to that. It must mean money.'

'Yes, indeed. More money than Avalon was offering.'

'Difficult situation for him.' Ironically.

'I understand it very well. I've been in academic life myself.'

'You probably know already that I haven't.'

'Jim Yavner told me about the course you're teaching at Prince Consort and you've been a schoolmaster. I've studied your entry in *Who's Who*.'

'The Prince Consort job interests me – it's fun! My first effort... Jim thought I ought to be doing a more regular sort of job – a better-paid job.'

'Such as teaching for us at Avalon.'

'My course at Prince Consort is only one class a week. And only for volunteers at that.'

'What we had in mind is two classes of an hour and a half each per week. For regular students.'

'Distinctly more prestigious.' I hoped to keep the irony out of my tone of voice.

'More appropriate to your reputation.'

There was a pause. He said:

'I'm a great fan of yours.'

For an instant I caught a different twinkle from those bright brown eyes – I wondered if what he'd said was strictly the truth. I decided there was no reason why it shouldn't be the truth – people at parties often told me they were fans of mine, and from time to time I received a letter from somebody who committed his or her fan-hood to writing. (I admit to being encouraged by fan-letters, especially when they came from foreign countries – I always acknowledged them immediately, sometimes fulsomely.)

'I particularly admire the sequence of three novels...'

'There's a fourth one – a companion-volume. Everyone in it is 70 or over. I wanted to sub-title it *Old Age and Surgery*.'

Gower laughed. 'You wouldn't get away with that.'

'That's what everybody told me.' I went on. 'You know the aim of my art – it's stated in one or other of those books you've read. Quoted from Horace. To speak the truth, laughing...' I shook my head lugubriously. 'I'm afraid publishers don't see any future for the truth spoken, laughing.'

'Too difficult for the masses, no?'

'It doesn't excite them... Publishers are not enthusiastic. By "a future" publishers mean a large and steadily increasing sale.'

'Publishers have got to live.'

'So have I!'

'Then accept an appointment with Avalon University London Centre!'

I knew that was the opening for me to ask how much Avalon University London Centre was prepared to pay? but I was too shy. I wasted my opportunity. I said:

'That's smart of you.'

He looked pleased with himself. Then generously he gave my opportunity back to me.

'Are you sufficiently interested to let us talk about your stipend?'

He named a sum: it seemed to me, with no experience of being an academic, not unreasonable.

'I'll consider it,' I said, meaning I'd discuss it with friends who did have experience of being academics.

'Thank you , Mr Lunn. That's encouraging, indeed. I shall be looking forward to a favourable answer. Yes?..'

We began to discuss the job . The Avalon course was on The English Novel. I said I should want it to be called The English Realistic Novel.

'The realistic novel is the one that interests me most.' I was recalling some of the numbers on Jim Yavner's "standard list". 'It's the kind I write myself.'

'With great success.' He paused, smiling. Then striking while the iron was hot, said quickly, 'You can teach one of your own novels, of course.'

I hadn't time to say Oh, Yes! when the telephone rang. The shutter opened and I could overhear his secretary saying:

'Call from Professor Yavner on the line, Will. Do you want to take it now?'

I calculated that it must be 9.00 a.m. in Avalon. Jim Yavner was not letting the grass grow under his feet.

Gower looked at me with a very sincere expression.

'I guess it's about you..'

I stood up. 'Then I think you'd better take it.'

'May I tell him I'm hopeful?'

'I don't see why not.'

'And that we're going to meet again within forty-eight hours for a definite answer.'

'Depends on how hopeful you are by nature.'

'Very hopeful I am.' He held out one hand to me while picking up his telephone with the other hand.

As I shook the hand I was offered I heard him saying, 'Hi, Jim! Your friend has given me permission to be hopeful. I'm super relieved.'

With the conversation in progress I left the room and was shown out of the building by a good-looking American girl who appeared to be on the staff.

'What d'ya think of AULC, Mr Lunn?' she asked in an unselfconscious matey way as we went downstairs. (She pronounced it as a single word, "Aulc".)

'Don't know yet,' I said. 'What do you?'

'I think it's great.'

When we were nearing the front entrance I said:

'There are two things perhaps you can tell me about AULC.'

'Go ahead!'

'One; is there a decent pub within reach? Two; is there a public swimming-bath within reach?'

She registered the questions without being in the least fazed, (as she would have called it.)

I explained: 'I'm not a devout drinker – rarely more than a couple of pints of beer at a time. But I am a devout swimmer – a thousand metres twice a week if I can manage it.'

'Great!' We were going through the front doors. 'If you walk along the main road over there' – she pointed to it – 'there's a pub on the corner of the second block. And if you walk a quarter of a mile down that street you come to a public swimming-pool – I sometimes use it myself.'

'Thank you,' I said warmly. 'I consider AULC to be most desirably situated.'

She smiled at me and we parted. I went out into the afternoon sunshine. And thence home.

I was having my tea when Elspeth came in from her work. We kissed.

'You look cheerful, darling,' she said. She sat down beside me and took hold of my hand. 'Are you cheerful?'

'More or less. We've got to think about this Avalon job.'

'Will you be a Professor?' She was teasing me.

'I hadn't thought of that. I don't want to think of that.' It was one of my party-tricks to see professors as figures of fun, recommending that they should wear gowns and mortar-boards all the time – Prestige Attire, I called it.

'What was Gower like? Was he Welsh?'

'Gwilym? Now I come to think of it, it's possible.' I described his physical appearance, finishing up – 'Shrewd, and I wouldn't rule out wily... A nut-brown Welsh farmer.' I gave it further thought. 'You can see him sitting round with his mates, putting away the pints of beer in a local pub on cattle-market day, somewhere up in Brecon.'

Elspeth laughed. 'I suppose that's all imagination.'

'I should call it invention. I've no cause to believe he's Welsh... I have no experience of a local pub on cattle-market day; and I have never been up to Brecon – though I don't doubt it's a beautiful countryside. So far as I know, he's English and a gent.'

'A nut-brown Welsh farmer... I like that.'

'The n-b W f.'

She was smiling.

'With no basis in fact.'

'It makes an interesting picture.'

'Exemplifies Peter Ackroyd's advice – Don't write about what you know: write about what you don't know!'

'Did he really say that?'

'Something of the kind. It must describe what lots of people do – that's why there are so many absurd books around.'

She squeezed the hand she was holding. It indicated that I'd said enough.

'Are you going to see Gower again?'

'Within forty-eight hours, I told him. You and I have got to do some thinking, my darling. And I must ask the advice of our real academic friends. James, Fred... I'll ring them tonight. I must find out what university teaching is supposed to mean, nowadays, and what you get paid for it,'

'What about George Bantock? You'll have to make your peace with him.'

'I know that, too.'

She stood up. 'I must go and see about something for us to eat.'

'That suits me. You know my belief – what are the two main things in a man's life? Eating and – '

'I do know,' she said and turned towards the door.

Chapter V

Careers

The following morning.

'Dear Boy, we don't want to lose you!' His enthusiasm came over the telephone.

I had nothing to say to that.

'I congratulate you on having an offer from... where is it?'

'Avalon University.'

'Avalon University.' He repeated it thoughtfully. 'I'm sure they're richer than we are.'

'The actual terms haven't been settled,' I said. 'Still less agreed.' I wanted to head him off a diatribe about the persecution of our universities by Government in the form of insufficient funding.

'How much teaching do they want you to do?' he asked.

'That hasn't been settled yet, either.' Then unable to keep up prevarication, I said, 'Probably two classes a week.'

Instantly I knew what I'd let myself in for.

'Two classes,' George echoed. 'With ours it would only mean three. You are a great success here, Dear Boy.' He repeated with great emphasis, 'We don't want to lose you.'

'But George, I've not been teaching at Prince Consort for very long.'

'Look at the number of volunteers you're getting!'

'I got a fair number to begin with – coming in to see what it was all about. And when they discovered I was expecting them to read *Emma*, the number promptly fell off.'

'Since then it has risen steadily.'

George Bantock was not an easy man to defeat in this sort of argument – after all, he had been winning arguments about pay and position for a lifetime. And in fact I had to admit my number of volunteers was now staying up very well.

'Please consider not resigning, Dear Boy! I know of no other college doing a course like yours. It's good work.' He paused. 'I'm sure we can't equal the stipend the Americans are offering you.' He paused again. 'If you'll let me know what it is, when it's decided, I may be able to use it to lever a bit more out of our people.'

'Thank you, George. I promise to let you know. It's very good of you.'

'I hope I shall be in a position to announce how good it is of you to stay with us.'

I laughed. So did he. End of conversation.

At the Underground station on my way home I telephoned the news to Elspeth at her work. It happened to be an evening when the girls were coming in to dinner – to report on their progress. We had a lot to talk about.

Elspeth arrived home from her job with the Housing Association late.

'Architects are a pain in the neck! They see themselves as artists, and spend the day fiddling about with their rulers and set-squares – forgetting they've got to write reports on what they're doing. Then they come in with half-written scripts at the last moment and expect everyone to fall into line.' She paused for breath. 'Did you put my cottage pies in the oven?'

'Yes, I did. At the time you prescribed.'

She appeared to be satisfied.

'I'll make the drinks,' I said, and dashed out of the room – then had to come back again to greet the girls.

'What are you doing?' asked Virginia.

'I'll make the drinks,' said Viola. 'You sit down, Daddy.'

Three of them in a small kitchen seemed to me too many, but it was pleasant to be left on my own, to sit on a sofa and contemplate my situation in peace. Meanwhile in the kitchen Elspeth was acquainting the girls, I presumed, with that situation. In due course they all came back to the sitting-room.

'You must do it, Daddy,' said Virginia.

Viola was handing round the drinks from a tray. 'It just shows how wrong you were when you said nobody wanted you.'

'What did George say?' asked Elspeth.

'"Dear Boy, we don't want to lose you."'

Small burst of laughter all round. George, when he came to our parties, was always the subject, with his nose pointing eagerly up in the air, of entertainment to the girls.

'So that means two jobs!' Virginia.

I didn't say anything.

'Does it?' Elspeth.

'I don't know.' I explained what they could all see for themselves. An hour-and-a-half's class was all very well; but I was lucky if, with preparation and travelling, it didn't take a very substantial bite out of that working day.

'Getting on with your novel comes first,' said Elspeth.

'That's right,' Virginia.

'You must get on with your novel.' Viola. 'But...'

'I know, I know.' I looked affectionately round at the three of them. What a family! Do you wonder I was a male chauvinist? Yet I felt that they had to experience it personally, the anguish of being kept from getting on with a novel, to know what it was like.

Elspeth rested her hand on my forearm.

There was a pause. We had our drinks.

Virginia said, 'What about giving all three classes a trial? To see how it works out.'

'I've seen enough of these things, my darling girl, to realise that if you don't say No before you jump in, it's much harder to say No when you're drowning.'

'And he's tired already,' said Viola. She sipped her Noilly Prat and soda.

'I know he's tired.'

There was a pause. I drank some whisky.

'I wanted to know what you all think.'

'If you weren't writing a novel, and weren't tired already, we should all say, Try it!' Elspeth, half-amused.

'That's right.' Virginia. I could see she was in favour, anyway.

'That doesn't tell me what you all think about it when I am writing a novel and am tired already.'

Virginia. 'That's fair enough. When we decided to make a change we wanted to know what you thought about it.' She drank some of her weak beer – she was driving afterwards.

'And now the boot's on the other foot.' I laughed. 'How are you two getting on with your affairs?'

'What would you be teaching at this place?' Viola, as if she hadn't heard me.

'The realistic novel. I've stipulated that from the start.'

'Including yours?' Virginia.

'One of them.'

'Not enough, Daddy!' Virginia was laughing.

'It's OK.' Viola, sensibly.

Virginia said, 'Think who it means cutting out!'

Elspeth observed, 'Jim Yavner knows your line about literature. About post-modernism and literary theory and all that.'

'As he proposed me for the job, he can't feel that the Avalon boys and girls are going to be overwhelmingly subjected to evil propaganda.'

'Aren't they?' Virginia.

'Are they not!' I laughed.

'That's right,' said Virginia, sympathising as an artist with me in my resistance to "post-modernism and literary theory and all that." She said, 'I think you ought to take this job. You owe it to yourself to put your point of view across to as many people as possible. Especially young Americans.'

'That's right.' Viola. 'You must say what you believe. It would be wrong not to.'

'Goodness!' On the face of it I was surprised by such strong unanimous support – on consideration not surprised. They had not been deaf to my strictures about current trends, in particular post-modernism. ("It's the Idea that matters, not the Execution".)

I looked at Elspeth. 'What do you think?'

'Even if Jim does know, and does put you up for the job, you shouldn't set the cat among the pigeons straight away.'

'I'll try not to. I'll go at it gently to start with.'

Viola. 'You will get found out...'

'Sufficient unto the day,' I replied.

'We don't want the day to come too soon,' said Elspeth. She drank some of her Noilly Prat and soda decisively.

Virginia. 'I think Daddy can do it cleverly...'

We all smiled.

I kissed her on the cheek.

'In the meantime it will be fun, doing something that the post-modernistical faction in the Avalon department would strongly disapprove of if they knew what was going on.'

Now I came to think about it, the prospect was not just fun – it was intolerably alluring. The element of mischief; the thought that I might be playing a subversive role. What an opportunity!

I said, 'George Bantock doesn't want to lose me. But when we sees me doing a more recognised job – for a more recognised salary! – he'll get used to the idea.'

'And the sooner the better?' Viola.

'That's the way it will probably work out.'

Elspeth said, 'Come on, girls! It's time to get your father's dinner...' She stood up.

They all picked up their drinks.

I thought there was very little for them to do in the kitchen. I leaned back luxuriously in my chair and swigged my whisky.

'Isn't it lovely to be a male chauvinist!' I said provocatively as they went out of the room.

'MCP,' said Virginia in mock denunciation.

'If I'm an MCP, what does that make you as my daughter?' (The P in MCP stood for Pig, of course.)

She turned her back on me.

Viola looked at me, laughing, as she followed her sister.

Left to myself I set about telephoning Fred and James. Both university lecturers, they viewed Avalon's proposals with very moderate raptures. They counselled me not to make trouble for the time being over the meagre pay I was being offered; but to make my own terms – they insisted – about the size of class I was prepared to teach. As I wanted to teach my class as a seminar, both specified it should not number, for comfort, more than 15.

'At most 17,' said James.

'You mean 17 for discomfort?..' said I.

Elspeth called me into the dining-room and we sat down to dinner, Elspeth's cottage pies, of which we were all very fond. It promised to be a jolly dinner. And then I realised to my chagrin that I had monopolised the time so far with my own concerns, when the girls had come to discuss theirs.

As soon as we had embarked on the meal I said, 'And now, how have you two been getting on with your affairs?'

'Not bad.' Viola. As predicted, the course at Queen Anne's would take three years, with the possibility of specialising on nursing children. After that it would be open for her to take a fourth year, studying for a degree. 'It means exams...'

We all smiled sympathetically, yet hopefully. From her tone of voice it sounded as if she might have got over some of the nervous apprehension that formerly paralysed her.

'She'll manage those.' Virginia, characteristically settling it.

'What about funds?' I asked Viola.

'I'm looking into that. Some funds are available from charitable institutions, for instance the International Red Cross...'

'Isn't there such a thing as Macmillan Nurses?' I said vaguely.

'I haven't got to that yet.' Viola paused. 'But I don't think you have to worry.'

'That's good!' I found it a bit hard to believe all the same.

I turned my attention to Virginia. 'And you?'

'Not so satisfactory as Viola's. Not yet...' She paused. 'You don't get governmental support for a medical training if you've already got a degree.'

'That's a fraud!.. Doesn't your degree in science count in your favour?'

She smiled cynically. 'It doesn't matter what the degree is in. It cuts you out of getting a grant. Just the same if it's in geography – or even English!'

I didn't comment on that. I said:

'Won't it shorten your course?'

'You begin with a three-year university degree course – I suppose it has to be the same for everybody. Then another full-year's course at least.' She rounded if off. 'Estimated cost, £5,000 a year, in London anyway.'

I glanced at Elspeth and suppressed the impulse to exclaim Good God! It would be three years before Viola qualified, four before Virginia qualified. Virginia went on.

'It's cheaper out of London. I'm thinking of trying Edinburgh – the Medical School there is affiliated to the University and is very good: and the fees are said to be about half.'

I thought of having to try and find £2,500 – and still felt the impulse to exclaim Good God!

Reading my alarm, she went on. 'There's a possibility of me applying like Viola to charitable institutions. I'm applying to our Local Council, who are supposed to cough up £800 a year for the first two years.'

I found it difficult to believe that as well.

'And everybody,' Virginia went on, 'suggests student loans for the last three years. They go half-and-half.'

I didn't care for the idea of her starting a career in debt, but I acquiesced.

'Don't be worried,' she said. 'I shall get through it all right.'

'She will,' said Viola.

Elspeth said 'I shan't be able to stop working.'

'Poor Mummy!' Viola.

We drank some wine.

It turned out to be a jolly dinner after all.

I had telephoned Will Gower to tell him I was looking forward to taking our negotiations further and I had an appointment to see him the following morning. Elspeth and the girls all thought I was going to accept his offer.

I set off for the Avalon Centre cheerfully. 'You're in negotiating mood, Joe,' I said to myself while I was riding in the Underground.

Actually there didn't seem to be a great deal to negotiate – negotiating is largely about money and I had already reconciled myself to accepting the stipend Gower had named. I supposed I might conduct myself now in such a way as to make myself terribly desirable and then spring it on him that I wanted more money than he'd named. Neither Fred nor James believed I could carry that off.

The only occasions in the past when I'd wrung more money out of anyone were when I'd employed an agent to do it for me. I had a gift for writing books well enough, but no gift for wringing money at all.

I was greeted with engaging enthusiasm by my opposite number in negotiating, in his small cluttered office with its view of green trees and white Regency mansions. His bright twinkling eyes looked brighter and twinklier, his apple cheeks applier. He sprang up from his revolving chair and shut the shutter in the wall.

'This is great, Mr Lunn. Have you come to say Yes?'

'I've come to hear more.'

'That's great, too.' He gave me the most engaging of all smiles. 'Yes, indeed... May I call you Joe?'

'By all means.'

'Joe.' He held out his hand. 'Will.'

We shook hands as if the bargain had already been struck, our friendship sealed.

'Have a cup of coffee, Joe.'

I accepted.

He pressed a button calling his secretary who miraculously cleared a space to accommodate a coffee-making machine.

The coffee was very good.

Then he sat down again in his revolving chair, while I dumped on the floor a pile of journals from the end of his small sofa so as to make room for me to sit down.

'Let me recap what I said yesterday, and then we'll take it from there.'

'Suits me,' I said in what I judged to be the same idiom, while feeling minimal enthusiasm for detailed discussion of what my former employers referred to as Pay and Conditions of Service.

Two hour-and-a-half classes per week for a semester of twelve weeks at the stipend already named. (No pause for negotiation!) Title of the course already provisionally agreed. The English Realistic Novel.

'That means I shall have to make a list of twelve novels,' I interpolated – he didn't contradict me, though I was soon to learn that he should have.

'You will be styled Adjunct Professor,' he said.

I was too taken aback to protest. "Adjunct" – a word nobody with an ounce of literary taste could possibly have chosen. Think of the sound of it to start with! Adj-unct... Two awful sounds in succession.

'That's usual here,' he said. 'Professors from the home campus – such as Jim Yavner – naturally retain their full title.'

'I see.' I said. I saw that I was destined for a lower level. What had become of that "negotiating mood" on which I had congratulated myself while I was sitting in the Underground train? Pull yourself together! I exhorted myself, while I was sitting in the actual negotiating position.

I drank some coffee. He did the same.

'I should like,' I said. 'to discuss the size of my classes.'

'Of course.'

'I want to teach them – it seems to me the most satisfactory way in a case like this – to teach them as a seminar.'

'I agree.'

'That means a class of 15, no more.'

I watched for the cunning element in the twinkle, and saw it not.

'For comfort,' I went on. '17 at most.'

'I think there should be no trouble about that, Joe.'

I could do nothing but indicate satisfaction.

He seized the moment. 'If you are agreeable, Joe, I'll send you a draft contract immediately. The semester begins in ten days' time.'

'OK.'

There was a momentary pause. We both drank sips of coffee. He said:

'I haven't disguised my enthusiasm for your joining the staff here...'

'That's fair enough.'

'Apart from the urgency of my need to get somebody, you fill my bill most completely and most happily. Just the sort of man I should most like to get.'

'What's that, Will?'

'Someone who can teach a course on the novel because he can write it, not someone who teaches it because he can't.'

I laughed. 'Shades of Bernard Shaw!'

'Exactly.'

There was a longer pause, during which we both finished our coffee and I recalled a moment in our first meeting when he'd said he'd concur with my view of literature if there were no persons on the Avalon Faculty listening. I wondered if he were running some kind of minor feud with those persons. I began to like him.

'What else has to be said?' I asked.

'We begin the semester with Registration Day. A Holy Day in the University Calendar.' He gave me an oblique glance. 'It's a day when the students choose the courses they want to attend. In the morning of Registration Day they're all gathered together in a main lecture theatre, where they're addressed by each Professor in turn, who gives them a three-minute outline of his course.'

'Three minutes!' I laughed.

'That's the theory. The practice is that students can see the Professors in advance, in the flesh... And choose the ones who take their fancy.'

'What a beautiful idea! So I'm going to be on show...'

'That's right. Actually it's referred to here as The Horse And Pony Show.'

I laughed again. (I guessed Horse And Pony Show was his invention, up in Brecon.)

'You have nothing to worry about,' he said. The bright brown eyes twinkled with shrewdness, cunning and, I thought now, genuine friendliness.

'In the afternoon,' he went on, 'you sit at a little desk and the students queue up to register with you for your course.'

'I see the idea.'

'Any questions?'

I shook my head. 'Not at the moment.'

'Then what about another cup of coffee, Joe?'

'You offer a very good cup, Will. Thank you. Yes.'

'You will get a draft contract by the second post tomorrow. I should like to get a reply by return...'

'I shall want to discuss it with my wife.'

'Of course.' He gave the impression that in my shoes he would so the same. Perhaps he would. I knew no more about the state of his marriage than he knew about the state of mine, but I imagined it to be satisfactory – he looked the sort of bright-eyed, apple-cheeked fellow who'd be a pretty lively bed-mate, a good husband apart from the occasional lapse. For my part – I had been happily married for nearly thirty years, more than happily married. No lapses to speak of. My wife was the centre of my existence.

I said, 'My wife will probably welcome getting me out of the house two mornings a week.'

I was already forgetting that I was still pledged to a third morning at Prince Consort; and that if Elspeth found she had to go on working, she would be out of the house herself most mornings.

'I hope she'll meet my wife.'

He looked at me as if he thought he'd hooked me.

And by the second post on the following day a contract – not a draft, but a final version, arrived.

That night, with Elspeth looking over my shoulder, I signed the contract.

Chapter VI

Registration Day

'I've put you in to bat first for the English Literature Faculty, Joe. Next after this man.'

Will Gower and I were standing just inside the university lecture theatre where all this semester's entry of American undergraduates were assembled. 'You've got three minutes, no more!'

Up on a podium, behind a huge bench, an American professor was already launched on a resumé of what he was going to tell his pupils in a course on International Finance.

'How long has he been going?' I asked.

Will glanced at his watch in the manner of a man who has taken careful note of the time at which the present speaker began speaking.

'Two minutes.'

I guessed it was the first figure that came into his head.

All the way up a very steep rake rows and rows of young men and women appeared to be taking in what the professor was telling them. I listened, too.

'This is quite good, Will. This course wouldn't do me any harm.' My claim that I had no head for money was proved by the fact that I had never made any.

'I'm sure he'll agree to your auditioning it.' (I took "auditioning" to be American for "sitting in".)

The international financier went on for at least another minute and a half, if not two minutes. Then he came down the steps from the podium, saluted the Dean and made off.

'You next, Joe.'

'Right.'

I didn't go up the steps, but took up my position down below, centre-stage, leaning my back against the podium. I waited while the audience settled down – a few more came in and a few left, perfectly decorously. I was idly surveying them when I suddenly realised that my gaze had been caught in a somewhat un-idle way by two hundred twenty-year old young men and women, hair glistening from being washed, eyes bright with attention for what I was going to say, lips eager and rosy from the last conversational exchanges between each other... Something had come into the atmosphere which made me recall the favourite dictum of one of the dottier of my colleagues when I was a schoolmaster, a dictum he frequently repeated in the staff-room –

"Teaching is the most erotic of professions."

Something had come into the atmosphere, something exciting, stimulating. I felt an instantaneous temptation to entertain myself and entertain them by saying surprising, provocative things. (I didn't doubt my ability to do that: in my own university days I had liked to fancy my chances as a self-appointed iconoclast. That liking could be revived like a shot.)

The last exchanges died out. I made a start –

'Ladies and gentlemen!' (That must have been new to them.) 'I should like to introduce myself. My name is Joe Lunn.' I paused a moment. 'And I'm not a professor.' I grinned at them. 'Never have been... I'm not even a literary guy. I'm just a writer.'

I liked their silence.

'I've published about fifteen novels – I think it's fifteen. I've always had to count them up on my fingers – much to the amusement of my daughters when they were little girls. The total wasn't fifteen then, so I had enough fingers.'

Some quiet laughter. I wondered if Will Gower was thinking I was finding my feet. Actually I now used my feet to walk a couple of yards from centre-stage. I announced that my course was entitled The Realistic Novel In England. I didn't expect them all to know what a realistic novel was – but those who took my course would know by the time they reached the end-of-semester examination. (Menacing!..)

'I'm asking you to read 12 English novels that I call realistic. I will discuss each of them in turn with you in class – with the aim of helping you to get through it in the first place. Some of them are very long, and if you are not used to reading long novels you may well find them hard going. *Middlemarch*, by George Eliot, the centrepiece of the list is 700 pages long! It's there, in spite of being 700 pages long, because in my opinion it's the greatest novel in the English language.' I looked round the class. 'Has anyone read *Middlemarch*?'

One hand raised diffidently in the air by a girl in the front row.

'Good!' I hadn't expected any of them to have read it. Will Gower had told me the bulk of AULC students were "majoring" in a host of subjects which ranged from Stage Directing to Fashion Retailing – a range where you'd scarcely expect to find *Middlemarch*.

'I'm delighted!' I beamed at the girl. (She was quite comely.)

I ran through the reading-list and told them to get copies of it from the Dean's office.

'You'll notice,' I said, 'that my list is rather weighted in favour of the 19th century novel; that's because the classic period for the realistic novel is the 19th century. As you must all know, they wrote better novels in that century than we write in ours.'

I paused a moment to observe how that had gone down.

'You want to know my aim? In the first instance it's to help you get through the books, to understand what they're about. And, I hope, to appreciate what they're about – about real people such as you may recognise as being like yourselves; following their destinies in the real world, the sort of world in which you are going to follow your destinies. Reading these books will help you to understand yourselves, I hope...' I gave them what I hoped was a hopeful smile.

'But you are going to find it hard going, as I've already said. And if you find it too hard going, my advice is – Don't shilly-shally: register before it's too late for one of the other courses! Painting and Acting must involve less reading, but it would be improper of me to suggest them.'

There was a faint stir in the audience, presumably among those who were registering for Painting or Acting.

I looked at my watch and crossed the room to the other end of the space below the podium. Half a minute to go.

'One thing I must say, even at the risk of throwing the Dean's schedule out of gear... This is not, repeat not, a course in Creative Writing. I wouldn't dream of teaching such a course. It might influence you to write like me – than which nothing could be less desirable!.. On the other hand, when we come to passages that I think are particularly admirable, I shall try, as a writer myself, to show you How The Trick Is Done...' I looked round at all those shining young eyes and lively red lips... What an erotic profession!

The Dean said:

'You have another half minute.'

I turned back to the audience.

'You may have noticed that I'm given to irony. My wife is always begging me not to be ironical in public. "People believe what you say," she declares. That's her warning to me. So let this be my warning to you! If you are impetuous enough to register with me, Don't believe all I say!' I smiled at them sideways. 'If you believe all I say, the CIA may never let you re-enter your native land again.'

I gave a curt nod of my head. 'That's all. Thank you!' And I turned to the way out, where Will Gower was twinkling shrewdly. As well he might. There had never been a word about Literary Theory, never a mention of even one of the sacred names which Jim Yavner had told me were sweeping the campuses of America: Derrida, Foucault...

I grinned at him. 'How was it?'

'Jolly good, Joe.'

I was tempted to ask 'Was it subversive enough?' but for the moment my nerve failed me.

I went out of the building, along the main road that the friendly American girl had pointed out to me, to the corner of the second block – where there was a White Lion. I gave myself a pub-lunch to fortify myself for the last item on the Horse and Pony Show schedule, the award of rosettes, i.e. my acceptance of the signatures of those young men and women who wanted to take my course.

The ceremony was held in a large hall, round the periphery of which there was a row of card-tables, each with a folding chair behind it. On each chair sat a member of the faculty. Beside each table were the first members of a queue of young men and women waiting to be signed up.

I took my place on a chair behind which was a placard saying REALISTIC NOVEL. To hand on the table a sheaf of set-book lists for me to dole out; in front of me a form to fill in with the names of ponies honoured with rosettes of acceptance. The huge room was buzzing with voices and a slight unidentifiable smell of cooking.

I glanced briefly at the aforementioned form. Spaces for 25 names. 25! I ought to have been provided with a form with spaces for 15 names. There must be some mistake. I searched round for a sight of Will Gower. He was not to be seen.

Will Gower would certainly rectify the mistake.

There were some three or four undergraduates queuing up at my table.

I surveyed the room. For SHAKESPEARE 1 and SHAKESPEARE 2 there were queues so long that they had to fold back upon themselves. Well, they'd all heard of Shakespeare: none of them had heard of me – yet... (Envy is the occupational vice of artists. Sad, but that's the way it is.)

I got on with registering my three or four, inscribing in the spaces of my form their names, universities, subjects they were reading – sorry! majoring in. I handed each of them a copy of my list of set-books.

'Start reading now!' I exhorted them.

After four there were no more waiting.

I observed that the next table, INTERNATIONAL FINANCE, had only a couple more. ADVERTISING, on the other hand, had a queue of at least twenty, joyous youths and maidens conversing animatedly – I presumed they had been told "It Pays To Advertise."

There was a break of a quarter of an hour in my string of waiting clients. Then another two or three lined up. Like the first ones to register, each brought a form that I was required to countersign, showing that I accepted this person for my class: it enabled me to read which courses they had registered for before mine. I realised that they must have spent the intervening period in the crowded queues SHAKESPEARE 1 and SHAKESPEARE 2.

My total number so far grew to 10. Then to 13 – including one who had already enrolled for a SHAKESPEARE. The SHAKESPEARE queues, though no longer folded back upon themselves, were still long. It dawned on me that they might include recruits destined later for my queue.

Desperately I looked round for Will Gower. No sign of the nut-brown Welsh farmer, that clever, successful, Welsh farmer... No wonder he was successful! Where was he?

I was up to 15. My number for seminar-teaching – in comfort, anyway. Fred and James would know what they were talking about. For reassurance I quoted Will's very words to myself –

'There'll be no trouble about that.'

15 and another two in line. I felt my first intimations of alarm.

I reached 20. Second intimations of alarm.

Then 25 – the supposed maximum number of seats in the class-room if the form meant anything. Too late for intimations of alarm; I needed the direct help of Heaven. Where was Will?

I had to cope with two more waiting. 'I'm terribly sorry. The class is full. I can only put you down on a waiting-list.'

'Oh, Professor Lunn, I'm an English major and I've got to take this course.' A girl with a most appealing expression – while she looked at me she enhanced the appeal by producing tears... What could I say?

The formal answer to the question turned out to be "Nothing".

When I finally ran Will to earth I learnt that it was a rule of Avalon that no student would be refused a course. They had paid, or their Mummies and Daddies had paid, for them to come over to AULC; thus entitling them to their money's worth of teaching in the subject of their choice. They had a Right to it! (It showed how justified I'd been in shying away from Students' Rights in the first place.) Education and Money! I had a lot to learn.

Unless some of the young men and women on my list changed their minds, I was in for a class of at least 25. I realised that my waiting-list had, could have, no validity whatsoever. I'd have to accept the lot. With a certain simplicity of charm the man who was English and a gent confirmed that straightly.

I might have expected to be led up the garden path by an n-b W f. But by a man who was English and a gent!

Chapter VII

Beginning at AULC

On my first morning I arrived early at my class-room, a pleasant room with windows on two sides, one window looking out over a stretch of grass – rather ragged grass yet nonetheless a beautiful sight for the middle of London. The September sun was shining brightly through the windows on to "serried ranks" of students' chairs. (Why "serried"?) Already half a dozen of the chairs were occupied by young women, chatting in a friendly fashion.

Will Gower's office had provided me with a list of names of the students who had registered for my course. There were not 15, not even 17, but 32.

However all was not lost. From the commotion of fresh arrivals three singled themselves out to approach me in order to break the news that they had inadvertently registered for two classes which were simultaneous; they apologetically wanted to drop mine. As if apologies were necessary for that! 29. I received the news with touchingly good grace. (At this juncture I didn't know that two more were going to turn up at the end of the morning and ask if they could join the class – illustrating the fact that one should never tell oneself precipitately that all is not lost!) So it was to be 31.

This morning I found myself facing 29 fresh bright faces: in fact the faces of the young women were very fresh and bright, the faces of the young men slightly less so, as they hadn't yet found it necessary to acquire the habit of shaving every morning – with the exception of one who surprisingly had a beard. Out of the whole class there were only 7 young men, confirming my idea that English Literature is a girl's subject: after all, among novelists there's a preponderance of women, while publishers' offices give the impression of being peopled by women.

To my horror I observed that one of the youths was wearing a baseball-cap; and two or three of the girls appeared to be chewing gum! That had to be stopped, for aesthetic reasons if nothing else.

So, a beginner, I faced my first class. I saluted them and then took out my class-list and said very politely:

'I should very much like to know who's here. Would you mind if I called out your names and you answered?' I was still haunted by the shadow of the 1968 Students' Revolution – even though it was more than ten years ago – according to the final terms of which no Avalon student was compelled to attend a class if he or she didn't feel like it.

'It will also help me to know your names. There are rather a lot of you, but I've promised myself to learn all your names by mid-semester.'

At this several pairs of them exchanged looks of surprise or disbelief or both.

'So I beg you, please don't take offence if I keep asking you outside the classroom to remind me of your names. It's in a good cause!'

I saw no signs of surprise and disbelief changing to rebellion. I imagined that several of them were accustomed to being members of a lecture-audience numbering 100. I went through my list. (It reminded me of my own teacher's "calling the register" when I was a child at elementary school seventy years ago.) They responded.

My list gave their universities: 70% of them were from Avalon, the other 30% from universities all over the USA, one of them from as far afield as Berkeley, California. Encouraging.

Having got to the end of the list, I asked how many were Majoring in English? 8 were.

'Good gracious!' I said; 'I'm daunted.' I explained. 'If you were present on Registration Day and heard me deliver my commercial for this course, you'll know why I'm daunted.'

For the moment I couldn't remember if I'd told them I gave up formal studies in English when I was aged 14, (thinking I should be more usefully occupied going on with more French). But I did remember I'd told them I was not "a literary guy". I said, 'You may know more about English Literature than I!'

One or two smiles of amusement among my audience. Some of them must appreciate irony, which was a blessing.

'Now it's time to begin.' I looked round at them. 'Who's made a start on *Emma*?'

No more than a third of the class. Some hadn't even yet got a copy. I told them to go up to the office as soon as the class was over and make a start on the book immediately.

Speaking of when the class was over reminded me of something else. I told them that after my class it was my intention usually to go and have a beer in the local pub, after that to go and have a swim at the local baths. I said I would invite them to join me in both. (I expected a fair number of takers for the first, few for the second.)

It really was time for me to plunge into my first experience of trying to teach English Literature. I was glad that nobody from the Department at Avalon was listening to me – it was bad enough that their Maker was. As I'd discovered that few of my audience had read more than the first pages, I decided to devote myself to the opening paragraph of *Emma*, reading it to them twice over; for the first time as an example of marvellously conveying information in an astonishingly small compass; for the second time illustrating the pulse in the prose-rhythms. I recommended them to learn the paragraph off by heart – if they could recite it it would always help them to create an impression in literary society.

When we came to the end of that, I broke it to them that I proposed to incorporate into my course some notes on the life and nature of the author of the novel they were studying.

'An Artist and his Work are indivisible, like Body and Soul – though it may make it easier to talk about them if you pretend they are separate.' I paused. 'I think you get more out of a novel if you know something about the author and the author's life.'

(I hadn't realised how inquisitive they'd be, when they ended the course with a novel by me, about my life...) By the time I had imparted a little preliminary information about Jane Austen's life I saw that they were beginning to look tired, so I ended the proceedings. I discovered I was somewhat tired myself.

When I was on my way home, I found myself harking back to the dictum of that erstwhile schoolmaster colleague – "Teaching is the most erotic of professions." Ridiculous. Yet it wasn't so much that he was a ridiculous fellow as that he was the sort of fellow who habitually overdid things. I always jibbed at being bulldozed by things overdone – taking my cue from Aldous Huxley, I called it in literature Vulgarity. And I couldn't resist jumping in to counter it. Thus could I be lured into argument, passionate argument, where I had no strong feelings on either side. Also ridiculous. I felt embarrassed, ashamed of it. In this case it was probably the shame of it which led me to go over our actual argument. Relying as usual on comparative thought I had retorted:

'Teaching must have its competitors.'

'What are they?'

The Law? Medicine? Stock-broking? I had no immediate answer. Too late I thought of Dancing, Film-Acting...

'You agree that in teaching there's an element of initiation?'

'How do you get from initiation to the erotic?'

'What does 'rites of initiation' make you think of?'

Again I did not answer. From a cursory reading of *The Golden Bough* years ago I should have had to say "Tribal circumcision of adolescent boys".

Instead of leaving the argument alone, I said;

'That's for primitive societies.'

'That's bloody patronising, my friend. Are they so primitive?'

As I thought some of them probably were, I didn't answer. I said:

'Suppose the word "initiation" does have sexual associations – when one uses the word for non-sexual activities in civilised society, those associations are refined away.'

'A tincture remains.'

'In all teaching?'

'Of course.'

I doubted if I could ever make him understand what "overdoing it" meant. Weakness of character led me to persist –

'Would you claim that an element of sexual initiation infuses my teaching of physics to Form IVC?' (Form IVC was known in the staff-room as "the sink form".) 'I assure you that it doesn't.'

Then, summoning up remembrance of their oafish pubescent faces, it struck me that sexual initiation was about the only kind of initiation I might have had any success with – certainly I was having none whatsoever with initiation into electromagnetic induction.

By the time the Underground train drew into my home-station I had reached no conclusion, other than the original conclusion that I ought to have kept out of the argument in the first place.

On the other hand, now that I had found myself at close quarters with 30 young men and women I couldn't deny that I had noticed that little something which came into the atmosphere, exciting, stimulating – provoking me to say provocative things.

When Elspeth came home she wanted to know –

'Didn't they object to your calling the register? Setting yourself above them. It's elitist!' Ironical.

'But I am above them. I am elitist.'

Elspeth looked sceptical.

'Anyway, I've got something truly elitist in store for them. I'm going to ask them to stop chewing gum in class and stop wearing their baseball caps indoors.'

'They'll say you are anti-American.'

'That's as may be. I merely think the girls look so much more attractive when their jaws are not on the go; and the boys when they're not wearing those baseball caps – even when they're wearing them back-to-front like the sainted Holden Caulfield.'

Elspeth shrugged her shoulders.

'Tomorrow,' she said, 'you've got Prince Consort."

'Yes.' I made no further comment.

The young scientists and engineers were morally deserving, but I had a feeling that I was going to find the young Americans more fun – which was unjust. (It did strike me that the young scientists and engineers were all male, while the young Americans were nearly all female.)

On my second morning at AULC, after I'd called the register – now numbering 31 – I launched into my campaign for the elimination of chewing-gum and baseball caps.

'It's a matter of aesthetics,' I said. 'The human face looks its best in repose. You may risk a Mona Lisa-like smile and still look beautiful. You simply must take care about laughing. As for mastication – that's strictly for private! Chewing makes you look ugly.' I mimicked exaggerated mastication. 'You see!' And I went on. 'If you don't see that or don't believe it, look at yourself in a mirror while you are chewing gum.' I shook my head. 'Especially if you do it with your mouth open.'

Now the next step. 'As for baseball caps' – I was addressing the young men – 'I admire them as a symbol of your athleticism, but I look with disfavour on any attempt to play a game of baseball in class. Therefore in class baseball caps are un-necessary if not otiose.'

In my audience there was an exchange of glances. I was criticising the American Way of Life, if not attempting to subvert the Constitution of the USA itself. No actual student riot broke out.

'Now we must get on with *Emma*. How many of you have read 50 pages?'

Two hands raised. Young women. I looked at one of them. 'That's good. Keep it up!' The other young woman volunteered, 'I've read it before.'

I remembered the girl at the Horse and Pony Show who said she'd already read *Middlemarch*. The presumption that they were 100% illiterate was wrong! On this showing it was only something over 90%. (At Prince Consort I'd had one engineer who had already read *Mr Polly*.) Life was not as bad as it was painted. Though perhaps nearly so...

'Who has read 20 pages?'

Several hands, male and female.

'That's good. My first question will always be, Do you find it readable?'

Modified assent.

'My next question will be Do you find it believable? As this is only your second class, it's too early to ask that. But be prepared for it!'

Too early it was. It was going to take them at least two weeks to get through *Emma*. Even if I summarised parts of the story for them. When I compiled my reading-list I'd based it on one novel per week. What a mistake!

On the other hand fewer novels on my list would mean fewer to be read in advance. Having had no experience as an academic I hadn't beforehand tumbled to the good old practice of mugging up each novel on the night before I was due to teach it. I tumbled rapidly. There were protests from Elspeth –

'Do you have to read a book every night when we get to bed?'

'Yes. I shan't be long...'

Actually I was enjoying reading the book again. But I was not long.

Chapter VIII

Going On At AULC

I tided over my first semester at AULC, then my second. Will Gower persuaded me to go on. I developed a habit of dropping in on Will from time to time at the end of my class. He was very anxious to keep me. I suspected he hadn't got anyone else to hand if I did resign. I was happy to stay. The only cloud on my happiness was the size of my class. I frequently saw fit to remind him of it.

'How many is it you've got this semester?' As if he didn't know!

'30. It's too many.'

'Your students are happy with it.' Will kept his finger on the pulse of AULC. He went on, 'If you're willing to teach for us another year, Joe' – he gave me a twinkling brown-eyed smile – 'perhaps for several more years...' He paused, as well he might. 'We'll see what can be done about it to help you.' (With the twinkle having changed to a steady look of utmost sincerity.)

I didn't believe for a moment that anything could be done, even with utmost sincerity. At Avalon University refusing students was tantamount to refusing fees. Though I was not paid according to the numbers in my class, how would Avalon regard my stipend if the number were halved? My first contract had been renewed as it stood. When education is run on business principles, what was I to expect? He went on –

'I'll make some enquiries,' inadvertently disclosing that so far he had not made any.

'OK, Will.'

I thought he might as well get on with it.

I realise I must interpolate here that my staying on at AULC had led to my withdrawing tactfully from Prince Consort.

'If you ever want to come back, Dear Boy, you'll be received with open arms, wide open arms. Don't forget that!'

I judged my friendship with George Bantock had not moulted a feather.

So, back to AULC – from Will's office I went down to the entrance where a little knot of pupils was waiting for me. I was well into my stride of recruiting a small party to accompany me after the class to the White Lion, stipulating a party of not more than five. I asked them to select themselves – it was important not to be seen to have favoured pupils. Consequently four or five were usually waiting for me, standing outside in the sunshine or sheltering inside from the rain.

On this occasion there were five, three young men and two young women. I had already noticed that when they came out of class the young women – not the young men – were inclined to light up cigarettes immediately.

I rehearsed with them their names and then we began our trail down the road.

'You don't like us to smoke, Professor?' One of the young women.

'Killing yourselves. What do your Moms say?'

'My mother smokes.'

The girl beside her gave her a look of admiration. For a moment I was quiet. We walked fairly briskly, though I was limping a little – my replaced hip-joint was beginning to give me trouble – and they moderated their pace.

The interior of the White Lion had recently been got up, rather surprisingly, to look like an Italian tavern: it was now, in current parlance, a "theme-pub". (I was expecting its name to be changed any day.) There were red-and-white checked table-cloths, candles in straw-covered Chianti bottles. The ceiling was painted over with vines fruiting copiously. A huge picture-postcard view of a sunny coastal landscape entirely covered the main unbroken wall. A french window opened on to a tiny patio, which in winter appeared to be used for the storage of crates filled with empty bottles.

My first move was to ask the barman if he would be kind enough to turn off the piped music. 'I've brought my friends here so that I can talk to them. I do want to hear what they say – I'm slightly deaf.'

The barman obliged. As the time of day was still before noon, the pub had not accumulated its lunch-time regulars who had to have music wherever they go.

My next move was to order a round of drinks. I announced that I would buy one each for everybody, including myself. 'After that if you want another drink, or something to eat, you're expected to fend for yourselves.'

One or two of them were clearly on the point of offering to pay for their first drinks. Most of them were apparently not short of money – in due course, I had observed, they would order food seemingly without concern about the price. (I suspected that some of them ate pretty frugally in their apartments.) I took their orders for drinks. The young men ordered Guinness – perhaps they were picking up local habits.

'And now what about the young women?'

The young women remained true to their native habit and asked for sweet, cocktail-y drinks, some of which I'd never heard of.

'*Not* picking up local habits,' I said with amusement. 'Nice English girls don't usually drink pints – with the very special exception of my daughters, whom I persuaded to make a start with modest half-pints of lager... But then, what father's daughters are not very special exceptions? Both very nice English girls.'

'Are they in College, Professor?'

'The elder is at the local university hospital training to be a nurse. The younger is at Edinburgh University studying to be a doctor.' I broke off to make sure the barman had taken the order. 'Let's sit down!' I paid the barman and asked the young men to carry over our drinks.

We all settled down to enjoy ourselves. I suppose I was as new to them as they were to me. Actually I took steps to look, as well as to be, new to them. Though I was going to treat them in a very free-and-easy manner, I had no intention of trying to masquerade as one of them. For my classes I resumed my dress as a former government servant of some seniority: dark suit, shirt with collar and tie, black shoes with a polish that would have done credit to an Air Force officer, a formal overcoat. An elitist should look like an elitist, especially if he is out to tease nice young Americans.

All parties round the table were shy to begin with. I looked idly at the coastal landscape, with Italian sun shining on trees and waves.

'Where is it, Professor?' Her name was Marion – she was the one who told me her mother smoked. I had a suspicion that she was trying to tease me. Her flat-mate was called Louise.

'It's an idealised view of the Italian coast somewhere. Probably meant to be Sorrento. '

'Would you call that realistic art, Professor?' She definitely was teasing me.

'If it's idealised it can't be realistic.' One of the young men, Jason. Possibly a bit of a smart arse. On the other hand he must have some intimations of what I was trying to teach them.

'The coast of Italy looks idealised in reality, wherever you go, Jason.'

'It must be beautiful.' Jason's flatmate, Robert.

'It is.'

Pause.

'We're going to Italy in the mid-semester break.'Marion and Louise.

'Then you'll get your bottoms pinched in trams and buses.'

'I got my bottom pinched in Venice – standing in line outside a theatre.'

'That shows how little respect Italian men have for the drama.'

Delighted laughter from both young women, restrained laughter from the young men.

'Anyone else going to Europe at mid-semester?'

'We are.' Jason for himself and Robert. The third young man remained silent – was he one of the few who were short of cash?

'Where are you going to?'

'Amsterdam.' Robert.

'Oh, not Amsterdam!..' I failed to restrain my feelings. 'Why on earth do all you people make for Amsterdam first of all when you get here?'

'What bugs you about Amsterdam, Professor?' Robert again.

'Amsterdam is the European centre for Pot and Sodomy. Everyone knows.'

The young women looked amused, the young men huffed. I didn't suppose Jason and Robert were going to Amsterdam for sodomy, but I did suppose they might be going there to acquire supplies of cheap hash.

'Amsterdam for Pot and Sodomy,' I repeated for the sound of it.

'You're a poet as well as a novelist, Professor Lunn.'

'Just what I thought, Marion.' I drank some of my beer.

The boys and girls drank small amounts. (Boys and girls? They were young enough to have been my grandchildren!)

'It's time for a short homily,' I remarked. They all listened. 'If you do invest in supplies of cheap hash when you go to Amsterdam, for God's sake don't try to smuggle it into this country!' I gave them what I hoped was a menacing look. 'The Customs people are on constant look-out for students. That means you. So take heed! Get caught and you're in what you would call deep shit.'

The young men didn't seem to have taken my homily in very good part: that's one of the hazards of standing *in loco parentis* – as it is with actually being a father. They'll get over it, I thought. There was a temporary hush. The young women looked amused in a slightly superior way.

'Have you been to Amsterdam, Professor Lunn?' Louise.

'My wife and I went many years ago. There are some marvellous pictures to be seen there. And some marvellous Dutch East Indies dishes to be eaten there.'

'We are going to see pictures in Italy.' Marion.

'And hopefully grab some real Italian food.' Louise.

'Do you do any painting yourselves?'

'My mother does.' Marion.

'Is she a professional painter?'

'Not really. She teaches school.'

'Is that what you're hoping to do?'

'Hopefully not.'

The young men smiled patronisingly.

'What are you hoping to be?'

'I'd like to be a university professor. If I'm good enough.'

Without her noticing I made a self-deprecatory gesture at the mention of a university professor having to be "good enough". Robert and I caught each other's eye. I picked up my beer: picking up his Guinness Robert gave me an ironic look. I was pleased.

I went cheerfully on to talking to them separately, asking them where they came from – mostly New England – inviting them to tell me about their families, which they did. Finally what they were proposing to do "hopefully" after Avalon, and what, even more hopefully, they wanted to be?

'My dad wants me to go to Law School.' Jason. How appropriate! I thought.

'I don't know yet.' Robert.

'I shouldn't worry about that,' I said to him. 'Lots of people don't know till they graduate.' (And lots don't know afterwards, I thought.)

I turned to the third young man who had scarcely uttered. 'And you?' I wondered if in this company being without money inhibited him?

'I want to be a Professor.' A speech worth waiting for. All I had ascertained so far was that he came from Detroit and his father was an engineer with General Motors – "blue collar"? I didn't ask him what he wanted to be a professor of, lest he should say English Literature.

When the party broke up it was later than I'd expected, but I went down to the Baths all the same. No volunteers to keep me company there. All the same, I didn't give up hope. Some day I'd get a volunteer.

Chapter IX

Another Family Dinner

Viola and Virginia had come home to spend a week with us together. Viola had completed her three years' training and having negotiated a whole string of examinations successfully was now qualified as a nurse. She was pleased yet rather shy about it. As she was working in London at Queen Anne's, she could drop in and see us whenever her shift-timetables allowed it. The rail-fare from Edinburgh was too much for Virginia to fork out regularly from her modest allowance: anyway she seemed devoted to Edinburgh – we were destined to learn why.

Elspeth had come home early from work in order to cook a celebratory dinner. Both girls were looking well and happy. Viola arrived first.

'Have you been reading your *Times* with care?' she asked me, smiling.

'I have. I know that Ali Baba has been arrested. At last.'

'I should have been out of work if I hadn't already resigned.'

'I wonder if he'll go to prison.'

'He's very wily. Virginia was always saying he'd do a runner.' (Virginia's idiom was recognisable.)

'Is he more wily than the Serious Fraud Office? That's the question.'

'We shall see.' She was in high spirits.

Virginia was just joining us. Putting commonsense before shyness, she said:

'I always knew you would.'

Viola gave her a look of not entirely unmixed affection.

At that Virginia dropped out of the conversation to assist Elspeth in the kitchen.

We all sat down at the dining-table and Elspeth brought in the plates of soup which we began to eat.

Virginia returned to the fray. She looked firmly at Viola.

'What are you going to do next?'

Viola said, 'I'm going to take the specialised course in child-nursing – that's what I want to do most of all. Get the full paediatric qualification.' She paused and then added in a diffident tone of voice, 'They've asked me if I want to take a university degree.'

Elspeth and I exchanged glances. Memories of examination paralysis...

I said, 'That's all to the good.'

'I think you ought to do it,' said Virginia. 'Think of all the exams you've got through already! I'm sure you'll cope with a degree course without any trouble.'

Viola did not say anything. A slow colour rose up her neck; she bent quickly over her soup-plate. Then she looked up and said:

'When people make these proposals they don't say where the funds are to come from.'

I dismissed that idea immediately. 'I don't propose to let the question of funds stand in your way,' I said, though I wasn't at all sure where the funds were going to come from.

Elspeth said to her:

'It will be all right, darling.' It meant her working for still more years with the Housing Association.

We finished our soup. Elspeth went to the kitchen to serve the next course and Viola went to help her.

I was left facing Virginia. She smiled at me as much as to say You do agree I was right in telling her to take a degree?

I melted.

'And what about you?' she said. 'How's the novel?'

'I soldier on.' It seemed to me a happy way of referring to the process of creative art.

'It's turning out much more difficult than I thought.'

'Mummy says you've given up Prince Consort.'

'That is correct.'

In the past I had warned her about saying "I told you so". People don't like what you say the first time round, when they think you are wrong. When you say "I told you so" on the second time round, implying that you were right the first time, it adds insult to injury.

Virginia restrained herself from telling me she had advised me to give up Prince Consort... or had she? Didn't she first of all favour my doing both Prince Consort and Avalon? I didn't remember and didn't try to remember.

'Are you still enjoying Avalon?'

'Very much. I like my pupils. And there's some evidence they like me – when their Moms and Dads come over to London to see them, they sometimes invite me to meet them.'

She looked at me sharply. 'I suppose they're mostly girls?'

'They are. But that's not the reason. I like the boys as well. They're all pleasingly independent, self-reliant... When they get here at the beginning of a semester – in what is for many of them a completely strange city – they all find somewhere to live during their first week with very little help from the office.'

'Are there no hostels?' A hostel was what she was living in at Edinburgh, though she had threatened, against my advice, to find cheap lodgings.

I shook my head. 'No.' I corrected myself. 'Actually Will Gower has compiled a list of widow-ladies who want to make a bit of pin-money by taking in students.'

'Company for them, I suppose.'

I hadn't thought about it before. 'I guess that being a widow is pretty lonely.'

I recalled its having crossed my mind when I married Elspeth, so much younger than me, that there would be someone to look after me in my old age. (Not an idea to be proud of, yet sensible, though who was to look after her in her old age?..)

We were interrupted by Elspeth and Viola coming back from the kitchen with the next course. I hastily got up and filled the wine-glasses. Elspeth served us and we began to eat. She looked at Virginia and me.

'What have you two been talking about?'

I shouldn't have said Elspeth was jealous of what went on between me and the girls, but she did want to know what it was.

'I was talking about my pupils at AULC.'

'Confessing your infatuation with them?' Meant in fun.

'More or less.'

'No, he isn't,' said Virginia.

'We are waiting,' Elspeth said to her, 'to hear your views on your fellow-students at Edinburgh University School of Medicine.'

'I'm enjoying them. I'm willing to talk about them ad infinitum.'

'I'm sure you are,' I said to her. 'What about a few thumb-nail sketches, if I may coin a phrase?'

'OK.' She paused and ate a small piece of beef. Then she went on. 'They're quite a good lot. Most of them are very serious-minded, very determined to "get there".'

'Scottish,' said Viola.

'All the better for that,' said I.

'Not so much fun.' Virginia.

Viola laughed at her.

Virginia began to entertain us with stories about her fellow students which lasted through that part of the meal. (Although Virginia possessed a gift for the thumb-nail sketch, and Viola wrote an excellent letter, I'm bound to record that both of them declared they were never going to write novels.)

We all noticed, couldn't help noticing, the frequent appearance, in the course of Virginia's amusing rigmarole, of a new name – Alastair Strachan, a just-qualified young doctor, former University prize-winner. "I went with Alastair to see this" or "Alastair thinks that", or "Alastair suggests the other".

Alastair was starting a career in General Practice and was suggesting that Virginia, when she qualified two years hence, should do the same.

I intervened. 'Do I take it that this chap called Alastair is your current boy-friend?'

It was unthinkable that Virginia should be installed for three years anywhere without acquiring a boy-friend. (I deplored the terms "boy-friend" and "girl-friend" for persons who had grown out of girlhood or boyhood, but at the moment there was no help for it.)

'Yes. He's a good bloke. You know?.. We've been together for a year now.'

There was a pause.

'Do you mind?' She asked Elspeth and me, 'if I bring him home?'

'Of course not.' Elspeth and I exchanged glances. Viola was busy eating – it looked as if she knew about this already.

'Thank you.' Virginia gave us a smile. 'Do you mind if we try to fix a date, after dinner – Alastair is going to be very busy – he's joining a very busy practice in Edinburgh.'

Elspeth and I exchanged glances again. 'Yes, let's!'

I had a feeling that we too, were going to think Alastair was "a good bloke".

Elspeth and I had not always approved of Virginia's choices, which she had begun to make at an early age – too early in our view, though not in hers.

'Best not to take it too seriously,' Elspeth had remarked as a general principle in those days. We both trusted in Virginia's good sense.

'I agree. But...'

Elspeth had to concede to me a little when Virginia took to bringing home during university vacations a fellow-undergraduate and taking him up to her room, where they listened to pop music and smoked pot and must have made love. They were very discreet about the latter: nobody could miss the sound of the pop music; and to cover the smell of the pot they burnt joss-sticks.

Now to anyone, and certainly to me, who in my travelling days in the USA, as a bringer home of bright young scientists and engineers, had regularly been to San Francisco in the Haight-Ashbury days of Flower Children, the smell of burning pot and joss-sticks was as immediately identifiable as the smell of frying hamburgers.

'I don't know what we do,' I said.

'Nothing,' said Elspeth.

'This one,' I said, referring to the young man then in question, 'is so wet.'

'He's quite nice.'

'Agreed, he's quite nice. I can't imagine Virginia choosing anyone who's quite nasty.' I paused. 'But as a mate he's so lacking in backbone.'

I read the expression, touched with a grin, which crossed Elspeth's face. I said:

'I suppose he isn't lacking in that.'

Elspeth smiled, shaking her head – acquiescing to what life brought in its train. (Acquiescing, anyway, to what our daughter brought in her train.)

'I don't think there's any danger of her wanting to marry him.'

'I should think he'd want to marry her,' I said. 'He'd be a fool if he didn't.'

'She's a sensible girl.'

'Like her mother...'

So the pop music, the pot and joss-sticks and the etc. went on. Till the pair of them came down from the university and it all fizzled out.

On second thoughts I've just realised that when parading my aphorism, *You can't do anything about your children*, what I meant was you can't do anything about them without making matters worse. The crucial qualification!

And for more second thoughts I must add to what I've already said about Elspeth. When I married her she was young, shy (of me, at any rate), unconfident in her capacity for living among the sort of people I frequented: she wore unbecoming spectacles and her teeth were not all they should be. Acquisition of contact lenses and the attentions of a first-rate dentist made a difference to her self-confidence – all this to such an extent that an old scientific colleague of mine had the nerve to say to me one day:

'What a beautiful woman Elspeth has turned out to be. I never realised it when you married her.'

Male response to Virginia didn't appear to pass through a cycle of that sort. After a party it never surprised me when one of the male guests came up to me and said:

'That's a very attractive daughter you've got, Joe.'

I was not displeased. The days had passed when she provoked those headlong collisions with me, especially those collisions about serious things such as judging human behaviour – what's right and what's wrong, what's good and what's bad. I remembered a spell when judging, itself, of anything, was ruled out. Those days had now passed.

We duly arranged for her to bring Alastair Strachan home for a weekend as soon as she had a break in her course and he could get away from the practice.

The dinner ended amicably. As usual Elspeth had made a delicious pudding and I brought out a bottle of Baume de Venise that I'd been bamboozled into buying by the fashionable Sunday newspapers.

I looked back on the evening with a mixture of hope and sadness. I was hopeful about the future of Virginia in medicine and in marriage. I was moved to sadness when contemplating Viola's future, devoting her life to healing other people's children when she was unable to have any of her own: the inexorableness of the genes became hateful to me. I warned myself that I wasn't through with them, either.

Chapter X

About Marriage

Alastair Strachan had a great success with us.

It was the following New Year when Virginia brought him home to meet us. He was tall and well set-up, had dark curly hair with reddish glints, and was generally good-looking – firm jaw and fine legs, perfect materials for a Scottish beard and the kilt. It was not long before Elspeth and I were convinced they would marry.

Virginia was a clever girl and we thought, (perhaps I ought to say in view of some of her earlier choices), that she should never marry a man who was not as clever as she was. She had a strong character, as I have already implied – when they were at school she had constantly competed with Viola, and out-shone her, Viola diffidently and un-selfconfidently withdrawing from the competition. Nowadays they were leading lives apart, and it had dawned on Elspeth and me that Viola had "come on" – to the extent of the disparity between her and Virginia no longer being visible.

Now that Alastair appeared on the scene we saw that he too had a strong character and was as clever as Virginia, if not more so. (I know one's not supposed to talk about whether one's children are clever – it's "elitist". From which one is tempted to infer that it's democratic for them to be stupid.) Anyway, Alastair's medical career so far had been most impressive. Prizes and suchlike, which I've already noted. Just recently he had quit the medical practice to go in for Hospital work, and he thought he had a good chance of being put in charge of the Casualty Ward – entirely suited to the boundless energy and practical ingenuity which he had already proved. It was at a time when the public row about the long hours worked by young hospital doctors was just beginning – 83 hours a week, said some of the more knowing newspapers. Alastair was confident of surviving it, was fascinated by it.

What Alastair lacked – not uncommonly among doctors, I was told – was "culture", especially in its literary guise. Alastair was unconcerned, or even, so far as he knew about it, un-infected with any awareness of being at a disadvantage. A medical training does not exactly call for specialisation in the works of Conrad, Lawrence, Joyce and Woolf: if it actually had, there would have been precious little time in a medical training for the call to be answered. (Lucky for us, as we depend for our lives on the thoroughness of medical training!) Alastair had given himself up entirely to acquiring the necessary knowledge and necessary techniques for his chosen career – especially useful in a Casualty Ward – and for acting upon them, for answering the calls on his concentrated flow of interest and his highly practical bent, which led some of our academic literary friends, later on, to call him the Boy Scout. (Academic literary friends can be snotty!)

'You don't suppose,' I said to Elspeth one evening after they'd left, 'that Alastair and Virginia have married each other already without telling us.'

She gave me a wry smile. The truth of the matter was that she and I had married each other without telling our parents, (chiefly because her father was a clergyman and would have wanted to marry us in a church-service).

'I don't think so,' she said. 'Have you asked Viola? She might know.'

'Time will tell.'

(In fact they hadn't already married and it took quite a long while for time to tell us. They waited until Virginia qualified. In the autumn of that year they married unrebelliously in a Registry Office near where we lived. Alastair's parents came down from Scotland – his father was also a doctor, also tall and good-looking, active, able no doubt, but somewhat deficient in sense of humour, I thought. Alastair's mother was a pretty middle-aged woman, at every moment The Doctor's Wife.

Elspeth and I attended the ceremony. Viola was the bride's attendant. Alastair's father brought some flowers to Elspeth.

A happy day!)

A few days after Alistair's visit I got a message from Will Gower asking me to go and see him. I went after my class.

'I'm still thinking over your problem, Joe. How would you feel about dividing your class into two. We do it regularly for Julie Maxwell-Jones. She has a class of 40 or more.'

'Yes, I know,' I said. 'But she takes them to galleries and theatres all over the place.'

'You take yours to the pub.'

'For an hour or so after the class, when I'm wanting a pint of beer myself. Much as I love them, Will, an hour or so of them is enough for me.'

Will Gower was not a man to be put off easily.

'Think it over, Joe. In the meantime, if I have your permission, I'll put the idea up to Avalon.'

Silence.

'Have I your permission?'

What could I say but Yes?

In the Underground I thought it over. The idea of being paid twice my stipend for teaching the same thing twice over had its charms. The consequent idea of being robbed of twice as much of my writing-time had its counter-charms, but I decided to let Will get on with it.

When I got home I discussed the proposal with Elspeth.

'It means you'll be out even more.'

'Yes...'

We were sitting side by side on the sofa, holding each other's hand – when we were not disengaging it to lift our pre-dinner drinks glass to our lips. The room was quiet.

We looked at each other. I sighed. She smiled.

As I have already remarked, it was usual for me to think of my marriage to Elspeth – I'd heard it referred to thus among our friends – as a "closed marriage". In our sort of society, in literary society, anyway, people spoke of two kinds of marriage, "open" and "closed". In our sort of marriage you stuck more or less permanently to your spouse; in an "open" marriage you slept around, both partners slept around, with anybody and everybody. As I had married when I was forty and she was twenty-five, we had now been living together successfully as one for nearly forty years. As one? We were two different human beings with different personalities. Yet we had come to a certain one-ness of existence. Neither of us would have claimed that it was on a par with Cathy Earnshaw's "I *am* Heathcliff." Nevertheless there was a constant resonance in emotion and even in thought, sometimes distant, sometimes passionate. Each of us thought of the other many times a day – sometimes telephoned each other during the day. Not in an obsessive fashion; but just for the comforting, often merely casual, sense of being in touch.

We loved being in touch in the physical sense; in feeling the pleasure of passing manifestations, we were aware that the source which energised them was the physical experience of happy marital union. I couldn't imagine marriage without that. Nor could I imagine marriage without children. We had our two girls whom we adored with a steady, stable love. I was wont to say that for my own part I would have loved to go on having children indefinitely. (Elspeth said that for her part she wouldn't!) Having children, I thought, can make the experience of two satisfactorily married people complete, can make them – why not risk saying it? – One.

We had several friends who were satisfactorily married pairs, (not to mention quite a few who weren't). One day one of the former pairs, the wife, was speculating on what there was in common between us pairs – apart from comparable age and social status, she fixed on the particular criteria which defined our marriages as "closed". Elspeth and I agreed there was much truth in it. We were not such dolts as to doubt that there was a lot of fun to be had through the freemasonry of the "open" bed, but for us... Well, we knew where we stood – in a position jointly to shrug off the minor distractions of life, each of us in a position along with another human being to take on with fortitude the turns of Fate. At the time about which I'm making these ex cathedra statements we were all, (apart from me,) in early-to-middle middle-age: for us ageing was still a piling up of tiny permanent disadvantages, of minor irretrievable losses. Any grave blows of Fate were still to come... How do people survive any of them, all of them?.. God knows. It seems that the pulses just continue to beat.

It happened that I was due to learn how the pulses continue to beat.

When I got home one evening a few months later, Elspeth confided to me that she was worried.

I waited.

'I've got a slight swelling,' she said, touching her abdomen.

'How long have you had that?' I was suspicious. 'Why didn't you tell me before?' I was ashamed of not having noticed it.

'I didn't want to disturb you when you were getting on with your book.'

'You should not have done that.'

'I've made an appointment to see Edward.'

Edward was her gynaecologist whom she saw regularly – a very distinguished gynaecologist whom she knew from his family being friends of her own family. Elspeth had known Edward since they were both young.

I was temporarily satisfied, but only temporarily. The shadow prevented my giving her an amusing account I'd planned of the afternoon's scene in the Italianate White Lion.

The shadow remained with us until the appointment with Edward came off. (As Elspeth was a favoured patient, she was only held up for a few days.) The appointment was during the afternoon when I was at home, waiting...

She telephoned from the Underground station –

'Edward says he can't find anything wrong.'

'That's odd.'

She sensed that I was not satisfied.

'There's nothing wrong in his province,' she said.

I immediately thought of other specialists' provinces.

'Are you satisfied?' I asked as gently as I could.

She was thoughtful. 'I have to be.' I could imagine her smiling faintly, an ironical smile as she said:

'Actually the swelling more or less went down when I made the appointment. Like toothache disappearing when one's got an appointment with the dentist.'

I was unable to smile with her. But I managed to say: 'That's a relief.'

There was a long pause. We listened to each other's breathing. The thoughts that passed to and fro between us were so complex that I couldn't even analyse them on my own side.

I murmured, 'Then I suppose we can relax.'

'I suppose so...'

Chapter XI

A Swimmer At Last

It was not until the following Spring semester that I found a regular swimming-companion among my pupils – or rather, one of my pupils regularly found me.

As usual I had opened my first class of the semester with an apology for always being slightly hoarse and slightly deaf. 'It means that you can't tell what I'm saying and I can't hear what you're saying. It's the result of constantly going to the swimming-baths – and I don't intend to stop.' At that I opened my stock invitation to any of those present to accompany me. (I had expected this invitation – not the one to join me at the pub – to have fallen on stony ground as usual.)

First I went up to Will Gower, who said he had news for me. He was standing behind his desk, resting his particular rotundity on the edge of it, when I went in. His secretary outside told me he was expecting a visitor at any moment. He was looking brown and bright and intelligent, not to say pleased-with-himself.

'I got a reply from Avalon, Joe. They're willing to split your class into two.'

'That's interesting, Will.' I paused and then asked artlessly, 'I presume they'll double my stipend.'

Instantly there was a flicker of not-so-pleased-with-himself. 'I put that to them but they haven't yet replied. It will have to go before one of their committees. You know?'

I have to say that there was in me a flicker of not-believing-a-word-of-it. Perhaps I was unjust. I said:

'Of course. It means money.' He could take that as he pleased.

He was clearly undecided on how to take it. He hesitated. I said in a kinder tone:

'We'll wait and see what they say.'

'OK.' He gave me a slightly suspicious glance.

He was right. I actually was very suspicious. Anything to do with Avalon University and money couldn't help but make me suspicious.

'I hope to let you know very soon, Joe.'

His telephone rang, his secretary telling him his visitor had arrived.

I made my exit promptly.

When I got to the bottom of the stairs there was a young man, a member of my class, waiting to speak to me.

'Professor Lunn.' He smiled. 'Where do you swim?'

I told him. 'Are you interested?'

'I'm on the Avalon swim-team.'

'I usually swim after my class. I always ask if anyone would like to join me.'

'Sure.' The young man was clearly interested, if not intrigued. A professor who united the eternal virtues of swimmer and novelist?

'I'm afraid I'm not sure of your name yet.'

'Paul.'

'Paul what?' The first response of all my pupils was to answer as if they had only a Christian name.

'Oh... Paul Dugan.'

I grinned at him. 'You can give me some coaching, Paul. My style is still far from perfect.'

The young man didn't say, as I would have expected his English peer to say, "So is mine". He said:

'What do you swim?'

'Front crawl. What do you?'

'Butterfly.'

'A master!'

A smile of modesty. 'My girl-friend swims front crawl. She's on the university swim-team as well. We coach when we're back at Avalon – it brings in a few bucks.'

'Good for you! Is she here, too?'

90

'Yes. We share an apartment. You know?..'

I did know what he was telling me. I said:

'What is her name?'

'Liz.'

'Liz what?'

This time he laughed. 'Liz Jennings. She's in your class, too, Professor.'

'That's why her name is slightly familiar to me.' Pause. 'Perhaps you would both join me. She can polish up my front crawl and you can inaugurate my butterfly.'

'Sounds great.' Pause. He looked me up and down. 'Butterfly's pretty strenuous, Professor.' A warning that I found touching.

'I can see what you mean, Paul.'

We exchanged glances – mine was still amused, his was embarrassed. I guessed he was wondering whether he ought to have shown at the start that he was aware of our great difference in age. But he was not troubled all the same, that was clear.

'There's no secret about how old I am, Paul.' I paused an instant. 'Anybody can look it up in *Who's Who*.'

'Right.' I couldn't believe he was conversant with *Who's Who*, but he clearly meant to give the impression that he was.

'Old enough to be your grandfather,' I said. 'When we get into the bath you'll find me inconceivably slow.'

'That's OK, Professor.' He couldn't help laughing. Then suddenly with a spontaneous movement he held out his hand to shake mine.

A crowd of pupils were surging round us. We arranged to meet after my next class, both of us equipped with swimming-kit. I led off a small party to the pub.

After the next class Paul Dugan was waiting outside, accompanied by a young woman, his co-vivant, fellow-swimmer, Liz Jennings – a nice-looking, friendly girl, slightly shy – unlike her lover, to whom shyness, it turned out, happened to be unknown. Paul and I changed together and met Liz in the pool. The two members of the Avalon swim-team had the typically good-looking bodies of crack swimmers, tall, well-proportioned with square shoulders and narrow waists, elegantly muscled, smooth.

Paul said to the girl, 'Whaddya say, Liz? The professor doesn't look so old as we thought.'

Liz looked more shy than ever, Paul less so – in fact Paul was quite pleased with his comment. He was expanding his chest while I was pulling in my diaphragm. Liz's chest was a source of attraction to both of us: her body was substantial yet beautifully streamlined.

'Shall we swim?' she said.

She and I dived in and swam up and down: Paul stood on the side assessing my performance.

'Yeah, you roll a little, Professor. And your head's too low.'

'Let me watch,' said Liz.

I repeated my performance.

'OK!' Liz jumped in beside me and the lesson began. Meanwhile Paul did a couple of lengths very dramatic butterfly.

'He can't keep it up for long.' Liz said surreptitiously.

'I can't do it at all,' said I.

'You don't need to.' She smiled in a comfortable way and I was immediately delighted with her as a teacher. I was stirred to swim a few more lengths: meanwhile Paul did another couple of lengths butterfly.

When it was time for us all to leave it transpired that my lessons could not be regular as Liz followed the Realistic Novel class with Psychology immediately – she had managed to come today by cutting the other class.

'I doubt if it would justify your missing a Psychology class in order to give me a swimming class,' I said.

Liz smiled with seemingly amused acquiescence. I wondered if she always smiled with seemingly amused acquiescence to Paul's *démarches*.

'I have to leave you now,' she said. 'Take it easy, Professor Lunn.'

'You do the same, Liz!'

She walked away with a graceful, fluid gait, her long straight silky hair flowing over her shoulders as in a television advertisement for shampoo.

'OK, Professor,' said Paul. 'Let's shower and get dressed!'

We went into the changing-room, showered, dried and got dressed, talking the while; packed our kit, collected our valuables from the office, and paused on the pavement outside.

I recognised my cue. 'What about dropping in at a pub for a drink, Paul?'

'Sure. I was hoping you'd say that.'

'Then I'm glad I said it. Let's go!'

We went back to the White Lion, glowing with thirst after our exertions.

'What's it to be, Paul?'

'A Guinness, OK, Professor?'

'Sure.' I was mimicking him. 'I shall have one myself.'

'Since I've been in Britain I've gotten a taste for it. It's all I drink now.' He was laughing. 'Must be the Irish blood in me.'

'Have you actually got Irish blood in you, Paul?'

'When I'm being a pain in the neck to my Mom, she says I have. She's thinking of my Dad.'

'A pint, Paul?'

'Sure.' He was mimicking himself. 'Thanks.'

I produced the money and Paul collected the pints.

We drank a little. I was thinking over whether he looked Irish. He had characteristics which I was inclined to regard as typically Irish – a pale, strong-featured face, (easy to imagine pinched by famine,) very light grey eyes with very dark eyebrows and eyelashes. Altogether comely.

'What do you think of Avalon London campus, Professor?'

I gave a tactful answer. 'What is your opinion, Paul?'

'It's OK. You give us too many novels to read.'

I had laid myself open to that. I retaliated. 'You can't do a course on novels without reading any – at least I don't believe you can, though the matter may be treated differently elsewhere.'

'Like the US?'

'I didn't say that, Paul.'

The conversation lapsed while we drank a little. Then I asked him about himself. He came from Boston, where his father was an attorney: and he was majoring in History. He hadn't decided yet what he wanted to do in life.

'My Dad wants me to go to Law School.'

Many Dads do, I thought.

He was saying he thought he'd find the Law boring, though his father assured him he wouldn't.

'I wouldn't trade places with him, Professor.'

'You haven't got a place to trade, yet.'

'You know what I mean.'

'It'll bring you a certain living. You'll be able to marry, buy a house, raise a family.'

'Oh, shit, Professor!'

I laughed at him.

Paul said:

'Liz wants me to marry her. I don't want to.'

I gave a faint shrug of my shoulders.

'I'm not in a position myself, to set you an example,' I said. 'I didn't marry till I was forty.'

'Wow!' His light grey eyes opened to a maximum, and he laughed at me.

'That sure is an example!'

'Maybe, Paul. But I doubt if you should enthuse over it to your Mom and Dad.'

He looked at me sardonically. 'Yeah. I guess you're right.'

We were silent for a little while. Time was passing.

'Do you go to the pool after every class, Professor?' It was obvious, what he had in mind.

'Not after every class – but when I am going, I'll tell you in advance. If that will suit you.'

'That's great!'

'I think today was a success,' I said. 'We will do it again.'

'My first swim since I came to London. Really great!.. Thanks a lot, Professor. Let's do it again!'

I went home to Elspeth in high spirits – which were dowsed... Something was the matter.

'What?..'

'The swelling has come up again.'

We looked at each other in silence.

Then I said, 'What are you going to do about it?' I paused. 'Are you going back to Edward?'

She shook her head.

'Then what?..'

'I can't go back to him.'

'Why not?'

'It would look as if I'm not satisfied with him.'

'We're not.'

'You don't understand...'

She said nothing for a moment.

'Doctors must get used to this sort of thing,' I said.

'In Edward's case it's different.'

I realised what she was getting at. She said:

'I should feel I'm imposing on him. Taking advantage of his good nature...'

I didn't say That's exactly what you ought to do. It would upset her too much. Her innate diffidence made her in many respects a delightful, affectionate woman. She was thinking of Edward, at the peak of his profession, charging his grand patients enormous sums for a consultation: he treated Elspeth, as a childhood friend, free of charge.

'I don't see that that matters,' I said. 'You've got to get the best possible advice.'

She shook her head and said nothing.

I didn't think there was anything to be done. It was a pity, which I'd reflected on before now, that the diffidence which went towards making her so affectionate and loveable also went towards making her, on occasions such as this, darned obstinate.

In the past I had challenged her diffidence – and had now met my match.

We thought for a long time.

'What courses are open to you?' I asked.

'I shall have to make a start with our GP.'

We had no particular criticism to make of his professional competence, but we did not like him. He was a tubby red-faced middle-aged man who frequently wore a bad-tempered expression.

I acquiesced to her making a start with him.

Elspeth exerted herself with the GP's secretary and got an appointment rapidly. At least it was a help not to have to wait long.

I was at home waiting for her when she returned from the surgery.

I could see that things had gone ill.

Neither of us knew that the man was on the verge of a colossal heart attack, which might to some extent – only to some extent – account for his behaviour.

'Well,' I said. 'What did he say?'

'He told me it's wind.'

I was too taken aback to say anything.

'While he was stripping off his surgical gloves he said, "What you need, Mrs Lunn, is a bloody good fart."'

My speech returned in such black outrage that I won't print what I said.

Some minutes later, when we had calmed down a little, I said quietly – we were sitting side-by-side on the sofa:

'What are we going to do?'

Elspeth managed to reply, though her voice was tremulous.

'Nothing for the time being, my darling.' She paused. 'After all, neither Edward nor the GP found anything wrong.' She repeated, 'Nothing for the time being, my darling. The swelling will probably go down again.'

At that I withdrew from active conversation. Her earlier diffidence had been replaced, I felt, by a sort of evasiveness, almost a desire not to know the truth. It is very difficult to force someone you love to take the sort of steps I had in mind – to go to a doctor and ask directly, "Is it cancer?" – though a suspicion of it, a sort of pre-cognition of it, has passed unspoken to and fro between you.

Chapter XII

Leading Two Lives

The abdominal swelling did not go down. But during the next week a sudden change of fortune favoured Elspeth – but not the GP. He had his heart attack and disappeared from the scene for several months. His place was taken by a locum, an energetic serious-minded young woman whom Elspeth went to see immediately – they hit it off at once.

'She said,' Elspeth reported, 'that I must see a surgeon before the end of this week. She made an appointment for me while I was there.'

'That sounds more like it,' I said, my spirits rising a little at the thought of something definite being done – at the same time falling back much further at the thought of the situation most likely being not only urgent but dangerous.

Our feelings went through a spell of stasis while Elspeth was going to see the surgeon; then at his request being X-rayed; and then being referred back to him for diagnosis.

'He thinks it's an ovarian cyst,' Elspeth told me with what I thought was admirable sang-froid. (There are not many people who've heard of an ovarian cyst who haven't heard of ovarian cancer.)

'It's quite common, and it's treated by surgery,' she went on.

'When's the surgery likely to be?'

'He wants it to be as soon as possible.'

'Oh God!..'

I kissed her fondly. 'It's a ghastly blow, but at least something's settled.'

'Yes.' She rested her head against my shoulder.

There was a long pause.

'We must let the girls know,' I said.

'I saw Viola in the hospital – she was on duty. And we'll ring Virginia tonight.'

Viola had got her paediatric qualification and was working towards a surgical qualification.

'I'll ring her.'

'No, it's better if I do.'

'I was trying to save you.'

She smiled at me. The atmosphere had lightened. We decided not to miss our modest pre-dinner drinks. Life has to go on, even if it doesn't necessarily deserve to.

After dinner I telephoned Virginia in Edinburgh and told her the whole story. Like me she was impressed by the expeditiousness of it all, when hospitals up and down the country had enormous lists of NHS patients awaiting surgery; it argued for Queen Anne's being one of the more fortunate – or for Elspeth's complaint being one of the more desperately urgent.

There was a pause.

'I feel such a long way off,' Virginia said.

I thought she was a long way off if anything serious were going to happen. I could tell that that was what she was thinking. However she injected a tone of brightness into her voice. 'Give Mummy my love, and tell her I'll come down to see her as soon as I can.'

'Poor Virginia,' Elspeth said as she put the receiver back for me.

After that we went to bed straight away – I had some reading to do.

The following morning, with my domestic affairs a bit more settled for the time being at least, I gave more attention to AULC; for instance by going through the contents of my pigeon-hole for correspondence. There was a note from Will Gower, wanting me to go and see him –

'I'm glad to see you, Joe – you got my note?' He stood up, rosy and rotund as usual.

'What did you want to see me about, Will?'

He sat down and flustered among a pile of papers on the corner of his desk. Finally he fished out the document he was looking for. (I'd have a bet he knew exactly what was on it without finding it.)

'Reply at last from Avalon about our proposal to split your class in two. They approve, and they give their consent.'

'Good.'

He now gave me an apple-cheeked smile, an encouraging apple-cheeked smile; rather like the smile, I thought, of a man who's out to sell you a herd of sheep in a cattle-market up in Brecon.

(Let me interpolate: I liked him and we were beginning to be friends – I regretted my first mischievous designation of n-b W f. We lunched together now and then in an unfrequented pub, where he brought me up to date with all the internal gossip of AULC.) He held the letter in his hand –

'Avalon thinks it will be advantageous for your class to be split in two.'

I bowed my head.

'Advantageous for the class, advantageous for the Department.'

'Very nice, too. And what about me?' I spoke on a louder note. 'Advantageous for me as well?' I went on. 'What else do they say? Are they going to pay me a double fee?'

'Not exactly.' His glance flickered.

'What do you mean by "not exactly"? I can't imagine anything more exact than a factor of two.' I looked him in the eye. 'Can you?'

'Actually they argue that the research and preparation of the lectures is already done. For repetition of the classroom-teaching they propose to pay you in addition half your original fee.'

I blinked. Then I exploded.

'Well, fuck me!'

The energy and coarseness of my response clearly surprised Will – it surprised me too.

'The sods!' I did not subside readily. I ranted on –

'What a nerve! What impertinence! What the hell do they know about it? Bloody insolence.'

'I know, Joe. I know... Their case is that with the preparation already completed, a second performance of the lesson will be merely repetition.' It was meant to be a pacifying speech. It was not.

'Merely a repetition! That's the one thing it won't be, I can tell you here and now. They must think I have a lot of notes that I read out every time – I suppose that's what some of them do, lazy bastards...' I took a breath. 'I do have some notes,' (not saying how scanty they were,) 'but I scarcely use them. I give my lectures extempore.' Spoken with moral fervour. I went on. 'Not like some of my colleagues, who nurture their notes with the intention of publishing them as a text-book – they seem to regard their classes as a captive public of potential purchasers.' I gave him another hard look. 'The only books I publish are novels. I have my pride, Will...'

'I appreciate that.'

'I make my lectures up – if you call them lectures – as I go along. No two of my lectures are the same. Remembering what to say, inventing fresh quips to keep them on their toes – it's exhilarating while one's doing it. But it leaves one exhausted, really exhausted, if one's pulling it off successfully.'

I was thinking that I gave my lectures off the top of my head, which is the best place for lectures to come from, since it gives them freshness, spontaneity – and more importantly enables one to incorporate any incidental ideas that occur to one on the spur of the moment; such as the truth of Darwinism, or the instability of Capitalism, or the fundamental flaw in Freudianism... I was able to touch on all or any of these in a twelve-week semester. My aim was to stir my pupils up, not to turn them into little know-alls. I enjoyed it, and there was plenty of evidence that they enjoyed it.

I summed up.

'My case is this, Will – the important things to me about giving a second run of my lectures are , one, the slice of my writing-time it will rob me of, and two, the creative energy my sort of lectures takes out of me. That's what Avalon have got to pay me for, to recompense me for!'

Will paused in drinking his coffee. 'I'll make that case to them, Joe. It's a good case.'

I drank some coffee myself. I didn't believe my case would be accepted by the accountants of Avalon, and I hadn't the slightest intention of accepting their present offer. A typical accountant's ploy! At Avalon they were probably all accountants, from the Chancellor downwards. A business consideration!

'What about having lunch today, Joe?'

I knew that in the circumstances I ought to say Yes. I had to say:

'Sorry, Will. I'm already committed to the pub with five of my pupils and then a trip to the baths with one of them.'

'Paul Dugan?'

'That's correct.' As if Will Gower could ever be incorrect about such a thing! (I didn't deign to ask him how he knew.)

'OK.'

We were preparing to part. We finished our coffee.

'I wish I had better news for you, Joe.'

'That's all right, Will.'

I hoisted my shoulder-bag onto my shoulder.

'How is Elspeth?' He knew she was unwell.

I smiled wryly. 'I wish I had better news for you, Will.'

'I'm sorry. What's the diagnosis now?'

'An ovarian cyst.'

His glance flickered. 'That can be treated.'

'By excision, I'm told.'

'When is the operation to be?'

'Quite soon.' I didn't tell him urgently.

He held out his hand.

'Give her my best wishes... You already have mine.'

We shook hands and I went down to begin the next part of my routine.

It's no use pretending I didn't enjoy having at last someone to go to the baths regularly with me. From the beginning of my teaching at AULC I had been attracted by the spontaneity of most of my pupils – spontaneity it seemed to me in the absence of my experiencing for comparison the behaviour of other young people, apart from my daughters' and that of their friends, in particular Virginia's. (I was going to see less of Virginia's friends now she was married to Alastair Strachan.)

It was difficult to imagine a young man more spontaneous than Paul Dugan. If anything interested him he remarked on it; if he wanted to know anything he asked.

During a rest period between my lessons on the defects of my crawl we were standing up to our waists in the water, chatting. He suddenly looked into my face with an inquiring friendly expression and said:

'Which of those teeth are yours, Professor?'

'The bottom ones,' I answered, before the indelicacy of the question struck me. When it did strike me, it was too late – and, come to that, who cared?

That interchange was typical of future conversational exchanges in which indelicacy was spontaneously relegated in favour of intrinsic interest – relegated on both sides apparently without the slightest difficulty, it seemed.

The trips to the baths became regular, as did the trips to the pub afterwards. As long as he kept an eye on me I contrived to hold my head a little higher in the water and to roll a little less. I was not sure I could keep it up when I was left to myself . It amused me to notice that when he were left to himself, he rarely swam more than a couple of lengths of his dramatic butterfly: I discovered it was the crawl he swam for Avalon.

On our visits to the pub afterwards it was clear that he could handle two pints of Guinness without a tremor – I couldn't say the same for myself . It would not have surprised me if he could be found to be able to handle a third pint, but discretion held me back from offering it.

On the second pint our conversations tended – by external criteria, at least – to become increasingly indelicate. I discovered that it didn't inhibit me any more than it inhibited him. He liked to talk about what he did and to ask me what I did. Well, well... He had a description of an early exploit that was positively poetic. (He was shocked to hear that I hadn't made a start till I was almost twenty, and looked as if he were going to pass a very unfavourable moral judgement upon me as a consequence.) Aged fifteen, he was being enthusiastically welcomed for the first time into a girl he was in love with, while they were lying on the floor of an open sailing-boat, rocking gently in the sunshine on some American lake or other. It sounded beautiful. At the risk of breaking the spell, I said:

'What did you do about contraception, Paul?'

'Nothing. We were lucky.' He looked at me over the top of his glass of Guinness. 'I don't trust to luck now. Liz doesn't.'

I thought that was good news.

Thinking of Liz stirred him to further recollections.

'We like it standing up,' he declared.

'Isn't that rather awkward?'

'She folds her legs round the back of my waist.'

'And you support her?' I thought Liz, streamlined or not, looked quite heavy. 'You must be strong.'

'It's good.'

I realised that with fifty years of experience under my belt – literally there – I was nevertheless short of things to declare in return.

Paul said thoughtfully: 'I haven't met your wife.' I wondered if he was speculating about her weight – and should not have been surprised if he'd asked.

'I think it's rather unlikely you'll meet her,' I said. 'For some little time at least. She's ill – what you call sick.'

'What's the matter?'

'That's as yet undecided.' I looked at him. 'I'm rather afraid it's going to be serious.'

'Gee, that's bad news. I'm sorry, Professor.' He paused sympathetically.

'That's all right, Paul.' I raised a smile. 'What about another Guinness?

'I got a class.'

'Then I'm happy to see you mean to go to it.'

We drank up.

'Do you want any help in marking the mid-semester quiz, Professor?'

'That's an offer, Paul. I'll think it over.'

'Let me know after the next class?'

'Good idea.'

He hastened away from the pub to his class, and when he had gone I thought the offer over. I could see no harm in it.

The quiz was a list of a hundred or more one-line questions each calling for an answer of not more than a word or two: marking them was purely mechanical if the marking-person were supplied with a list of answers. Paul Dugan had worked hard on the set-books – possibly to impress me – and he was bright in the first place. I decided to accept his offer.

For somewhere to do the marking I settled on the flat one day after class – Elspeth would be at the hospital for tests. The kitchen would be the most suitable room – where we could spread out the papers on the extended plastic working-top. I abstracted Paul's and Liz's papers to mark myself, and shared the rest with him.

We sat down to a meal first of all – bread and cheese and fruit and a couple of the recently-introduced cans of draught Guinness. Paul's glance moved round the room. I waited for some uninhibited comment.

It came –

'You keep your kitchen very clean, Professor.'

'That's the way I keep my person.'

He took the reference on the spot – to a subject on which we'd already had arguments that allied utmost indelicacy on both our parts with the maximum passion on his: the relative advantages of being circumcised and uncircumcised, the former for him, the latter for me. He was incapable of listening to any case other than the one which I judged to have been instilled by his mother.

You may wonder how on earth I had come to be discussing this subject with a young man fifty years younger than myself. Every time it happened I wondered too. But there it was. I allowed myself to be lured into it, the way I allowed myself to be lured into that argument with my fellow-schoolmaster about teaching being an erotic profession – when I wasn't deeply engaged by the argument on either side. Commonsense was eroded by the excitement of disputation. Yet I'm not a particularly disputatious man. Anyway, in this case Paul Dugan argued with the maximum passion from the start; and regularly he induced it in me, God knows why. I began to see the Foreskin as Paul Dugan's King Charles's Head.

I had endeavoured to meet his case with "You don't know what you're missing!"

'Infection!' Delivered like set-point if not match-point.

So it went on. I concluded that American Moms must be obsessed with keeping their boys clean. (Actually I have read somewhere that Dr Freud imputes another motive for their having their boys mutilated.) Mutilated they are on the widest scale in the USA, even granted the high percentage of Jewish people in that country – in New York phenomenally high. One evening I had sat on the edge of a swimming-bath in New York – there being a notice saying "For reasons of Hygiene the Wearing of Swimming Trunks is Forbidden" – conducting a count. In a fifteen minute survey I and one other man were the only men not mutilated, out of a total of twenty-odd. Astonishing.

Paul Dugan was adamant. I became as adamant as him. Ridiculous! One day when the showers at the baths were being remodelled, with the result that we had to make do, in turn. with a shallow rectangular trough to stand in and a dribbling rose overhead. I took first turn. Paul stood waiting, watching me soap myself, and saying with devastating self-righteousness when I reached the critical point –

'That way you get cancer.'

'I don't know how you can say that when you can see perfectly well that after seventy years and more I still haven't got cancer.'

He shook his head in what could have been a gesture of disbelief, if disbelief in the circumstances weren't ruled out by evidence.

I rinsed off the soap, stepped out of the trough, and said:

'Your turn! You have nothing further to fear – what you've lost you've lost already.'

I was being no less ridiculous than him, and considerably more ill-advised by drawing a parallel with my keeping my kitchen clean.

'You can renovate your kitchen, Professor, but you can't renovate your body.'

'That's what I call implacable, Paul.'

He let it go.

We got on with our lunch and began to think about marking quiz-papers.

It was late afternoon when the marking and totting up of scores was over. (Both Paul and Liz had got some of the highest marks.)

'That's a boring job over,' I said as we produced the final list. 'You've done a marvellous job, Paul – and saved me a very tiresome one. I'm most grateful to you.'

'My pleasure.'

I grinned at him. 'Another can of Guinness?'

He grinned back.

'You were hoping I'd say that?' I said.

'Well, yeah...'

Chapter XIII

"He thinks I want him to marry me, but I don't!"

Will Gower did not succeed in getting Avalon to pay me double the stipend – he went on trying "in case you change your mind."

I said. 'Not a hope, Will. Four classes a week is too much for me, even for ready money.'

He smiled ruefully, 'And?..'

'I think we cut out the idea.'

'I'm sorry, Joe.' He glanced through the window. 'So that's that.'

'But that isn't all, Will. I've come to see you about something else.'

'We'd better have some coffee.' Not only was he proud of his machine for its brew; he often relied on it for an ameliorating effect in a difficult situation.

'That's good.' I was very devoted to his coffee, and had no objection to a certain amount of amelioration.

When we'd got the coffee, I said:

'It's another choice for you, Will. I want to cut down my list of set-books again.' I paused. 'The little darlings simply can't keep up with the reading.'

'Again?'

'Yes, again. They are not used to protracted reading. They've been brought up on Visual Aids – that means they're shown a page of the book projected on a screen and told what the page is saying.'

Will laughed. 'Joe!'

'I admit that's a bit of an exaggeration. But...'

'The reading-list is your choice. I shouldn't have thought there were any objection to your cutting it down. Even to cutting it down again. What does the number stand at now?'

'I began with 12 – one for each week of the semester. Fatal miscalculation. Made through ignorance or inexperience... you can choose which. Then I reduced it to 10; and now we're down to 8. I'm proposing to cut it down to 6 – final reduction! It's the only hope, but I think it will work out all right. The news of the day is that they want me to cut out Dickens. Very embarrassing.'

'Dickens. Not *Middlemarch*?'

'Surprisingly not. They like *Middlemarch* in spite of its length. It has even been known for some of them, who haven't managed to get through to the end of it here, to take it back with them to the USA to finish it there. I must say I find that encouraging!'

I think he realised I must have taken a vote on it. He said:

'So it's Dickens they want to eliminate...'

'I suppose I gave them an excuse. They latched on to the fact that I don't consider Dickens to be a "realistic novelist". Nobody but a fool could think he is – admittedly there are passages of powerful realism; equally there are passages of powerful child's eye grotesquerie and caricature – not to mention of sheer fantasy!..'

Will laughed. He was obviously thinking that if I'd said this sort of thing to my pupils it was not surprising they were making it a reason for dropping the book from the list.

'Skilful teaching, Joe.'

'No need to be sarcastic.'

Will went on laughing, his eyes small and brown, glinting, his cheeks gleaming. I said:

'Are that bloody Department going to object when they see Dickens dropped from the list – even when that's what their treasured students are asking for?'

'They may not notice.'

'So deep in their studies of literary theory, eh?'

He did not permit himself to be drawn.

The disappearance of *Martin Chuzzlewit* from the list was agreed in London. I thought that Avalon, if they wanted to keep me on their books, would be struck by the tactical advantage of acquiescence.

A few minutes later I departed from AULC to the baths.

Paul Dugan was waiting for me.

'I have to apologise to you, Professor.'

'What for?'

'For Liz and I coming in late to your class this week.' He paused a moment then gave his explanation.

'Liz is into it first thing in the morning, nowadays.'

'Oh,' I said.

'We hoped you wouldn't notice us coming into class late.' He blushed very faintly. 'We were trying to be very discreet. Not discreet enough, though, I guess.'

'You guess correctly. Of course I noticed you both.'

'I'm very, very sorry, Professor.'

He was looking me in the eyes as contritely as could be. I said:

'There's nothing to be sorry about, Paul.'

His expression turned to surprise. I said:

'Surely you must know me well enough by now to know that I always put First Things First.'

A moment of incomprehension and then a burst of laughter.

I joined in.

When we parted after our swim Paul gave notice that he would have to miss the baths next time. When I came out of my class it was Liz who was waiting for me.

'Can I come with you today, Professor Lunn?'

'Of course,' I said. 'There's nothing like a lesson from a different teacher. As you'd find if you were taught The Realistic Novel by somebody else, even anybody else.'

Paul would have laughed. Liz smiled nervously. I have to admit I was a little surprised by her volunteering to come with me. She must be cutting Psychology.

We arranged to meet at the baths after I'd taken a party to the pub: she was already in the water, swimming like a dolphin, when I arrived. She took up the Instructor's role, which Paul nowadays neglected. I thought there must be something in the wind, but I had no idea what it could be.

Afterwards. Would she come to the pub for a quiet drink? In the ordinary way I should have half-expected her to say No. Blushing, she said Yes.

The pub was quiet for once, and we drank our drinks in silence for a few minutes.

Then we began to talk a little. Not long before the subject was Paul. She pushed back the long, fine, silky hair from her forehead and looked down at the table.

'There was something I wanted to say to you, Professor Lunn.'

'About Paul?'

'Yes...'

'What?'

A moment's hesitation. Then –

'Paul's a wonderful guy...' This was the preliminary. Then with an effort she came out with – 'But he thinks I want him to marry me.'

'And?'

'He's got me wrong. I don't want to marry him.' Her eyes reddened as if she were restraining tears. Yet her voice had become less tremulous.

I looked at her.

'Have you told him?' I corrected myself. 'I mean have you conveyed this to him?' I paused. 'It sounds as if you haven't.'

She shook her head.

I was thinking about what Paul had confided in me about not wanting to marry her... Neither of them able to broach it with the other! I said;

'The situation doesn't seem to me to be insoluble.' I looked at her seriously. 'You must just tell him, Liz. Give him to understand, anyway...'

'He doesn't understand! He's not open to listening to me.' She burst out with her trouble. 'He doesn't respect my point of view!'

I believed every word of that. On her lips, though, it sounded too close to the Feminist Message of the day for me to make the observation that he didn't show much respect for my point of view, either – that would have seemed to her, in her present mood, either irrelevant or a sign of my male chauvinism, distracting attention from Paul's all-important incapacity for respecting her female point of view. I kept quiet.

She was waiting for me to say something.

'I'm sorry,' was all I could manage.

One of her hands was lying on the table. I clasped it.

'I believe what you're telling me, Liz. I can well believe he doesn't respect your point of view. And I agree that a happy marriage depends on each person having respect for the other's point of view... A corny speech but sensible – like so many things that are corny.'

She did not withdraw her hand. I said:

'Paul is intelligent, but he's very young. He'll change.'

'We're both too young. You know?.. It's true a lot of people marry at our age. But I think it's too early... For Paul and me it's too early...' She was looking at me intently.

'I think so, too, Liz.' I had thought of a way of relieving the solemnity of the conversation. I said, 'I didn't marry till I was 40.' I saw her startled look, and said playfully, 'Would you have waited for me, Liz?'

'Did your girl-friend wait, Professor?'

I laughed. 'She didn't have to wait. I was already 40 and she was 25.'

The solemnity was relieved. Liz smiled. She left her hand in mine.

'I guess I'll wait till I'm 25,' she said. With an amused look – 'Or maybe 23.'

I smiled back. It was a sort of pact.

Chapter XIV

Operation

The first of May – "*the merrie, merrie month of May, when birds do sing Hey ding a ding a ding...*" Hey ding a ding to you! I thought bitterly, Elspeth was about to undergo surgery.

Paul Dugan, some time after the conversation I had had with Liz, had invited me to go over to visit him in the States, and to go touring in his "old clunker" of a car, as he called it. I gave Elspeth's health as my reason, hoping thereby to let him down lightly, for telling him that I couldn't accept his invitation. I couldn't have accepted in any case. I'd enjoyed having him as a regular swimming-companion – quick-witted, helpful, energetic. But for my taste he lived too near the surface of his nature: I couldn't have faced the prospect of day-long, one-to-one association with him over a distance of 3,000 miles or more, assuming the "old clunker" held out. We parted with regret. During the next three years he was to write to me occasionally a letter of news, but then the correspondence fizzled out. It was like the end of a holiday friendship. (By the way, he never married Liz.)

Beforehand the surgeon asked Elspeth and me to go and see him together. He described in a friendly simple way what he intended to do, with the aim of defusing some of our anxieties and fears. What he succeeded in doing, instead, was fusing our liking and admiration for himself. That was all to the good. He would speak to us again after the operation.

The operation came and went without a hitch.

Viola was working in the same hospital, so she was able to keep an eye on her mother's progress. When she dropped in to her mother's ward she made it her business to hobnob with the Staff Nurse or whoever was in charge at the time. They were able to check that the surgeon did want to speak to me again, and to check when he would be doing his rounds of the Ward, so that I could lie in wait for him.

Viola had sailed through the process of getting her paediatric qualification with such success that Virginia had rallied her into improving her professional chances by following it up with the surgical qualification – necessary for treating children in Intensive Care, for instance.

It had to be said that, launched into nursing children, Viola was showing less diffidence, more self-confidence, than any of us had ever seen in her previous jobs.

'It's so much more fulfilling,' she said to me, not scorning a cliché even if I did happen to be a litterateur. 'So much more worthwhile than being involved in schemes to enable Ali Baba to evade the Serious Fraud Office.' She smiled sourly. 'He hasn't done a runner... Not yet.'

'Do you think he will?'

'I don't know. The only way of knowing, now I've left the company, is through radio and television – where you get a choice between crime-reporting and civil war-reporting.'

'True. I'm fed-up with them myself.'

'Crime-reporters don't tell you why people did the things they're supposed to have done. And what they're likely to be doing next.'

'That's true.'

'It bores me.'

'That's crime-reporting. They can't tell you things outside their scope.'

She frowned. 'Those are the things I want to know!'

'D'you think I don't? They're what I want most to know.' I laughed at myself. 'I'm a novelist!'

The frown disappeared. She said:

'I'd get equally bored with the civil war-reporting night after night if it didn't worry me so much.' She paused. 'The civil war in Ethiopia... Night after night. All those children starving, babies dying... It stops me getting to sleep.'

I listened attentively. There were constant appeals for nurses to go out there to help. I said:

'I can understand that. I find them terribly upsetting myself. I can't imagine anybody seeing those pictures of tiny children with bellies like footballs...'

Viola gave me a steady, penetrating look – I noticed the dark blueness of her eyes. I waited. 'So?'

'I should volunteer myself. To go with one or another of the various organisations – Nursing Aid Overseas is said to be very good. If it weren't for Mummy...'

'Yes,' I said, thinking Thank God for some dispensation!

There was a lull. Viola looked at her watch. 'I must get back to the Ward.' She kissed me and left.

Later, at the specified time, I lay in wait for the surgeon. Elspeth had been moved out of the main ward into a small private room, glassed off from the corridor leading out of the ward. While I was waiting I could see her through the glass; and could also look down the ward – to see women lying in beds, flowers on tables, nurses moving about, bright sunlight shining through the windows.

The surgeon recognised me.

'Your wife is doing very well, Mr Lunn.'

I hesitated. 'The swelling of her stomach hasn't gone down completely.'

'We are hopeful it will. There was a tremendous amount of air as well as of fluid in the abdomen – it made operating more difficult.'

'Yes.' I shifted on my feet and he appeared to think the seance was over. Glancing nervously through the glass window, to make sure we were not overheard by Elspeth, I put out a hand to detain him and said:

'There's still one thing. The most important of all...'

'What is it, Mr Lunn?'

'Was it cancer?'

Looking at me directly he gave his answer – in a tone of voice for description of which I could only think of the Trollopian word "manly". 'It might be cancer, though there are the results of tests to come in.'

'So it might be,' I said.

'Yes.'

'But it might not?'

'Yes.'

Pause. He said:

'I'm afraid in this hospital the results of biopsies are very slow to come in.'

I was silent. Then I said:

'Were you able to excise it all?' Not a very reasonable question in the circumstances.

'At present, Mr Lunn, we can't be certain.' He paused. 'After an interval I may want to have another look-round inside...' It was clear that he was trying to give me an encouraging smile. 'In the meantime I shall be wanting your wife to be put on chemotherapy.'

'I understand.'

'Our senior consultant in chemotherapy is based in the Royal Essex Hospital. So we shall ask your wife to attend there. Every week for blood-tests. And probably once a month for chemotherapy – that will be for the chemotherapy consultant to decide.' His tone was now conclusive. It conveyed that I had had my allowance of his time.

'Thank you.'

We shook hands and parted. I went in to see Elspeth. The ward was still brilliant with sunlight.

On the following day Elspeth was moved into the main ward. Other sides of her personality came into play. She became increasingly absorbed in "ward-life". In practically no time at all she knew all the nurses, and in scarcely more time than that many of the patients. She knew them by their Christian names and they – plus the Caribbean kitchen-helps who came round with trolleys for serving tea and meals – all called her by her Christian name. She began to find out what the other patients were suffering from, and, as soon as she could get around, called on them and chatted with them, made friends... How different from me! After my hip-replacement operation years ago, my temptation was to spend most of my time with the curtains round my bed drawn a little – when I had the courage to draw them, for I could sense faint disapproval from the nurses as well as from my neighbours. The nurses wanted to be able to keep an eye on me, the patient; the patients in the next beds wanted the comfort of a neighbour's interest and feeling – which I seemed to be unable to supply as it were by turning on a tap. A failing on my part. Elspeth was an example to me of what a fellow-human being should be like. I wished I could be like her.

This phase lasted another couple of weeks, when Elspeth's recovery was such that she was told she could go home. The results of the tests, biopsies or whatever they were, had still not come in – and were not expected for an unspecified period. (The National Health Service not coming up to standard – but then there was no evidence of the laboratories' having come up to standard before the NHS was instituted.)

Being home again was cause for a subdued celebration. Viola was on ward-duty and with a typical show of high-minded rigidity wouldn't ask for time off. Alastair and Virginia, who were down for a few days from Edinburgh, staying in Virginia's previous digs, came to dinner. With her Virginia brought things to eat. She unpacked a dish to show Elspeth –

'Dee sahl-mon,' said Alastair with a put-on Scottish accent. Then, 'And this is Virginia's lean cuisine mayonnaise.'

'Thank you. I should like some of it.' Elspeth looked up at Virginia. 'I don't know how you find time to cook.'

'We have to eat, Mummy.' When addressing her mother, Virginia's tone of voice nowadays was often tinged with "you don't seem to understand, quite". In my opinion Elspeth probably understood things better than Virginia, being older for one thing, a little gentler and more reflective for another. Gentleness and reflection are a helpful basis for understanding anything, in my opinion.

Virginia handed the dish to Alastair: addressing her mother –

'Can you drink a glass of Sparkling Saumur?'

Virginia knew we had a stock of it – we drank it as a substitute for champagne.

'A half glass.'

'OK.' Virginia bustled off to join Alastair in the kitchen.

Elspeth and I stayed put: we smiled at each other – when Virginia was around we knew our place, and it was not in the front line of the action.

As it was a celebratory meal of sorts, we had set ourselves up in the dining-room. At the first pause Virginia looked round the table and said:

'I have some news for you.'

I had to admit that my first thought was that she was going to say she was pregnant. Elspeth and I glanced at each other.

For once Virginia did not guess what we were thinking. She said:

'A vacancy came up for another junior doctor at Alastair's hospital.'

Pause.

'I've had an interview for it,' – she and Alastair looked at each other, all smiles – 'and they've appointed me..'

Elspeth and I smiled rather differently.

'It means we shall both be working under the same roof. In different departments, of course. But we shall be able to meet in the canteen and travel to and fro together.' She was triumphant.

'What marvellous news!' I jumped up and kissed her warmly. 'I congratulate you, my darling girl.'

Elspeth, still a long way from being recovered, gave a less energetic performance. Was she not as happy about it as I was? And I – wasn't my happiness tinged with anxiety, as I knew Elspeth's was, about Virginia having let herself in for a job in which she was likely to be grossly over-worked? Junior doctors...

We all raised our glasses to Virginia.

'In the absence of champagne,' I said, 'Sparkling Saumur is fully acceptable.' An appropriate remark as it was I who had laid in the stock of it.

We ate the rest of our cold salmon with gusto; and then some chocolate eclairs which Virginia had brought from her local patisserie.

At the same time we all knew that Alastair and Virginia could be no more certain – in fact were probably less certain – of Elspeth's future than Elspeth and I were ourselves. Yet, whether Elspeth had cancer or not, here we were, eating cold salmon followed by chocolate eclairs, washed down with Sparkling Saumur – and enjoying them.

As soon as the meal was over Elspeth went back to bed: Alastair and Virginia went home to seize an opportunity for getting a bit more sleep than usual. I was left to clear up the dining-room, stack the dish-washer and so on. Left on my own, I could hear Elspeth's radio from the bedroom. I wondered if she, too, had thought Virginia was going to announce the prospect of having a baby; and whether it stirred in Elspeth a recollection of the difficulties in her own second pregnancy. May Virginia be spared that! I thought.

Suddenly – quite irrelevantly while I was polishing a clear water-jug – I was pierced by the recognition of how very dear to me Virginia was! A darling daughter in the here and now; a part of life in the future.

Chapter XV

Hope And Fear

'What do you think of Virginia's news?'

Elspeth was speaking. I was lying beside her later that evening. I said:

'I think it's good.' Nevertheless I couldn't keep a certain caginess out of my voice.

Pause.

'You don't think it's so good?' I finally said to her.

'How will they ever see each other?'

'See each other? Oh, I know what's troubling you – you're still hypnotised by the Press hullaballoo over long working-hours. Junior hospital doctors supposed to be working every minute of their waking day and all that.'

'Many of them do – enough for their Union to have made an official protest to the Department. We knew when she took up with Alastair that he worked excessively long hours.'

'Partly from choice. He's fascinated by casualties – all different, all urgent. Great experience for a young doctor!' I rolled on to one elbow and stroked her forehead. She said;

'Maybe. It is his choice... I'm worried by the thought of both of them getting swept into a maelstrom.'

'Virginia isn't going to be in charge of a casualty ward.'

'All junior hospital doctors work too long hours – sometimes they're so tired they scarcely know what they're doing. Even Alastair concedes that.'

'I agree it's worrying...' I changed tack. 'One could have thought the medical profession as a whole wouldn't let it go on.'

'The consultants don't give as much support to the junior doctors' cause as they might give – so Alastair says.'

There was an anguished note in Elspeth's voice – after all, she was still unwell, her resistance to anxiety low. And it was clear that Alastair had inadvertently made matters worse: he was too young to have learnt to dissimulate. I didn't know she had discussed the subject with him at this length. I stroked her forehead again –

'It's time we stopped this agitating conversation at this time of night... Especially when we both know there's nothing we can do about it. We've got two junior hospital doctors in the family now.' I paused, then went on kindly: 'And if that's what they want to do with their lives... it's a pretty honourable thing to want to do.'

I went on stroking till I felt the tension relaxing in the skin of her forehead. 'And if I were you I shouldn't worry too much about their never seeing each other.' I looked down into her eyes. 'I guess love will find a way.'

A pause while she thought it over. Then she slowly looked up into my eyes, the corners of her mouth went up, her eyelids flickered... I was leaning close to her; the same thought was going through both our minds at the same time. Love will find a way – how we should like to! In the present circumstances it was not to be – I noticed that she had not got her usual gentle grasp of me.

'Not yet,' she whispered.

'Oh Lord, how long?' I cried.

This made us both laugh. I kissed her lightly and then rolled back into my place.

'Good night, darling.'

'Good night...'

Looking back on it now, I realise that I felt intimations of things going well with her. There was hope.

This turned out to be the case. Elspeth progressed: weekly visits to the Royal Essex for blood-tests – white corpuscle count; an overnight stay once a month for chemo-therapy – commonly known as "chemo".

The senior consultant in chemotherapy was impressive; tall, lean and incisive; with the confidence of a man who is on top of his job and knows it. His manner struck us at first as a shade brutal, but we came to recognise that it overlaid a nature which was thoughtful and considerate – as shown by his appointing a young woman doctor to watch over Elspeth's case; another intelligent, sympathetic young woman who knew his methods and was familiar with the drugs he was treating Elspeth with. Elspeth took to her and as the treatment went on the young woman was to become a personal friend... Everything had been thought of.

I realise I can't resist writing here and now Long live the NHS! in spite of the fact that it's not the sort of thing one is supposed to write in a novel – like many other things I've wanted to write into novels. And have actually written, despite knowing there were EngLit professionals around the place who were ready to say I shouldn't do it. It was my aim to make novels out of my experience of living, in a blend of three elements: things I had actually experienced myself – "too autobiographical", the pros said; comments and reflections on what that experience had taught me – "too opinionated"; invention of characters and incidents necessary for the telling of my story – "short of enigma, metaphor, symbolism."

Oh dear! This was the particular Art-form I had chosen for myself and I meant to stick to it; it was my Art. It might not conform to the current mode favoured by some EngLit pros, but I'm not sure I didn't see that as a point in its favour. You couldn't read a page by me and think it was by anyone else...

But no! Confronted with it, conscientious objectors immediately leapt on their high horse and furiously rode away in the opposite direction. I have to confess that I hoped they'd fall off.

Of course they didn't fall off, but it was a pleasing distraction to think about. And we needed a pleasing distraction from what was becoming the constant tenor of our lives in those days, a constant fluctuation of mood between Hope and Fear. Hopefulness for continued living, apprehensiveness of death.

Into this situation broke a summons from Queen Anne's Hospital for Elspeth to undergo the "look-round inside" examination. The surgeon, as before, talked to me afterwards. He answered the crucial question: Was it cancer? It was. I felt a powerful spurt of fear.

The bulk of it, he said, had been excised. He had found a certain number of "seedlings" which he had removed. ("Seedlings" – could a metaphor be more inapt? I thought. Seedlings in one's garden one nurtured to help them to grow: one looked forward to when they would spread out their stems and flower.) But there was one relic of cancer, he said, which it would be too dangerous to excise – this relic he trusted to be suppressed effectively by another course of chemotherapy.

'I understand,' I said.

I understood through having been inducted into the subject by Alastair and Virginia.

Chemotherapy suppresses but does not cure.

Nevertheless this knowledge encouraged Hope. Chemotherapy can suppress for a considerable period, which may even turn out to be indefinite.

Comfortingly I reminded Elspeth, 'I understand that chemotherapy can be very effective.'

'In some cases.'

I was sitting beside her. As I took hold of her hand she gave me a tremulous smile, and repeated what had become a family-saying ever since it was uttered by a hospital registrar to me ten years ago, when things went what could be grievously wrong after my ur-hip-replacement.

"Don't look on the black side, Mr Lunn!"

There was something comical as well as desperate about it. Don't look on the black side, Mr Lunn! – I did my best to smile. It was a message of Hope. Yet along with it there was subdued Fear...

We were both silent. Yet hope was blossoming.

Chapter XVI

A Nonconformist Conscience

The Royal Essex had warned us that the chemotherapy might make her feel ill – the chemotherapeutic drugs being used to kill off the cancerous cells were liable to begin to kill off the non-cancerous, i.e. the healthy, cells, as well. To start with it actually had made her feel ill; but the effect was now worn off and she was beginning to feel better, to look better: she was eating well, sleeping well, feeling well enough to return to her normal life of housekeeping – though not to her old job of work.

When I married her I had said I wanted her to give up her full-time career. I didn't say it was so that she could look after me full-time; but that was at the back of my mind – an idea that was commonplace enough in the 1950s and would be judged utterly reprehensible in the 1980s. When we agreed to have children, which was at the front of my mind, we didn't know that she was only going to be able with great difficulty and some danger to have a second child, Virginia; and then to be warned that it was inadvisable to become pregnant again. Now, in the 1980s we were perfectly satisfied with Viola and Virginia – Virginia came down whenever possible from Scotland. Viola dropped in frequently. Two of them made us happy.

Full-time housekeeping: going about London with me, well enough for a Spring weekend in Brighton –

'You're sure it's all right?' I enquired of the young woman doctor charged with over-seeing her case.

'I think it's a very good idea,' was the response. So the trip was settled.

Viola came in to see her mother before we left. Afterwards Elspeth said:

'Do you know what's biting Viola? With me recovering you'd think she'd be cheerful; yet she seems to be preoccupied with something... unhappy.'

'I don't know,' I said – which was not strictly true. Viola looked pale and worn: I suspected that what was "biting her" was her conscience, when she was not responding to the constant appeals for children's nurses in those countries overseas where there was civil war, famine, children dying... I guessed that Elspeth's not being fully recovered inhibited Viola from confiding in her mother. I felt sorry for her. How little one knows even of one's own children, what mysteries govern them!

We went to Brighton and came back in high spirits: the high spirits endured as did Elspeth's reassuring symptoms. She said in a moment of enthusiasm –

'Let's have a party!'

I smiled, half in astonishment. We were both smiling.

Chemo had brought us a stable infusion of Hope...

'Let's ask all our friends,' Elspeth said. 'We won't tell them about me if they haven't heard already.'

I pondered. Won't tell them what? The bright side happened to be shining gloriously, but the dark side remained at its reverse. I couldn't forget the difference between cure and suppression.

So the party was arranged for the autumn: 60 people invited – more, I contended, than the flat could possibly hold. Sunday lunchtime, food served by an excellent caterer, the finest wines. Everything set for success.

The party actually was a success. In the first place there was an unexpectedly large turn-out of guests; in the second it proved my contention that we had invited more people than the flat could hold – nobody seemed to mind that. (Overcrowding at a party promotes... shall we say, Togetherness?) Looking round at the assembly, *begeistert* by drink, Elspeth and I were pleased with our friends.

Two well-known lady-novelists, well-known for drinking a little too much at parties, drank a little too much and provided unscripted entertainment for the rest of the company. Two other well-known lady-novelists, well-known for selling modestly well, were overheard confidentially exchanging sales-figures of their most recent novels – an exchange far from notable for veracity on either side. (We were to hear some time afterwards that the lady-novelist with the lower sales-figures telephoned her publisher first thing next morning to lambast him for selling fewer copies of her books than the other lady-novelist's publisher sold of hers. The second publisher felt compelled to check with the first; then both publishers felt compelled to check with the lady-novelists themselves; and so on... all keeping each other occupied over a considerable period!)

The party was a great success and Elspeth was universally congratulated; only a very few of the guests thought she did not look well... I personally did not see sure signs of illness, though my powers of observation were no doubt twisted by wish-fulfilment. Elspeth claimed that she was feeling surprisingly well. Nevertheless I was not free from the shadows of "the black side". They were liable to come upon me when I woke in the night, Elspeth lying close to me, breathing... I would suffer an agonised moment, and wondered what she, in her profound resilience and courage, felt? One night the idea suddenly occurred to me that she might have proposed the party in order to make sure of seeing all our friends for the last time. Even in the closeness of our intimacy, perhaps because of the closeness of our intimacy, I could not bring myself to ask her. We had been given to understand that the period of recovery such as she was now enjoying, was not uncommon in cancer cases. It was known as "a remission".

To my mind the word "remission" told its own story.

And yet... Mightn't remission be prolonged indefinitely? Like the treatment itself?

When it seemed clear to us that the remission was not just a flash in the pan, that it was lasting, we began to feel we were living in a dream of old times. Elspeth called on all her resources of body and spirit. She enrolled herself in the corps of cancer-sufferers, she joined organisations which supplied them with information and advice about ameliorating routines of habit and diet – all to good effect, either physical or psychological, it was difficult to say which. At literary parties she made the acquaintance of fellow-sufferers and they encouraged each other with information about how long they and others had survived on chemotherapy. Five years, for instance. Rumours of ten years! It was a strange freemasonry: it had an inspiriting effect. Sometimes I felt a little left-out...

One night I had a telephone call from Viola. She wanted to see me as soon as possible.

'And I don't want Mummy to be there, really.'

I agreed, though the request was very unlike her. We arranged a time, the next day. I was going down to the London Library to return books, so I fixed on a café in Jermyn Street. I felt apprehensive.

At half past three in the afternoon – timed to coincide with a blank in Viola's roster – I arrived at the café and chose a table well away from the window which looked out on the street. It was a dull day and the window was slightly clouded by drizzle: the room was not over-lit at the best of times. Only one table was occupied so far, and young Greek waiters, with nothing to do, were gossiping together behind the Gaggia machine. There was a pleasant whiff of coffee in the air but no music.

Through the window I saw Viola arriving outside. She crossed the threshold, saw me, came straight to me.

'I hope this is all right?' I said, feeling as if I were being party to a secret rendezvous.

'It's OK,' – said in a dismissive tone.

I looked at her and saw that her face was pale, her eyes strained. She sat down and a very polite Greek waiter appeared at her elbow, leaning over her a little further than was necessary.

'Coffee, Madame?'

'I just want some tea,' she said peremptorily. 'No thank you, no cakes.'

Not an auspicious beginning. She realised that she was being unfriendly –

'I'm very sorry, Daddy. I'm a bit...'

'A bit, what?'

She drew a breath. 'I've been seeing Nursing Aid Overseas.'

We looked at each other – with apprehension on both sides.

'I had to do something, at least to make a start,' she said. 'There are lots of agencies in the field – the International Red Cross, V.S.O., Christian Aid, Save the Children and so on. It was a question of choosing the one which would be the best spec for me – the one most likely to be interested in my qualifications.'

Dismay made me feel that my heart had suddenly begun to beat faster. I hadn't realised she was so close to "doing something".

'And it was Nursing Aid Overseas,' I repeated. 'They must have fallen on your neck.'

'Not exactly.' A faint touch of amusement now. 'But nearly...'

I attempted irony. 'Perhaps when they know you better?'

'I was asked to bring my CV and a couple of references with me.'

Pause. 'They're terribly short of children's nurses, trained nurses. They need help.'

'I see. Did they accept you?' A foolish question.

I was corrected. 'Not on the spot. I filled in the forms they gave me.'

'The wheels of administration have got to go round.'

'You should know.'

'True. Time was when I was responsible for quite a few such wheels. People kept ringing up to know when the going-round would be over.'

'What did you say?'

'Soon...'

She smiled, a little more at ease. There was a pause. Then she said:

'I liked the woman who interviewed me.'

'That's a good sign.'

'She kept me nearly an hour. And promised to let me know as quickly as she can.'

'So it looks hopeful?'

Viola nodded her head. 'She asked me where, if I were made an offer and had my choice, I would like to serve.'

'Where did you say?'

'Ethiopia...'

I didn't say anything, but the degree to which I was devastated must have shown in my face. She broke out –

'Oh, Daddy!.. I've thought and thought about this – thought about nothing else for weeks.' She was twisting her fingers together. (Our tea was there, on the table, but I doubt if she was aware of it.) 'I don't know what to do!..' It was a cry of pain as well as indecision.

I waited. She went on.

'I should know what to do – I'd go anywhere I'm needed. If...' She was looking very agitated. 'If you didn't say No – and I don't think you would?'

I nodded my head in doubtful acquiescence. Then she cried out with great force –

'But it's Mummy!'

'I can see that.'

'If we were sure she's going to stay all right... You know?'

'We aren't sure.'

Suddenly tears came and ran down her cheeks. I took hold of her hand across the table – then let it go in order to search in my pockets for a spare tissue. I found one and gave it to her.

I was appalled by the thought of her going away, so far away from us all; and possibly in actual physical danger; above all by her leaving her mother at the present time... She clearly understood that. I could think of nothing to say.

'Would you object if Mummy were well?' She stopped drying her eyes and looked at me in appeal. 'It's the first time in my life when I've known so definitely what I want to do. What I must do.'

'To all intents and purposes Elspeth is well.' Tears came into my own eyes. (I had another tissue.) I meant to add, 'For the time being,' but I couldn't bring myself to do it. I looked at her directly, and said:

'I understand. I know what the struggles of conscience mean.'

Viola tried to smile. 'The Nonconformist conscience...' The phrase we used playfully in the family. 'I'm sorry I've landed you with...'

'You don't have to feel sorry,' I said. 'It isn't inherited.'

'I suppose it's inculcated!' Said with ironic force.

'Oh God!' She didn't blame Elspeth and me, but I was confronted with the thought that I might be in some way responsible.

She was recovering her equilibrium again. She said;

'What if I went abroad just for a limited period while Elspeth certainly is well? For as long as that happens to be...'

'And that still may be for a long time.'

She nodded her head. 'Daddy, I don't want you to be...' She didn't finish the sentence.

Not knowing what the last word of the sentence was, I murmured, 'No...'

There was a silence in which we looked down at the table, wordlessly exchanging thoughts that couldn't be put into words. I thought it was time to stop.

'Let's order some more tea,' I said. 'This has gone cold.'

In a trice the very polite young Greek waiter was beside her. I said:

'I think we had best postpone the next stage in this conversation until you've got some definite news from Nursing Aid Overseas. There's no point in breaking it to Elspeth until you know where you stand.'

Very quietly she said, 'Thank you, Daddy.'

In silence we broached our second pot of tea – it was very good tea but we scarcely noticed it.

Then we went home. And began to wait for the news from Nursing Aid. The wheels of administration went round with surprising speed – so I thought patronisingly.

The news when it came was in Viola's favour. Her application was accepted, (subject, as they specified, to last-minute checks. I thought Nursing Aid Overseas must have some retired civil servant on its staff.) They would offer her a six-month contract at an acceptable wage; the country, Ethiopia. They would procure the necessary visa for her as soon as they got her passport; and they would entrust Thomas Cook with arranging a medical, shooting the appropriate 'shots', booking a flight, and so on. Nursing Aid Overseas knew the ropes.

When she telephoned me with the news I was momentarily without speech – the chance from her side had come off, from my side it hadn't.

Reverting to our conversation at the café in Jermyn Street, she said:

'If there's the slightest sign of the remission wavering, I'll come back by the first flight. Otherwise I shall expect to work the six months out and then decide what to do next.' A mixture of decision and subdued excitement infused her tone of voice. I said:

'Now we shall have to tell Elspeth...'

'I will tell her.'

'That relieves me,' I said. 'Thank you.'

'It's my duty.'

That seemed to be final. She came back to the flat with me. As I was not present during her conversation with Elspeth I do not know what actually was said. (Elspeth knew already that Viola passionately wanted to do children's nursing in the cause of humanitarian aid somewhere.) The upshot of their conversation was presented to me later that evening – Viola's proposition had carried the day.

Elspeth discussed it with me. 'I understand it and you do...' she said. 'Ethiopia seems so remote, and it's probably dangerous with them having a civil war... Why, in Heaven's name, when they've got a famine on their hands, do they have to have a civil war?'

'There are civil wars going on all over the world,' I said, glad of a shift in subject. 'I suppose sociologists can produce an analysis. As a non-expert, I find civil wars sickening, next door to inexplicable – what is achieved by them in most cases? More people poorer, more people dead...'

We looked at each other, with Viola's leaving us momentarily overshadowed. But only momentarily.

'Viola says the organisation informs her that there are regular flights to and from Addis Ababa.'

We were quiet while we assimilated that information together. Elspeth was taking it very well.

When the time of departure was at hand, Virginia and Alastair came down from Edinburgh for the farewells.

I had little doubt that Virginia was not happy about it all. She looked at me searchingly without expressing her opinion; but her large grey eyes, usually excitingly splashed with hazel, looked unexcitingly unsplashed with hazel, a uniform grey...

'We,' she said, 'Alastair and I, will simply have to come down and work in London, and find somewhere to live here.'

The implication was clear. It would give me, as well as Elspeth comfort. I embraced her lovingly.

We talked of Viola. We had all noticed that her unusual pallor was dissipated, that her eyes sparkled again.

Finally Virginia said to me, 'Do you think it will all work out all right?'

To avoid the risk of being told not to look on the black side, I said nothing.

Virginia understood.

Yet Viola's parting words, whispered to me while we were kissing each other goodbye, stayed in my mind –

'If I only get my six months out there I shall know that I've done something...'

Chapter XVII

A Matter of Nomenclature

'It's no use sitting around moping.' Elspeth, now Viola was gone.

I agreed. 'Actually the Fall semester begins in a couple of weeks.'

'But what about me?' She was smiling.

'What about you?' (I simply didn't know.)

'I could go back to my old job, now... But you don't want me to.'

'I think it's really too soon.'

The immediate dilemma was left unresolved.

'I don't want to sit and mope,' Elspeth said.

'Of course not.'

However the immediate dilemma happened to be resolved for us almost immediately. By a letter from Spain, from an old friend, regular correspondent of Elspeth's, whose husband had decided he wanted to retire there – not to the Costa del Sol, that spot most favoured for retirement to a life of sun and pleasure by gentlemen being pursued by Scotland Yard; but round the other side of the Strait of Gibraltar, at Cadiz. The letter ended with the usual friendly invitation to go and see them – *Why not before the summer ends? The weather is gorgeous.*

I could see that Elspeth took it as a sign from Heaven.

'Let's go!' she said. 'We can't mope in Cadiz.'

'Not on tons of *tapas* and fifty-seven varieties of *jerez*.'

'And you know you like Joan and Bill.' A very wifely remark. It resolved my dilemma for me. 'Not to stay with them,' I said. 'Let's go to the Cadiz *parador*!'

'I'd love that! There's time for a good ten days' holiday before your semester begins.'

I realised I'd been feeling mopey over Viola myself, and considered that we did need something; but not necessarily fleeing the country for ten days or more. However I was swayed by Elspeth's enthusiasm, by a nervous pressure I sensed at the back of it – nervous pressure to get the most out of life?

To get the most out of her life... With no alternative I telephoned Joan and Bill, went round to Thomas Cook; and I rang up Will Gower to acquaint him with my movements –

'I think it's a very good idea, Joe. It means that you may miss the Horse and Pony Show – when we shall miss you.'

'Thank you. I'll be back in time.' I wanted to be there for Registration in order to get an early sight of my next semester's pupils.

'That has an advantage for you. An old friend of yours is visiting us for a few days as soon as the semester has begun.' He paused to keep me guessing.

I guessed immediately. 'Jim Yavner!'

'Yes indeed. He wants to see you.

I nodded my head in acquiescence. 'I have no fights with Jim Yavner in view.'

I imagined him at the other end of the line, nodding his head ironically in approval. 'I'm glad to hear it, Joe.' Then in a different tone of voice – 'Jim's talking of retiring at the end of this academic year.'

My boss!.. 'I hope they're not going to choose a successor who's cruelly post-modernistical.'

'Cruelly post-modernistical!..' Will laughed, as if it were a good joke.

I was not laughing. It seemed to me that he was not immune from *Schadenfreude*.

Next day Elspeth and I began our holiday. The Cadiz *parador* was superb, built on the cliffs with hard black Atlantic waves crashing on the rocks below, sunlight trapped in the spume; something of a light wind but not a single fishing-boat out... And then, from our bedroom window at the back of the building, a view over the local bull-ring, an oval of sand, glowing – to our way of thinking glowing sinisterly. We were not going to watch any bullfights: I, with faint hankerings after *machismo*, might have consented to watch just one: Elspeth, with no such hankerings, simply ruled it out.

Elspeth was much restored and rapidly fell into her old-girls-together mood with Joan. I discussed with Bill at somewhat greater length than I thought was necessary, "living in the south". He and Joan were Roman Catholics which must make "living in the south" more practical if not more comfortable. Though they kept going off to Mass or to Confession I discovered I did like them.

Interesting excursions, entertaining company, the hobby of figuring out quirks in Spanish grammar, sunshine and sea-breezes.

When we got back home it dawned on us that we had been happy.

On the following day we got our first letter from Viola.

'My first real letter of news, so it's going to be long. Please show it to Virginia. It's meant for all of you.

Addis Ababa, September 1st

It's sunny and cool and marvellously green – the big rains have just ended – but I've never been so scared in my life. Addis Ababa is a modern city in parts, but the outskirts – the suburbs even – are just a collection of mud-hutted villages, with stray donkeys in the day-time and hyenas howling at night. All falling to pieces. In the town centre there are holes in the roads, and the shops, which must once have been modern, are un-painted and there are no imported goods – the money is all going to arms for the beleaguered government's conscript army. Many of the troops are only boys, so it's not surprising that it's not disciplined. A rifle is a new toy to a teenager. At night the curfew keeps us indoors – just as well, it's safer. In the suburbs, where I'm staying, you can hear the constant sound of guns, though it's not even war, not yet in Addis anyway. Just people firing for what they think is fun. And dogs barking; and hyenas making their strange whooping sound on a rising cadence, terribly scary.

It's beautiful and ancient, and in some ways like living in the Bible. Priests in robes with fly-whisks, under highly coloured umbrellas on holy days – they even dance outside their churches to celebrate the festivals, dignified old gentlemen in white shawls, elegant beautiful young women in sophisticated expensive western dresses; and desperately poor peasants in rags. Women almost bent double under loads of sticks, and juvenile soldiers everywhere looking as though they might shoot on sight. You can't get a foreign newspaper – and locally there's no reliable news – only rumours and "Derg", (that's military propaganda.)

I'm trying to get out of Addis to help up north where both the civil war and the famine are at their worst. Most of the actual fighting is taking place far away from here. The hospital I'm temporarily working at is full of wounded soldiers, amputees, children blinded – most of them very young, but then so are the "rebels" or "liberation front", (depending on whichever side you are talking to). Although drugs are scarce, doctors at a premium, and hospital beds bulging, you can still get private treatment if you are able to pay. Addis Ababa New Market is a hive of black market smuggled goods at a price.

I'm doing my best to get out to where the drought and famine are doing most damage. It's just that even as a free volunteer with useful skills, getting permission to travel is virtually impossible. I have come across a young Ethiopian in the Ministry of the Interior who wants to be helpful, so I'm going to try through him, but I'm not confident of success.

I think of you and send you all my love.'

Somewhat reassured I plunged into the Avalon semester. Prospective pupils too many in number, attractive and promising in quality. The n-b W f buzzing round, his tan deepened by his summer holiday – in Jamaica, not Brecon – very busy, very efficient.

'Professor Yavner is due at the beginning of next week,' he said, grinning.

'What's he due for?'

Will looked at me sideways, bright brown eyes twinkling slyly. 'A "freebie", I should say, wouldn't you?'

'I should.'

'He's got some news about changes in the Department –'

'About his retirement?'

'In favour of someone "cruelly post-modernistical"? No – at least I have heard nothing about it. But he'll tell us, I expect.'

'What are the changes, then?'

'Mainly in nomenclature, I understand.'

'Nomenclature – what on earth?'

'He'll tell you.' I presumed that he was keeping me guessing, but I had no evidence that he knew. On the other hand, I could wait.

Everyone at AULC knew that Jim Yavner loved London, and of course they took it as accepted fact that his visit was a "freebie". Such visits were not rare from senior professors – and some not so senior – at Avalon U. We had a constant stream of visiting Deans, of whom there must be shoals on the home campus. (American universities seem to abound in Deans.) "Freebie" or not, Jim's visit was something I could look forward to.

We met in Will's room while Will was out at a meeting in the House of Commons, (a propos getting special permission for a troop of AULC students to visit the House during Prime Minister's Question Time).

Though I was delighted to see Jim, I was not in the highest spirits that morning, as Elspeth was not feeling as well as usual. My spirits fluctuated in parallel with her state. If she had not got cancer, what was the matter with her would have had no significance. Perhaps it hadn't now. As it was... A little of my worry should have been dispelled by the brightness of the September morning sunshine on the landscape seen from Will Gower's windows: for myself, I never tired of it – a row of trees shedding their leaves, a distant road with cars flashing by, a terrace of white-painted Regency houses; and the sky, a clear blue where it was not obscured by heavy greyish-white clouds.

Jim Yavner was addressing me. 'One reason for my being here is to sound you out as usual about continuing to teach for us. We hope you will.' He gave me a satirical grimace – 'Despite classes of 30 instead of 15.'

Before I could introduce the topic of what Avalon was prepared to pay me, were I to teach classes of 15, he went on:

'We appreciate that you are popular with the students – and with those of their visiting mothers and fathers whom they introduce you to.' He was being serious. 'Students who have taken your course pass the word down the line to the next bunch.'

(I was not entirely without admiration for the home campus Intelligence service.)

Giving him a satirical glance from the opposite side of the discussion, I said:

'Keeps the fees up, *nicht wahr*?'

I was putting down a marker that in view of my boosting AULC's income I was not expecting the academics to have me sacked for teaching incorrect ideas.

My satirical grimace came back with interest in the form of a super-knowing grin.

There ain't no flies on Jim, I thought. And I must say I liked him the better for it. His long jaw and penetrating grey eyes were beginning to look more mellow, the grey furrows down his cheeks even tinged with pink.

'I've also got some news for you, Joe, which may interest you.' (Sarcastic.)

'I'm all attention.'

'The title of the Department of English Literature is to be re-framed. To bring it into accord with modern practice.'

Instead of making the obvious facetious comment, I said, 'I'm all ears.'

'It's going to be entitled the Department of English and Textual Studies.'

A moment's pause to accommodate my stupefaction, then –

'That's magnificent, Jim! I do congratulate them. Those academic boys always felt they were held back by Literature – not being able to write it themselves. Now they're getting rid of it. What a triumph! Another great barrier gone.'

(The first great barrier, the author, had already been eliminated, his death publicly celebrated at the Sorbonne some years previously.)

Jim was too smart to ask me what further barriers remained for elimination; but that was not going to deter me from telling him.

'The last great barrier, remaining... The Text, of course! If they can get rid of the Text, after first the Author, then Literature, there's nothing to hold them back. They can advance theoretical studies in total freedom!'

As he was showing all the signs of disagreement, I went on. 'Somebody's got to say these things unambiguously, Jim.'

'No one more unambiguous than you, Joe.'

'Unambiguous Joe – that's me. I should like to be called that.'

We were laughing at each other. Back in our old playful sparring days.

Jim Yavner changed the subject. 'You haven't told me how Elspeth is.'

I gave him a brief summary of her medical history since the 1st of May that year. I could see him taking the information in and probably making from it deductions not dissimilar to mine.

'We're living on Hope,' I said.

His glance flickered. Then he said, 'I'm glad. Rosalind will want to know.' He looked at me. 'We're leaving tomorrow. But we'll be back.' A gleam of amusement at himself.

We were interrupted by Will Gower's returning to claim his office.

Will said, 'All well?'

Jim said 'Sure.'

Chapter XVIII

Several Bits of News

A few weeks after Jim Yavner had left, at mid-semester to be precise, Avalon University London Centre was shaken by drama – the Administration was stood on its head. Frank Moroni, one of my students, had been arrested at Harwich on his way back from Amsterdam. What for? What a question! For attempting to smuggle hashish into Her Majesty's United Kingdom, of course.

In the offices of the Administration all the telephones appeared to be in use at once. I had merely dropped in for a casual call on the Dean.

'What on earth's going on?' I said to him.

Agitatedly holding the receiver away from his mouth, he told me.

'The little fool!' I exclaimed.

Will completed his telephone conversation and turned to me.

'Every semester,' I went on, 'I give the Amsterdam party a warning about this.'

'I know.' A trick Will hadn't missed. He reverted to Moroni. 'Damned stupid thing to do.'

'Frank Moroni is the reverse of stupid.'

'He's one of your pupils isn't he?'

'He is indeed. I know little Frankie Moroni very well. He's damned clever – and knows it. He's under the impression that he's so clever he can get away with anything. I told him – I told them all – not to try any funny business with drugs! But no... Frankie Moroni has to try just that. He thinks he's the cat's whiskers...' I caught a flicker in Will's eye. 'Yes, I know that expression's out-of-date. I asked Paul Dugan what they say nowadays in comparable circumstances and he told me... I'm afraid it wasn't quite me.'

'What did Paul Dugan tell you?'

'It appears that you say nowadays in comparable circumstances "He thinks he's hot shit". I suppose I might have known the expression, whatever it was, would incorporate America's favourite word?'

Will gave a sarcastic half-smile. 'You can take it that Moroni, however hot he was, is getting the opportunity, where he is now, to cool down.'

'Where is he now?'

'In a police cell, waiting for his father to arrive to bail him out. I've just been talking to the police.'

'And then, what?'

'Back to the USA on the next plane. There's no place for him here, unless we want to lose students in the future. His father doesn't see it, but we do – AULC does.'

'If the father is another little smart-ass like the son, he'll probably demand a refund of Frankie's fees for classes missed.'

'He won't get it.'

I indulged in momentary reflection. 'It seems a pity to lose little Frank Moroni. He added gaiety to life. As well as being clever he's very handsome in a miniature Italian way – quite a few of the girls in the class were susceptible to him.'

'For God's sake, Joe, don't give me anything more about Frank Moroni!'

I shrugged my shoulders. At that moment both telephones on his desk rang simultaneously. I took the opportunity to make my getaway.

So that was that. But AULC was not the only one to provide me with dramatic news on that day. When I got home I found Elspeth waiting for me with a letter from my agent. It was about the novel I was supposed to have been "perfecting" for the last two years. I had sent the manuscript to him for an interim opinion on the present version, which I looked upon as re-written and re-written ad nauseam, (ad nauseam to me, anyway). It appeared that he had submitted it to a publisher without my knowledge or consent, and the publisher had accepted it at once without demur...

'You see,' said Elspeth, implying that the same result might have been obtained without all that nausea – quite likely, I now realised, it would. And quite possibly it wouldn't... Who was to know, apart from *le bon Dieu*?

'I think it's wonderful news for you.'

'Well, I admit it's...' I searched for the cliché, 'a weight off my mind.'

Elspeth put her arms round me. 'You'll get reconciled to it,' she said playfully. And kissed me on the cheek.

I knew she was right. I was relieved, even pleased by the news. But I knew I should not start another novel until we were more sure of where she stood in health. I have to say that I saw – or imagined I saw – signs of the remission faltering, and I suspected the hospital's being of the same mind.

The signs were touches of illness, increasing frequency of calls to the Royal Essex. The Essex decided the doses of chemo twice a week were having an effect on her health so deleterious – it was essential they be not reduced – that different arrangements must be considered. It was not an unusual state of affairs; everyone understood the downside of treatment with chemotherapeutic drugs.

Just before the end of the year the hospital carried out an ultrasound scan: they decided it would be better for her to move into the hospital and go home from time to time than to do the reverse routine.

Elspeth accepted the change philosophically, if that word could be used to describe acquiescing to something which is both painful and ominous. Ominous? Of course it was ominous, so ominous that we didn't discuss it at length with each other. Facts sometimes speak for themselves – in this case the fact was a fresh sign of the abdominal swelling with which the illness had begun. One day she said to me, 'I wonder how long it will be...' Was she wondering, I asked myself, as anyone would wonder who is caught for an undefined period in the maw of a hospital could not help wondering, Shall I ever get out again?..

'Depends on how the treatment goes,' I said briskly. I doubt if she was deceived.

I may say that Elspeth's nature, affectionate, friendly, totally lacking in "side" was finding wonderfully new expression in the hospital ward at the Royal Essex as it had done at Queen Anne's after the surgical operation. In her quiet way she circulated "the chemo ward" (in fact I thought it could only be called "the cancer ward") getting to know the other patients, listening to their woes, the woes of human beings cut off from their loved ones... It came naturally to her to console them. They knew how she was situated – they loved her for it.

On the other hand, when the hospital decided that her chemo should be administered by a continuous "drip", that is to say injected by gravity through a perspex tube from a flask clamped a foot or so above the head of the bed, there were spells when Elspeth was unable to move readily about the ward. She regretted it. And so did I. When I was beside the bed, talking to her or tiredly resting my head in her lap – which latter she self-consciously discouraged – a ward-friend might well come up for a few words of consoling conversation and was not refused. Were such an appellation as "Ward-Mum" to exist, I thought Elspeth would be 100% entitled to it. She was my heart's delight.

One day when I was disobediently resting my tired head in her lap, the lap suddenly shifted under my cheek –

'Get up, darling!' Momentary pause. 'Look who's here!'

I lifted my head at the urgency of her tone. Who should I see but Virginia coming towards us down the ward. In astonishment I said:

'What are you doing here?' (Meaning away from Edinburgh.)

Virginia's eyes were bright with excitement. 'I've brought you some news. Alastair's got a job in London – just the sort he was looking for! It's at the Evelyn Hospital.' (The Evelyn was a recently founded private hospital.) 'It's a super place – very state-of-the-art!.. It means we shall have to leave the NHS.' She gave me a sly look. 'The Evelyn is still recruiting people, so Alastair can put me up to them as a possible.'

I thought, I bet he can!

Virginia was smiling at her mother. 'So we shall both be here in London from now on.'

'Darling!..' Elspeth looked at her lovingly. She knew, we could all know, the move was to be nearer to her now that Viola was in Ethiopia. I was reflecting on Alastair's having twice-over landed the sort of job he wanted. I said:

'The luck of the Strachans.'

'I don't know about that, Daddy.' Said neither in reproach nor reproof, but with a stately matronish manner I had never observed before. 'Alastair is good at these things.'

Elspeth flashed me a grin of commiseration – put in my place.

'I'm terribly pleased to think it's likely that you and Alastair will both be coming to live in London.'

'The reason I'm down in London today – as well as to see Mummy – is to begin the search for somewhere for us to live.'

'Have you got an agent? Not that I'm pressing you to get one, though we had one ourselves. Actually we found the flat where we are now living: the agent did the paper-work and took his percentage.'

There was a short lull in the conversation. Then Virginia said to her mother:

'And now tell me about you! Staff Nurse wasn't around when I came in.'

Elspeth did her best to explain. Virginia listened. She said:

'It doesn't sound too bad.' Her tone was satisfied with the explanation: I was grateful for that – neither Elspeth nor I had got to try and explain medical detail we didn't comprehend to someone who did.

'It sounds as if the hospital is doing its job,' Virginia said. It was consoling. I wondered if she was cultivating a bedside manner – Elspeth was clearly born with a bedside manner. Inherited? Inculcated?.. I thought of Viola.

In a little while we said a temporary farewell to Virginia: 'It won't be long before I'm back,' she said. 'Hunting for somewhere for us to live.' She smiled at me. 'I'll get an agent today!'

We kissed each other all round and she left.

I found it difficult to tell whether Virginia thought the situation was stable, and if so how stable – I should have had to discuss it with her on her own.

Shortly after I had an opportunity to discuss it with the senior chemo consultant – confirming and deepening my impression of his being both effective and humane. (So he should be, you may say. I agree. But there was one of his registrars who struck us as effective and a bully.) The senior consultant confirmed also my impression of Elspeth's state, of the chemotherapy having an increasingly destructive effect on her appetite and digestion. Nevertheless he was hopeful. I imagined he had sensed my orientation towards the dark side of things. He did not conceal from me the possibility that in the event of Elspeth's being increasingly unable to eat, they might have to begin "drip-feeding" her for a spell to tide her over her present difficulties. It was obvious to me that he thought it was normal and might be successful.

That night I collogued with Virginia over the telephone.

'Don't look on the black side, Mr Lunn,' she said.

I imagined her smiling gently. Had I been there she would have put her arms round my neck. From Edinburgh she whispered to me:

'It will be all right, Daddy.'

Chapter XIX

Wigs

A surprising message from Will Gower – would I go up and see him in his office as soon as possible?

It was a nuisance. It disturbed my routine of class, pub, baths, hospital; and what's more I suspected it wasn't necessary, though Will was not the sort of man who wastes his time on meetings that are unnecessary. I went, returning to AULC between baths and hospital. I found him at his desk, with a bright provocative look in his eyes –

'Another letter from Avalon about you, Joe.'

'Really! What's it about this time?' I thought I'd settled Avalon's hash while Jim Yavner was here.

He held up the document under discussion but did not hand it to me.

'They didn't do themselves a lot of good with their previous letters,' I went on; then, feeling I must have sounded ungracious, couldn't think how to put it right. I imagined from his demeanour that he thought the present letter wasn't likely to rouse me to ire. 'What does it say?'

'Recently they've been having enquiries from students of yours, wanting to know if, should they stay for a second semester here, there'll be a second course in the English novel.' He laughed. 'Given by you, naturally.'

'They must be mad! Jim never mentioned all this.'

'It's probably come up since he retired. Anyway Avalon has never been a model for letting the left hand know what the right hand's doing.'

I was momentarily speechless.

'You've acquired a reputation, Joe.' No hint of irony.

'Very nice, too.'

'I think you should assume that if you were to give us a second course with a different list of novels, manifestly tailored for "double semester" students, Avalon would pay you a full repeat-fee without any trouble.'

'Now that's a proposition!' He wouldn't miss the irony in that.

There was a pause.

'I can see you are thinking it over, Joe.'

In that case he could see more than I could see. 'I think it's a dotty idea, Will, absolutely dotty.'

Apparently I had not convinced him that I'd got enough of AULC on my hands. After all that talk.

I saw an opening to play him up, just for the amusement of it. I said:

'I know these students. By the end of a semester I've taken most of a class out to the pub for a drink – where I talk to them individually about what they're thinking of doing next.' I paused. 'Out of a class of 30 I doubt if I've ever had more than two or three who say they're thinking of, or even interested in, coming back to AULC for another semester.'

'Then it would be a nice small class. Think of that!'

'Are you implying that Avalon would pay me a full fee for it?'

'You could claim for having to prepare an entire, fresh course. And you could claim for the teaching-time being the same whether it's a class of three or 30.'

I gave him a suspicious glance. 'It's a beautiful thought! Less arduous teaching; a fraction of the number of test-papers and examination-papers to mark. Don't you think all those accountants at Avalon would spot it?'

There was a private smile on his lips. 'I don't see why they should. Not until it's too late.' The smile changed to a laugh – a devious rural Welsh laugh. Once again we were both on the same side.

I realised that while I had been occupying myself with playing him up, he had been playing me.

I couldn't resist the pleasure of lingering over a new thought, fantasy though it might be, of Will and me colluding to trick the Avalon Department of English and Textual Studies.

'Do you know what's just occurred to me, Will?'

'What?'

'For my Course No 1, if we may call it that, I originally prepared to teach 12 novels. That had to be reduced by degrees to six, because the little darlings couldn't get through them.' I paused. 'For my Course No 2, all I should have to do would be to resuscitate the six novels I dropped, for which the bulk of the work is already done!'

Will had his shrewd brown head tilted to one side, thinking... I said:

'But the proposition to keep before us is the thought of my drawing a full fee for preparation and research, without doing any preparation and research!'

Will laughed outright. Shared laughter... In the game we were now playing with each other the irritations of the past were forgotten – by which I mean in particular my constant maunderings about time lost from my "writing", (which he must be pretty sick of).

Will said promptly; 'Aren't you overlooking the fact, Joe, that giving two courses during the semester would entail four days away from your writing?'

I didn't deign to reply – I was only prepared to take so much from him.

Anyway the joke had gone far enough for both of us. It was obvious that we were not going to collude in deceiving Avalon. What a pity! My plans for being wicked never got beyond being inflated like so many balloons – to be pricked a few moments later. In this case, though, our entire disputation, let alone its outcome, had had no basis in reality. I consoled myself that the story of it would provide me with gossip to recall for Elspeth – it's very important when regularly sick-visiting someone to have something ready to talk about. For the present, erosion of my writing-time had become a non-subject: my novel, finished and edited and all the rest of it, was due to go off to the printer's at any moment.

I didn't tell Will about the novel in order to keep something from him for once. Also it would have led him to ask me – people always do – what I was going to write next? I was too concerned about Elspeth to start another novel, even to think about it.

Will and I continued to look at each other with amusement for a moment. He stood up and went across to his coffee-machine.

While he was busy my thoughts suddenly switched: wasn't it time I gave up teaching Course No 1 instead of permitting self-congratulation on having turned down Course No 2? I remembered Will in those first early days – the nut-brown Welsh farmer – when we were pretty distant from each other: in the intervening years we had become friends.

His coffee was good, as ever...

While I was drinking it I was focussing on how I would recount to Elspeth the anecdote about teaching two courses, how to present the spectacle of Will and me each under the impression that it was solely he who was leading the other on. Two men making frightful asses of themselves... That would amuse her.

From Will Gower's office I went straight to the hospital, I found Elspeth was sitting up in bed; while sitting on a chair beside her was Virginia.

I kissed them both and said to Virginia –

'What are you doing here?'

'House-hunting.' She smiled at me just a touch sarcastically. 'You insisted I should go to an agent –'

'I never did! You're always saying I insist on your doing things, when all I do is suggest...'

Elspeth was laughing at us.

'You suggested,' Virginia said with an emphasis which indicated that she stuck to it that I'd insisted. 'I went to the agent you and Mummy used. The one who did the paper-work –'

'– And took the percentage...'

'Exactly. I think he's rather good at his job. I hadn't got anything in mind already, as you had. He hadn't got anything much on his books. Then this morning he phoned saying something had come in yesterday which he thinks is exactly what we're looking for. He was terribly excited about it. He says it's a snip.'

I felt I'd heard that story before, but I said nothing.

'What does Alastair think about it?' said Elspeth.

'Pretty excited, too. We both came down this morning. He's gone to the Evelyn for final negotiations while I came to see Mummy. Then we're both going to look at the place this evening.'

'Final negotiations with the Evelyn?..'

'Yes. Actually it's all sewn up, really. But he wanted to see them – to remind then that I'm in the market.'

'Two for the price of one.'

'Two for the price of two-and-a-half I hope!' She was laughing gaily. 'Viola would approve of that.' Elspeth and I joined in the laughter.

'Where is it?' said Elspeth.

'Hampstead.'

'Hampstead? I suppose it's reasonably convenient for the Evelyn, but isn't Hampstead one of the most expensive areas in London for you and Alastair?'

Virginia grinned. 'It's West Hampstead actually.'

Elspeth and I subsided. 'I wish you the best of luck,' Elspeth said.

'So do I,' said I.

Virginia subsided. We were all quiet for a few moments. The watery fluids in Elspeth's life-lines, chemo and nutrient, pulsated steadily through their perspex tubes. The ward itself seemed quiet.

Virginia noticed a brown cardboard box lying at the foot of the bed.

'What's that?' she said to Elspeth.

'You can open it – I haven't got around to opening it yet.' Elspeth explained: 'When I was put on chemo I was warned that it might make my hair fall out.'

Giving her mother's head a glance, Virginia said, 'It hasn't.' She was undoing the string round the box.

'This is just in case,' Elspeth said. 'Staff Nurse thought I might as well look at them in case it becomes necessary. The National Health Service supplies them free of charge.'

'So it should.' Virginia had the box open, revealing a collection of wigs. (I thought it looked rather creepy – all that hair...) 'Are you going to try them on?' She passed the box to Elspeth who said, 'Is there a hand-mirror anywhere around?' She was taking one of the wigs out. 'There's one in my handbag – will you get if for me?' She surveyed the wig, not absolutely sure how to put it on. Suddenly she looked at Virginia –

'Do you know what this reminds me of? When you and Viola were little girls you used to get me to take you to the Millinery Department in Harrods, to watch the Harrods ladies trying on hats. Then you both giggled at them.'

'Well, they looked terribly funny. Hats do look funny.'

'They do to you. They do to your father...'

I felt called upon to justify myself. 'It's because hats look to me so extraneous to the human form. Dresses and suits somehow fit round it and become part of it. (When they don't, they look funny, of course.) But hats – hats always look stuck on the top. That's my theory, anyway.' I gave then a mock-haughty look. 'I'm the theoretician of the family, doncha-know.'

'I suppose,' said Elspeth, putting one of the wigs on, 'I shall look funny.'

She settled the wig on her head. It looked awful.

'Yes, you do,' said Virginia, passing to her the small mirror out of her own handbag. 'Just a bit funny.'

Elspeth looked at herself and pulled the wig askew. At that she looked very funny and we all laughed.

'I doubt if this one will do,' she said solemnly and took it off.

'Daddy's got a point,' said Virginia.

Elspeth tried another, looked at herself in the glass, then twitched it to one side.

'Oh Mummy, if you go on like this, you'll look like Charley's Aunt!'

It was apparent that Elspeth was enjoying the fun of it. She took off the wig she was wearing and tried on another at an eccentric angle. She had always had a talent for this kind of thing: she wore an innocent look while she was doing it. By the time she had gone through the contents of the box we were all three given up to hilarity.

The fun died away and Virginia prepared to leave, to meet Alastair at the house-agent's. First of all she picked out one of the wigs.

'I think this is the best one, Mummy.'

Elspeth looked at her gratefully. 'Thank you, darling.'

'What a pity Viola is not here,' Virginia said, putting her choice of wig down outside the box. Just in case...

As we all felt the same no one said anything.

Virginia said her goodbyes. Then I went and sat on the side of the bed, close to Elspeth.

For a time Elspeth was silent. We were both silent. The mood had changed. Finally she looked at me with a tremulous expression and said:

'I don't want to leave you all.'

There was nothing I could say. She went on.

'It seems so soon...'

I bent close to her, looking into her eyes. I said:

'I shall always love you.'

Before I knew what I had done the tears were falling from my eyes; and then from Elspeth's too.

What I had implied was I shall still love you after you've gone...

For the first and only time we wept together over our fate.

Chapter XX

Viola Back

It was at about this time that I had an upsetting personal experience, afflicting me so privately that I could not even speak to Elspeth about it. I happened to read in my daily newspaper an authoritative article – the writer himself was suffering from cancer – saying that "the typical cancer-sufferer" is one who is "frustrated, suppressing anger." No matter whether there is some genetic element in the inheritance of the disease – Elspeth's father died of cancer – I found it then, have found it since, impossible to get the idea out of my thoughts; that Elspeth might have been in some way frustrated, suppressing anger. If she was, then the cause must be me.

Anger? Against the limitations of my nature, distantness and an absence of "give" in myself; a tendency to shy away from "give" in others – manifest already in some of the things I have written here about myself. Frustration?.. By a strand of the overbearing in me, exemplified by my insistence on her giving up her chosen career when we married. (She took up a lesser career later, when the girls became independent; but it was not the same.) The truth of it was too elusive and has remained too elusive, to be settled definitely; a mystery of existence which will no doubt haunt me to the end of my life. Was I responsible for the fate of the single human being whom I loved above all others? Who was, from the day I married her, more than half of my very life.

Meanwhile the inevitable, like a shadow in the doorway, was darkening... There was scarcely room for doubt – the remission was ending. The swelling came back; she was in physical discomfort, and finding it increasingly difficult to eat meals as an alternative to the nutrient solution. Courageous and stoical, she meant to take advantage of the hospital's offer to allow her to come home to the flat from time to time in order to see how we could cope. I now had some help from Virginia, whose house-hunting startlingly had come to a triumphant end: the house in West Hampstead was pronounced to be Just what they were looking for.

'Is it a snip?' I enquired.

'Well, yes...' Virginia said over the telephone. I heard doubt... I suffered from erosion of belief in "snips" where house-buying was concerned. I didn't ask how much Virginia and Alastair were going to pay for it – that would emerge later, when our benighted Government raised the mortgage-rate, or rather dickered about with interest-rates in such a way that the Building Societies were bound to put up their mortgage-rates. I had registered the fact that Alastair and Virginia were going in for a house rather than a flat, and, from the sound of it, a house rather bigger than they had intended. All this meant one thing to me – they were going to start a family.

Alastair moved into his job at the Evelyn Hospital, and the two of them moved into the house within a week. As yet there was no news of Virginia's being found a job at the Evelyn, but I now had great trust in Alastair's Scottish pertinacity.

Elspeth was cheered by the return of Virginia to London. She still missed Viola. Like me, she was happiest when both girls were within reach. At that time we had another letter from Viola.

Virginia and I mulled over the letter in the context of our having to call Viola back home –

"Maichuw, Tigre Province   April 14 th

Tigre is an arid land littered with boulders. The houses are made of stone, the natural building material for the region, which is too dry for building mud huts. These houses are rather impressive big square buildings – but empty. Most of the villages are deserted – people trekking into the towns for food if they can find it. The rains have failed yet again, and what little seed remained for next year's crop has been eaten. But the relief agencies – and us – are under constant military threat both from the insurgents and the government troops. In fact as far north as this it's difficult to know which side of the battle line in a guerrilla war one's on.

There are people dying everywhere, it's desperately sad. I've had to harden my heart or I'd be running to catch the next plane back to London. Mothers carrying dead or dying babies, small children with distended bellies begging for food. And there is no food. The land is bare and dusty and people are starving. We are based in a former Seventh Day Adventist Hospital, a handful of expatriate do-gooders and some lovely Ethiopian nurses, desperately short of drugs and doctors. We've been trying to save a life or two, knowing that these children will probably die from starvation even if we can contain the diseases that go with it. This is my world now for as long as I mean to stay – basic and awful and horrifying and tragic, with no apparent end to it. And yet it's a country that's beautiful and haunting as well, a people – or peoples, there are over seventy languages – of Old Testament magnificence under cloaks of rags and dirt. Just round the corner are strange mountains, the Seniens, jagged and bare like a moon landscape – Ethiopia is the highest land mass in Africa. And a life very near to death all the time. The opposite to like home.

Yet I know it's where I have to be, because I'm alive here, feel useful (a bit) and needed – every time we save the life of a child we feel it. Even any comfort we can offer the sick, the dying, the bereaved (we are all bereaved), seems of more value, more useful – each time I suddenly feel I'm more needed here than anywhere else. And that's a good feeling to have, it keeps me going amidst the horror in this particular "heart of darkness". (I know Conrad is not a favourite of yours!)

I think of you all. With love –"

'She has obviously settled down there,' Virginia said.

'We shan't have the heart to send for her back.'

'I think it's marvellous that she's settled down so well.'

'She's never done this before?..'

'Poor girl!..' I said, thinking of her simultaneously having to face the loss of her mother and having to leave the environment where she'd found her métier.

'She'll get over having to leave Ethiopia,' Virginia said realistically.

I had no feeling that I was looking into the future, when I said: 'Perhaps she'll insist on going back.'

Virginia said nothing.

Together we went over Viola's letter again.

At the Royal Essex Elspeth's condition was subject to ebb and flow. 'I'm ready to take the offer of a weekend's absit,' she said.

'Whenever you're ready.'

I could reassure myself that she was in better form at present. She was even able to rouse a spark of her old self when I arrived to see her at the Essex.

'Did you come by taxi?'

This was because of my painful hip. That, too, had got worse – I was now more or less permanently committed to walking with a stick. When I walked down the ward to her bed I tried to swing along athletically as if there were nothing the matter! Had I come by taxi? If I'd said No, having chosen to travel free on public transport, I should have been in for trouble.

'You know you can afford a taxi!' She could still raise momentarily a bullying tone. I had to find excuses. Occasionally I did travel by taxi so as to be able to answer Yes without lying.

In the background there were the usual dramas of ward-life. One day an elderly Jewish man was dying of cancer in the next bed, surrounded by huge family weeping and mourning vociferously. It made us realise that we, for our part, were not given to such displays. Perhaps we might have survived the better for it. I should, anyway... She took up the offer of a Saturday night absit on three occasions; this was to ease the monotony for her, the monotony of being, among other things, continually chained to those pulsating drips. On the first and third occasions she was feeling too ill to respond. On the middle occasion she walked into the flat, a top-floor flat with the evening sun shining into it –

'Doesn't it look pretty!'

Said freshly, appreciatively, as if she were seeing it for the first time, when it was she, herself, who had created it to look pretty: reposeful and lively with muted greenish blue carpets and curtains, brilliant white walls and large paintings mostly by our friends, a few inherited pieces of furniture made of mahogany, rosewood and sandal-wood... Pretty. As if she were seeing it for the first time, not as if she were seeing it for the last time... Can hail and farewell be dissolved into each other, spoken as if it were from two sides of a transparent wall? Her air of separateness, of separation – I don't know which is the better word for it – was becoming marked. I had first noticed it up in the ward. It seemed to me that when I was with her her attention showed signs of fading that were new. It was particularly noticeable when she was immersed in her guise as "Ward-Mum" – while I was talking to her she would catch sight of something happening down the ward and her attention would flick away, only momentarily, perhaps, yet when it returned it was weaker.

Virginia had noticed the same thing. In a sense it was not surprising: Elspeth's life with us was becoming more remote, superseded by her life in the ward. Was it really becoming more remote for deeper reasons? Could it be that when one was coming towards death the end of life was not absolutely sudden? More of a merging?..

Virginia and I had now recognised that our alternating states of hoping and fearing had given way – we couldn't ignore it any longer – to a steady state of recognising the inevitable. Was it the same for Elspeth? Could it possibly be different for Elspeth? Despite her courage, despite her longing to live...

The air of separateness, of separation – was it the beginning, I asked myself, of her final separating from Life?

'I don't want to leave you all...'

And so another stage was passed. Elspeth found it almost impossible to eat at all. She was permanently hooked up to the second flask – the first for saline containing the therapeutic drugs, the second for nutrient. It sustained her life but she was becoming weaker – too weak to be got out of bed, with all the humiliations that involved. It was impossible not to feel that she might be coming to the final stage. We must call Viola back.

I discussed it with Virginia, who said, 'I should have called her back a few weeks ago if it hadn't seemed such a shame to bring her away, when she's really found something...'

I discussed it with the Staff Nurse: she concurred. 'I think Mrs Lunn would be happier if her elder daughter was here as well.'

I telephoned Addis, was unable to get in touch with Viola as she was out of the head quarters on duty: I left a message – and waited anxiously until she called that evening.

'How long will it take you to get a flight back?'

'I'll check that now.' She hesitated. 'Is it very urgent? Tell me!..'

'Yes... My darling...'

Silence.

'I'll reserve a flight at the earliest moment – I'll tell the airline why. And I shall explain to the hospital here why. I don't know whether they'll stipulate any time limit for compassionate leave – if there's any difficulty I shall resign altogether. If Mummy wants me...'

I didn't ask questions about the conditions of her contract. Just waited anxiously till the next call, which was to say she'd been incredibly lucky and got a cancellation on the next flight out of Addis Abbaba. She thought people responded urgently to the prospect of Death. (I thought airlines responded urgently to the prospect of a "no-show".) Viola gave me the schedules and I resumed my anxious waiting. In the meantime I telephoned the Royal Essex and left a message for Elspeth, telling her Viola was on the way.

At the appointed time on the following day the telephone rang again –

'I'm back.'

'Darling girl!..'

'Do you mind if I go straight from here to the Royal Essex?'

'I should like that.' (I should have liked to be there as well, but that didn't seem to be part of the plan.) 'So will Elspeth.' I paused. 'What about your baggage?'

'I've brought the minimum.'

'I see...' What I saw was that she had not committed herself to coming home for good. My heart sank.

The day's arrangements unfolded under the hand of Virginia. Viola was going to stay the night with her and Alastair. The evening was to be occupied by Virginia cooking dinner at my flat for the four of us.

Viola and Virginia arrived together, carrying baskets of food.

'You'd have thought I had no food in the flat,' I said.

'You can't have enough for all of us,' said Virginia. 'Shush, Daddy.' She kissed me on the cheek.

'Since you're here,' I said, 'please tell me the latest news about your getting a temporary job, presumably as a locum.'

'It shouldn't be difficult. But we want one that suits us.'

'At the Evelyn for preference?'

'Naturally,' She paused. 'It's a super hospital. Alastair hasn't given up hope of their having something to suggest.'

'Will it be tricky for you, under private enterprise?' said Viola.

'I don't see why it should be.' Virginia gave Viola the special clear-eyed look she used to give her years ago – for instance when Viola enquired if she, Virginia, had seen that spare Mars bar in the playroom-cupboard. Seeing the look now I just managed to restrain myself from saying she ought to go in for medical politics – it was a look my dear old mother had been expert at delivering, though absence of opportunity to exercise it had kept it from national use. My mother, Virginia's grandmother... the same look.

It was clear that Viola thought Virginia was moving politically to the Right.

Virginia said, 'If Alastair starts to rave about the Evelyn – state-of-the-art and all that – give his ankle a sharp kick under the table!

Viola nodded her head – it was the last thing she'd do.

Virginia stood up and said, 'I must begin the cooking. Viola, you stay and talk to Daddy!'

I was looking forward to getting Viola on her own. I wanted to hear her private views on Ethiopia in the first place, about her private plans in the second.

Viola glanced at the open doorway into the kitchen.

'I want to talk about my plans first.'

'What are they?'

Viola laughed. 'Not as inchoate as they'd have been before I went.' She seemed amused by the change in herself. 'Does that amuse you?'

'It pleases me.'

So that was that. I looked at her for further signs of change, but first of all I asked:

'Are you glad you joined Nursing Aid Overseas?'

'It has transformed my life, Daddy. I thought it would. It has.'

'In what way?' I wanted to know what she'd say about it.

'Made me feel...' She hesitated... possibly in putting something which meant so much to her into such commonplace language. 'Feel grown up.' She stopped for an instant. 'That's it.' She smiled at herself. 'I now know who I am. And where I'm going.'

Clichés have become clichés because they mean something to the people who use them. Viola meant hers. And I understood them.

'So you're going to go on?' What I meant was did she intend to go back to Ethiopia?

To answer me she took on a completely different tone of voice – for a topic I couldn't remember her having spoken on for years, if ever.

'It's final that I'll never have babies of my own. I know that, will accept it... But I can still make a life – I can make a life, Daddy – caring for other people's.'

I had nothing to say. We were both silent.

At this moment Virginia came in with a tray of drinks. She looked from Viola to me –

'Well, Daddy, how have you been getting on with my dear little sister?' (She was the taller of the two.)

'I think we have avoided serious conflict.'

'I didn't want Alastair to turn up in the middle of a civil war.' It seemed a silly remark – provoked by uneasiness of some sort? 'He's due at any moment now, if he's not late. I expect him to be late.'

'When you get the sort of job you love,' I said, 'you won't bother about his working overtime on a job he loves.'

With a captivating grin. 'That's right.'

At that moment we were interrupted. It was Alastair.

'Not late,' Virginia said triumphantly.

Alastair's cheeks were ruddy, his eyes flashing.

'The luck of the Strachans,' he said.

'Is there a job for me?' Virginia cried. Then trying to climb down a bit – 'Or the possibility of one?'

'Caution, caution!' He put on a Scots accent.

'Listen to the Dominie!'

'My dear wife, you don't know what caution means.'

I thought it was unjustified, until I noticed the way they were looking at each other – dazzling-eyed. The subject of the conversation was other.

Viola glanced at me: she was amused.

I retired from the talking. I only hoped we weren't going to start calling Alastair "The Dominie" because I liked him very much.

Chapter XXI

A Pub-Lunch With Will

The following morning, when I made my usual telephone call to Elspeth's ward to enquire how she was, there was different news.

'Your wife seems a bit brighter this morning, Mr Lunn.' It was a little charge nurse whom I knew. She went on: 'I think having her daughter back home from Ethiopia has given her a lift.'

'I'll come out and see her this morning.' (I was allowed to visit at almost any time of day.)

'I'll tell her, Mr Lunn. And your daughters?'

'They can organise themselves.'

I heard a friendly little laugh and we rang off.

I was cheered by the news of Elspeth, but it happened that I was not in the brightest of spirits, myself. My replaced hip, which had been going through a relatively quiescent period, appeared to have come out of it – with some fervour. I decided to get a taxi to the hospital; be a good boy.

Elspeth was sitting propped up in bed, looking brighter –

'Did you come by taxi?'

'Yes.' I was triumphant. I'd got through the occasion without having to decide whether to lie or not. I waited for the indulgence that was my due. Instead –

'Do you think it's time you went to see the orthopaedic consultant at St Anne's about it?' That was more like her old self. 'You mustn't let it go on.'

'I don't let it go on for pleasure,' I couldn't resist saying. I hated the indignity of using a walking-stick almost as much as the enduring of a painful joint.

'I know that.' Tone of voice softened by tender concern.

Au fond the reason I was putting off being treated at present was one I could not come out with to her, though she probably guessed it. Orthopaedic treatment would involve more surgery, and I couldn't face going into hospital myself while Elspeth was in hospital.

'I'll see about it,' I said.

'It worries me seeing you in pain all the time.'

'The pain comes and goes, you know.'

'It doesn't go much, so far as I can see.'

I smiled feebly.

'I'd like you to do something during the next few days. Will you?'

I acquiesced. That was that. I said:

'It's good to see you in better form.'

She smiled wryly at me – 'You mean I'm well enough to bully you?'

I just leaned over the bed and kissed her on the cheek. Peace was restored.

That was all very well, but I had given my word. I had to telephone our long-suffering GP and ask her to make me an appointment at St Anne's. 'If they tell you there's a fearfully long waiting list I shall not write a letter of complaint to the Minister of Health.'

Needless to say my number came up after that almost immediately.

I was called to see the Senior Orthopaedic Surgeon, so to that extent my number could be called a lucky one – I had hit a jackpot.

As a start I was examined by his registrar and then X-rayed: then I was interviewed by the great man himself.

The great man himself was in his early fifties, healthy-looking and strongly-built. He was dressed with a touch of individuality very pleasing in a hospital – a touch more appropriate to country-life. A rather grand tweed suit and expensive buckskin shoes.

'So,' he said by way of introduction, 'you've already had a hip-replacement, Mr Lunn. What year was that?' I observed that he had what looked like a complete folder of my papers in front of him.

'1977,' I said. 'So long ago I call it my ur-replacement.'

'Exactly.' He was nodding his head and permitting a smile of some grandeur to illuminate his countenance. 'They always come to us after 10 years or so. The prostheses in those days had a limited lifetime. They wore out.' Transferring his attention more particularly to me, he went on, 'You seem a pretty active sort of fellow.'

'I suppose so.' Momentarily I felt shy.

'We shall have to do a "revision", Mr Lunn, if you are willing.'

'What's a "revision"?'

'Taking out the old prosthesis and putting in a new one.' That was forthright enough. And suited to my level of understanding. I felt that the degree of professional eminence he was nowadays enjoying must have relaxed him to the extent of his being happy to treat his patients as human-beings. Good for him! I said:

'It sounds to me as if a "revision" is a replacement of a replacement.'

'You could call it that.' His practised facial expression was touched by a smile of amusement.

'Why do you ask me if I'm willing?'

'Because it's a much more serious operation than the original replacement.' Clearly not a man who was given to leaving room for doubt.

'You have to saw out the old one?'

'And gouge out the cement.'

I imagined that as the patient had asked for it, he saw no reason why the patient – this patient at least – shouldn't get it.

'Jesus!' I cried.

He must have thought this patient was somewhat deficient in reverence for either the Saviour of Mankind or Modern Surgery. Or possibly both. It didn't appear to worry him – any more than it worried me.

'And you lose a lot of blood.' He enlarged on that. 'It's a very bloody operation.'

'I don't know if I've got all that much blood to spare.'

An ironic, friendly smile. 'We shall see, shan't we?'

I looked at him, weighing him up – and decided he was a good chap. Previously I had dismissed surgeons as a somewhat brutal breed, built like rugby footballers, (this one was), going around carrying their bags of carpenter's tools; drills, saws, hammers, gouges...

'I'm willing,' I said. 'I can't walk without pain as it is. Not that I'm mad about walking – swimming's my thing... But I don't feel called upon to put up with the pain any more.' I paused. 'I shall be able,' I asked, 'to walk afterwards, shan't I?'

'All being well,' A quick laughing glance. 'And swim...'

'How long will the new prosthesis last?'

'Indefinitely.'

'But I shan't!'

'Then as long as you last.'

He was looking at me appraisingly.

I looked appraisingly back.

It appeared that both of us were satisfied.

Another seance was over. We stood up and shook hands. We liked each other.

Of course I reported the seance to Elspeth immediately.

'Well, you see,' she said – meaning that the occasion displayed how correct she had been in her initial judgement.

In that matter she later got approval from the girls. In fact by my current *démarche* even I got – shall we say a "modicum" of? – approval from the girls.

'They'll put you on their waiting-list,' said Virginia.

'We don't know how long that is,' said Viola.

'It will depend for one thing,' said Alastair, 'on how urgent the surgeon deems it to be.'

I cut short a technical discussion with my own final word on the subject –

'I'm not willing to contemplate going into Queen Anne's for surgery while Elspeth is still in the Royal Essex.'

'None of us would ask you to,' said Virginia.

I glanced at Viola and Alastair – judged by the look of them, nor would they.

At that point the subject came to rest. For how long would it be?

I found myself discussing this latest topic with Will Gower.

'We noticed you were having trouble getting about,' he said. 'Thank God you are managing to keep up with us. If it becomes excessively difficult for you, please let us know! I won't say Avalon will propose to subsidise a taxi for carrying you to and fro, but that's a stone that won't be left unturned – I mean the proposal won't be left unturned, not the taxi.'

I was silent. He had brought me out to lunch after my class to an out-of-the-way little pub that was not far from the Centre but unfrequented by the students. We were eating toasted cheese-and-onion sandwiches washed down by lager. He said:

'I hope you know, Joe, in fact I'm sure you do know, how much I sympathise with you in all these medical... contingencies you have to cope with. It's noble of you to stick with Avalon.'

I said unrestrainedly:

'I wish to God all these contingencies were not so medical, in fact all medical! My existence nowadays seems to be packed with doctors, nurses, hospitals... I'm getting absolutely sick of it. It's all so conscribed... I long for a change. You must long for me to have something else to talk about!' I drank some lager. 'I'd even swap for a world of contingencies in Bible Studies.'

I didn't wait for him to consider that idea. 'Anything to get away from doctors, nurses, hospitals!..'

He gave me a lively, brown-eyed look –

'It's the luck of the draw that you've got two daughters and a son-in-law all in the medical profession.'

'Not my choice – they did the draw, not I.'

'Do you regret it?'

'Of course not. They're trying to do something for their fellow mortals; and they're succeeding. That's the most important thing anyone could hope for in these days.' I paused. 'In their different ways I believe each of them has found a solution to the question of what to live by.'

'It's obvious for Virginia and Alastair. What do you see Viola doing?'

'It's too early to say. I suppose she may decide to come home and look after me. More likely – this is how I've begun to see it during these last months – she'll devote her life to the rescue of suffering children in one part of the globe or another.' I took a swig of lager. 'A Kiddie-Winkies Mother Teresa!' (It was the painful thought of losing her which made me resort to a sadistic quip.)

Will was watching me. We were silent for a minute or two. (We had the toasted cheese-and-onion sandwiches to finish anyway.) Will said;

'And what about you, Joe? Surely you've found what you want to live by? Distinguished writer and all that – no complaints.'

'No complaints? Tolstoi was a distinguished writer complaining to the end!'

'That's no contribution to the argument. Tolstoi was complaining about other matters.'

I laughed. 'You're right there, Will. The poor old sod.' I picked up a sandwich. 'We'd better get on with these things.'

Will was thoughtful – clearly about me. He picked up his last sandwich.

'At present, Joe, I don't think you're in a mood or state of mind or whatever you call it, to...' He didn't finish the sentence but what he had in mind hovered over the unsatisfactory talk. 'I think, Joe, you're too thrown by Elspeth.'

'Of course I am. Her fate is the centre of my life – and furthermore it's taking up all the periphery as well. Doctors, nurses, hospitals, operations, treatments...' I ploughed on with neurotic insistence. 'I'm hemmed in by them, totally preoccupied with them. I long for the skies to break and rain down on me something different, some freedom and high spirits.'

'What about the literary part of your life? You have a niche in literary society, a niche in literary history, we're told. Isn't that consoling enough for you?'

'Literary society – oh yes...' (I was too modest to bring in the literary history bit.) 'You're thinking of my being on the Executive of the International PEN, on the Council of the Royal Society of

Literature, on the Management Committee of the Society of Authors and all that. You think that's a Big Deal?' I laughed at him. 'I have to tell you they don't deal me very much – if anything. They don't fill my soul with longing any more – other than longing for the Booker Prize of course.' I put every ounce of my irony into that "of course".

'Your literary reviews, your scientific pieces,' he suggested without conviction, (rightly). He finished his glass of lager and laughed at me. 'And what about Avalon University London Centre? What about us?'

'That puts me on the spot unfairly, Will. I like my pupils very much. But that doesn't fill my life with joy and companionship, I'm afraid.'

'It could help. You turn down their invitations to parties.'

'We've gone over this before, Will. I don't accept their parties because I have my own feeling for propriety. I'm not going to drink too much in my pupils' presence. And smoking their pot is out. I don't propose when in Rome to do as the Romans do.'

(The thought fleeted through my mind that I had probably expressed a profound truth about myself – I constantly refused when in Rome to do as the Romans do – at the same time expecting them to love me for it!)

Will went on; 'There's nothing wrong with pot. I've been using it for years – in moderation.'

I was not surprised – after all, he'd had a sabbatical at Avalon U, where according to all reports there was a time when everybody was smoking the stuff. "As a social habit", they were supposed to have said. Yet I was faintly surprised to hear Will, as the Dean of AULC, saying it publicly. How little one knows of people, I thought... Which precipitated a realisation that the concept of "the nut-brown Welsh farmer" must be one of the furthest from the mark I'd ever had. However the thought of what a frightful ass I'd made of myself amused me. The joke was on me but it was a joke. I'd thought of myself as hot shit and then turned out to be cold porridge. Luckily I hadn't shared the idea with anyone but Elspeth and the girls – it was not a joke I'd want to circulate round the Universe.

Anyway, Will's eyes were nut-brown, his hair nut-brown, and during the summer months his tanned complexion not far from nut-brown; and I'd have put money on his coming out top dealer in any cattle-market up in Brecon!

'Another lager, Joe?'

'Why not?'

'You're feeling a bit better?' He was laughing at me .'A bit more reconciled to things?'

'I'd never admit that to anyone but you, Will – who can see it for himself whatever I say.'

He went across to the bar to buy more drinks. At that moment some other patron precipitated a battering issue of noise from a machine against the wall at the other end of the room.

Will, carrying the drinks, cast a glance at the infernal machine –

'Do you want to leave, Joe?'

I cast my glance at the two beautiful glasses, with liquid golden as piss, froth white as yesterday's snow... Only a direct quotation from Gertrude Stein could express what had to be said –

'A drink is a drink is a drink, innit?'

Chapter XXII

Death

Message for me from the Royal Essex – "Your wife would like to see you and her two daughters together."

It was an afternoon when I was not teaching. I managed to get hold of Viola and Virginia at Virginia's new house, where they were working on the place. We met, all three, in the foyer of the Essex and went up to the ward together. As we entered it one of the nurses – we knew all the nurses by now – was waiting for us. She said;

'Your wife says she wants to have a heavy talk with you.'

"Heavy" was not one of Elspeth's words, but the message was ominously clear. We gathered round the bed where Elspeth was lying – too weak to sit up? She waited for us to settle down and then addressed us –

'I've told them to cut off the nutrient drip.'

After a moment's pause, with the emphasis of finality –

'It's my decision.'

None of us uttered. It was indeed final – without the nutrient she could not survive. Of course we understood. She was already suffering intolerable discomfort if not intolerable pain. She could eat nothing and was hopelessly weak. Of course there was no other outcome than the one she had decided to take immediately. In reply neither I nor Virginia nor Viola could say a word.

She began to tell us the things she wanted us to do after she was dead. She had left an explicit and orderly will about what was to become of her property, including instructions that she was to be cremated "at the minimum expense". (We had all agreed to the latter at the time, but regretted it after it had happened.) What she intended to talk about now was how she wanted her disposable minor property to be distributed. The fact

170

that there was something she was determined to say seemed to give her an access of energy.

She came to the obsequies –

'You'll have to have all my side of the family,' she said with wry humour. (All my own side consisted of one sister, her husband and children, far away in Philadelphia.)

'You'll have to give them something to eat afterwards. Get them some sandwiches from Marks and Spencer's.'

It was difficult to believe all this was happening, this matter-of-fact discussion of trivialities. Like much that had gone on during the last few days it had an air of unreality. Very strange.

The "heavy talk" was over: we were completely at a loss for conversation. The girls mechanically set about the usual chores of hospital-visiting – changing the water in flowers, collecting the washing to be taken home for laundering. It was past six o'clock, the time when we usually prepared to leave, when Elspeth was obviously more than ready for us to leave. The light of a May evening was fading from the ward, whose grey walls were never inspiringly bright. Elspeth had said everything she wanted to day: she lay back exhausted. There was nothing for us to do but leave.

On the way out we spoke to one of the two nurses, asking for a promise that whenever the end came in sight they would send for us immediately. They promised. They understood. When the end came we were all to be there, holding her... None of us asked the question, "How long is it likely to be?" They wouldn't have been able to tell us. It was Friday evening now. Which day would it be?

On the Saturday afternoon the girls and I went to the hospital again; and then on the Sunday afternoon, sitting quietly beside the bed in a sort of vigil. We could see that Elspeth knew we were there and time was passing. At the end of visiting-time she managed to address herself to Viola and Virginia in a kindly tone of voice – 'You can go...' After lingering embraces they left.

I, it appeared, was meant to stay. I stayed another hour, exhausted, reduced. As I left I reminded the nurses of their promise, though I didn't need to – they were so kind.

When I got outside I was powerfully called by the public-house across the road – I longed for a stiff whisky. (Most of the big London hospitals have a pub on the opposite corner of the street –

breweries know their business.) Many was the time I had sat in this pub, quietly reading the *Standard* after leaving the Essex for the night. At this moment I thought perhaps I'd better not, as the girls had said they would go on to the flat and make us some supper. A taxi came up and I got into it.

The taxi drove me home at speed. When I let myself into the flat the girls were waiting for me. 'The hospital has just rung up. Mummy's much worse.'

'We must go,' I said unnecessarily.

'Yes.'

We called a minicab and in a few minutes we were speeding back – thank goodness I hadn't gone to the pub – in the direction along which I had just come.

Virginia had succeeded in getting in touch with Alastair and we all four met in the foyer of the Royal Essex and then went up to the ward where the two nurses on night duty were waiting for us – the lights were out and everywhere was silent. We were escorted to Elspeth's bed where the curtains round it were drawn. We sat on chairs close to the bed. I sat close to Elspeth's head, Virginia sitting beside me taking one of her hands, Viola sitting on the opposite side taking hold of the other hand: Alastair sat at the foot.

We thought she knew we were there. She was lying on her side, her face sweating and distorted, her hair damp and awry, the sheets rumpled. She was breathing stertorously in violent gasps – a racking sound. From time to time she squeezed the girls' fingers. They couldn't tell if it was a voluntary effort to convey a message or an involuntary spasm. Each of us whispered to her, 'I'm here...'

She was fighting for breath, fighting to live, perhaps fighting not to leave us. So soon... It was agonising to watch, but all four of us were under control. After a little while a young woman doctor whom we hadn't seen before came through the curtains. Tentatively, with great tact, she put a question to us – would we like her to give Elspeth an injection to ease her on her way out?

'Oh, please do!..'

The doctor gave the injection. We went on holding Elspeth's hands – for a little while Virginia gave up the hand she was holding to me. The stertorous gasps went on without perceptible diminution. The agony persisted..

The doctor came again, with a second offer. 'Oh, please do!..' Still it persisted.

At last a third time. We went on holding Elspeth, our most loved one. And the gasps stopped. I thought she must have died and I closed her eyelids. The gasps started again, but only for a minute or so, and then they really stopped... I pressed my finger gently down her eyelids for the last time. It was over.

The doctor looked in, then the nurses. The girls and I stood up and clung to each other, weeping, for I don't know how long. At one moment they leaned their heads away from me and one of them whispered – 'We will look after you!'

At last it was time to give up. The nurses were waiting outside the curtains. They came in to ask us – would we like a cup of tea?

Of course we said Yes, and it transpired that the idea was that while we were drinking a cup of tea, they, the nurses, would make Elspeth look tidier for our last sight of her. So we sat, the four of us, in the nurses' little room off the end of the ward, where they had a tray with cups and tea-bags and an electric kettle of boiling water. We found it a very acceptable cup of tea. It was in the early hours of Monday morning.

We were led back and shown through the curtains one at a time – Alastair went with Virginia. The apparatus of the drips, the stands, the perspex tubes and the plastic bags of liquid had been swept away. Elspeth was still lying on her side, but her face had been wiped and her hair combed. I looked at her, stunned.

She had never had many lines on her face, just a few down her upper lip. Now every trace of life's storms had gone. She looked simply beautiful... I bent down and kissed her cheek for the last time: to my lips it felt as smooth and fresh as it did on the day I married her, thirty-eight years ago.

I waited while the girls each took the last turn with their mother, and then, with our arms round each other, we walked out, down the stairs and out of the hospital.

Alastair had been getting a taxi for us. We all got in and it took us to my empty home.

Chapter XXIII

Aftermath

It seems that one of the dispensations of Fate is to ensure, after the death of somebody close to one, that one is kept busy. One's mind is distracted from dwelling on grievous loss by being forced to cope with a sort of civil-servant's schedule of official necessities – collecting death certificate, negotiating with undertaker, arranging funeral. (Arranging a funeral in this case according to the will of the deceased, a cremation.) Then notifying relations; putting notices in the newspapers; arranging a wake – in this case, by order of the deceased, assembling Marks and Spencer's sandwiches and bottles of wine. The first days of desolation are occupied with the trivia of action. Perhaps it is as well.

We assembled, just Elspeth's brother and sisters, Viola, Virginia and Alastair, and I at the crematorium on a grey, faintly drizzly June morning. The specified minimum of expense; no religious service; a single bunch of white freesias on the coffin when it appeared; a wait outside afterwards presumably while the ashes were dispersed – no mounds of flowers, no crowds of mourning friends. One mistake after another.

One mistake after another? I only realised afterwards, when I discovered how many friends there were who wanted to come to the funeral, but were unable to do so because my newspaper notices had not said where it was to be: and they would have liked to send flowers, they told me reproachfully – my newspaper notices had asked them to contribute to the Cancer Research Fund. On those two simple counts to start with I had deprived them... And lastly the mistake in accord with our absence of all religious belief, the mistake of having a cremation. I wouldn't have believed I could have shared the common atavistic desire for a grave, some place to which I could always go, at the spot above where her remains would always lie, to leave a flower.

Alastair drove us back to the flat for the wake. Elspeth was right – M & S sandwiches are the best. The mourning company were kept busy, eating and drinking.

On the following morning I began writing answers to letters of condolence, which came in by the score during the next few weeks. I hadn't realised that so many people felt an affectionate regard for Elspeth – so bound up must I have been in my own feeling for her. When, in the past, I had written letters of condolence myself I had often wondered whether they were of the slightest use to the recipients: when I received them myself I discovered they were. They resonated in me with a response deriving unexpectedly from Elspeth's going through so many months of suffering and treatment in hospital. Painful though it was, the "hospital experience", as it was likely to be dubbed, finally disclosed a consoling, uplifting side – to see so many people, doctors, nurses, helpers, devoted to "caring" (another cliché) not necessarily selflessly, not necessarily because they were paid for it, but because an impulse to do so seemed to come from the depths of human nature, the human nature we all share; despite the end of its being, where we were concerned, death, the experience was uplifting.

A letter which touched me poignantly partly on account of its content but also because it was so unattended –

I am writing to express our sincere sympathies and condolences to you and your family at this very sad time. As you know Elspeth was more of a friend than a patient to us all and she endeared herself to everyone at the Essex who knew her during her long illness which she bore with tremendous courage and good humour. We shall certainly never forget her nor indeed the wonderful support which you and your family gave. I am only sorry we were not able to do more to help.

With kindest regards and best wishes –

From the senior consultant in chemotherapy at the hospital. A letter unattended by us, a letter astonishing in its ever being written by a man with so many cares and duties on his plate. A gleam of humanity from the hospital machine.

This was happening at the beginning of June. Immediately in front of me stretched, of course, a roll of "Things To Be Done" –

175

necessary Things which no man could want to do... Where to live?.. How to live?.. The girls set about helping me. Any why to live? When Elspeth was no longer there for me to live for? After a few hours I threw that question out of the door as too shameful and dishonest: so long as the girls were alive I had them to live for – and I meant to do just that.

Life was no longer going to be easy for me in any sense. Where to live? Virginia and Alastair nobly invited me to go and live with them for a while – nobly, I thought, because they would be going against their own inclinations for my sake. I settled the question –

'Darling Virginia' – I had my arm affectionately round her waist – 'it's lovely of you and Alastair to ask me. And lovely as it would be to live with you both, I couldn't possibly do it.' I explained. 'You see, I'm too "set in my ways".'

She smiled. 'You mean you'd be too bloody awkward?'

I hugged her. 'I knew you'd hit upon what Parisians call *le mot juste*.'

There was an absorbing moment of relief – she was not going to be called upon to go against her inclinations: I was not going to be called upon to go against mine.

She said, 'That doesn't mean we can abandon you. We must make some plans for you. I think Viola's got some ideas as well.'

Virginia was always supposedly chary about giving away Viola's intentions in advance – in their girlhood they'd had several tiffs over it.

I said on a different tack:

'What about her going back to Ethiopia?'

'She can't decide.'

'Doesn't she want to go back?'

'She'll tell you.'

'Of course... But she must want to go back, after having taken so passionately to it. It's a fulfilling way of life for her.' I realised I was speaking to my own disadvantage. Of course I didn't want her to go back.

A different kind of smile appeared round Virginia's mouth –

'Has she told you about the French doctor?'

Thinking – And you probably ought not to be telling me about him, either – I said:

'No. What's that?'

'He's one of a *Médécins Sans Frontières* team at her hospital.'

'Oh!' I exclaimed, in a sudden turmoil of emotions.

'She will tell you,' said Virginia, clearly marking the end of the conversation.

I felt sympathy for Viola, having her confidences hinted at, even for friendly purposes.

Virginia changed the subject. 'We must start looking around at housekeepers.'

'I don't want anyone to live in!'

Virginia grinned, as much as to say "There he goes, set in his ways"! I stared at her to make sure she'd registered my adamant intention. Steady, grey, hazel-flecked eyes...

'O.K, Daddy.'

I suspected that she'd decided it was Viola's turn to try her hand with me.

I was right. I didn't have to wait long for Viola to come and sound me. On the following morning she turned up at the flat, looking smaller than Virginia but no less determined.

'We can't let you live here entirely alone,' she said.

'Why not?' I was taking a chance to short-circuit the proceedings. No luck.

'I've been thinking it over – as well as Virginia,' she said firmly.

There was a pause. Then she said:

'I'll come and live here to look after you if you like.'

Dramatic; and so touching that it almost brought tears to my eyes... I was silent – for a moment I didn't know what to say.

Viola coming to live here at the flat with me would entail far less of a shake-up in "my ways" than my going to live with Virginia and Alastair in West Hampstead – especially if they were planning to have a baby.

There was a long pause. Viola must have glanced at the time – eleven o'clock. On a business-like swirl of air, without a word she sped out of the room to make two cups of coffee. I couldn't help noticing that it was pleasanter to have morning coffee made for me than to have to make it for myself. (When Elspeth was alive I should probably have made it all the same. When Elspeth was alive...)

At length I said gently:

'What about Ethiopia? Aren't you thinking of going back? Isn't that where you feel you've' – I recalled the expression – 'found yourself?'

I realise that against my own interest I was making it easier for her to say she wanted to go back. Yet if going back meant to her what I thought it meant – going back to a way of life that would fulfil her deepest needs for the next part, if not the rest, of that life – I'd got to make it easier for her to go. What else is being a father supposed to be about?

'I can go back,' she said, 'If I say the word...'

I noticed that her face had become a little paler, the dark blue of her eyes enhanced.

'I can choose my time.' She laughed wryly. 'They're so short of nurses they've more or less got to take what they can get.'

'They're darned lucky to get you.'

She nodded her head with an amused smile.

Another pause.

What's to be done? faced us both.

'They've not got enough people out there. Among those they've got, there are some very good ones. I should be adding to them, I hope.' She gave me a quick glance. 'Yes, Daddy I definitely should. They've made that clear to me.'

'Yes.' I was not surprised.

'They've got an excellent team of *Médécins Sans Frontières* at the hospital. Led by a French doctor who's super.'

'Yes,' I repeated. I must have smiled faintly. Viola picked that up like a shot –

'I suppose Virginia's told you I think he's super.'

'She has not told me that.' Literal truth is always useful to fall back on.

'He's ten years older than me. And married. And has never given me cause for the ideas Virginia has taken into her head.'

There was something so serious in the tone of the speech that I concluded Virginia really had read more into the situation than was permissible. Yet I wondered, all the same...

'He's super to work for,' Viola went on. 'The other nurses agree. He works us like mad. And he works himself like mad, too. Fewer children die. It's a wonderful experience.'

'Isn't it harrowing?' I asked, thinking of the television clips we were seeing on the BBC.

'Harrowing, yet consoling, Daddy.' Viola turned away from me a little. 'The little Ethiopian children and babies are particularly endearing – or they are particularly endearing to me. A lot of them have a sort of docile response when you do things for them – it's sweet.'

The colour had come back again into her complexion. Her eyes were shining. I thought, She'll go back! My spirits rose for her. My heart sank for myself.

'What about a compromise, Daddy?'

I couldn't help laughing at her civil servant-like tactics. I enquired –

'What could that be?'

'My coming to live here in the flat for a while, to tide you over... We could be looking for a housekeeper who'd come in and "do" for you every day or most days.' She hesitated. 'And it might help you get over the loneliness of Mummy not being here.'

'I shall never get over the loneliness!' I cried masochistically. 'I can only work at getting used to it!'

(Masochistic or not, it happened in the long run to be true.)

'Let me try to help, Daddy! And Virginia will try.' A slightly less emotional tone came into her voice – she was half-smiling at me. 'You don't want to think that. I think you will get used to it, Daddy, just a little bit... Don't give up!'

I couldn't help half-smiling back – if only to encourage her.

There was a pause.

Viola had not completed all she had come to day. She knew my sister had invited me to go and stay with her in the USA, at a remote summer place she hired in Vermont by the sea. Sunshine, swimming...

'I think you ought to go, Daddy.'

'I can't go anywhere at the moment.'

'Yes, you can.'

'My arthritic hip's too painful.'

'You could increase your dose of distalgesics.'

I thought it over. An attractive idea. 'It would get me away from this place,' I conceded.

'That would be good.'

'Yet think of the utter desolation of coming back to an empty flat!'

Viola sighed painfully. 'You go, and we will think of something.'

I telephoned my sister that evening.

I have to admit, though, to something which occurred to me in my solitary thoughts late that night. When bereaved of one's most deeply beloved of all, does one make a nuisance of oneself in order to draw signs of being loved from those loved-ones who remain?

Chapter XXIV

Some Fresh Pupils

Sunshine and swimming in Vermont dispelled some of my misery but didn't purge my masochism – when I got back to London I thought my hip was decidedly more painful. Virginia met me from the airport with her car: Viola was waiting at the flat for us with a collection of Marks & Spencer's most *choisis* dishes for a meal. With a bottle of Sparkling Samur the meal didn't after all celebrate utter desolation. (Desolation was further relegated by the fact of Virginia's having finally landed the job at the Evelyn Hospital – the luck of the Strachans, more particularly of Alastair Strachan.)Furthermore in my absence the girls had hit on the device of calling on an old friend of mine and his wife, who lived in a nearby flat, and seducing the wife into saying she would share with me the services of the cleaning woman who came in to "do" for her. (It's always dangerous to share a woman who "does" for you.) Thus set up domestically, and with the Fall Semester at Avalon University London Centre shortly to begin, I was theoretically settled for the near future at least. I began to notice the first signs of my hallucinating.

When I first came into the flat at the end of a day I imagined I heard a voice – I knew it was imagination yet I was sure I heard it in the flat – saying:

'Doesn't it look pretty?'

Elspeth's spontaneous comment on that last visit to the flat when she was still able to appreciate her surroundings.

Inside the sitting-room I could not prevent myself from looking first of all at the corner of the sofa where I used to find her, reading. No one there...

I could have sworn I heard her voice – I recognised it strictly as hallucination. I must remark that I didn't for one instant think it came from a "spirit" person of any kind. She was gone from me, gone for ever, like everyone else who was dead. It would have been consoling to believe in an "after-life". But false to everything I had ever seen with my eyes, recorded with any of my five senses – and I had no vestige of evidence for a sixth or any other sense. Unlike Alfred, Lord Tennyson, I was totally unable to join in "Believing where we cannot prove". Even though there was clearly a price to pay. (Galileo, for one, paid it.) She was gone from me, disappeared – to nowhere... It was as if her physical presence gave reality to the experience of the years we had spent together – someone always there to say "*Das war so.*" I had lost the living record which confirmed all my last forty years.

The Fall Semester at AULC was due to begin in a fortnight's time – I had chosen to return from the U.S.A. in time for Registration Day, the Horse And Pony Show and all the rest of it. Will Gower had told me I could be readily excused, but I felt it would not be acceptable (to myself anyway) to duck out of it on the grounds of bereavement. 'Get on with it, Joe!' was the mode in which I addressed myself. Bereavement was going to last a long time – for the rest of my life, in fact. I decided to concentrate my present lonely hours on re-reading the set-books for my course – what could be more sensible than that?

I was happy to find the charms of the first book on my list lasting – *Emma*. When I came to Trollope, I can't say I found anything in the least missing – *The Duke's Children*. On the contrary. And yet... When I put this novel on my list I did not know that in the end I was going to be a widower just as the Duke was. He was constantly missing Lady Glencora's presence in the context of daily life, as someone to talk to, to ask the opinion of, to unburden himself to so far as he could. All very true. Yet I had not much feeling that he was missing her presence in the context of life nearer the bone. Life nearer the bone? Life at the bone is what I mean. The Duke didn't seem to be missing it gravely with the Duchess. I felt I was missing it desperately, if not very creditably, with Elspeth; though I consoled myself with the thought that Elspeth would assure me that it was not discreditable. A moment in each day when I felt it with strongest poignance was when I got into bed at night – there was no welcoming hand to grasp me... Trivial it may sound, yet it had been a continuous part of my living. And now – the physical deprivation of the widower... That's not self-pity; that's fact!

I speculated on whether any of these thoughts would find their way into my future class-teaching of *The Duke's Children*: there was no reason why they shouldn't. When I had gone over *Middlemarch* with them they had seemed to be able to understand Mr Casaubon's delicately, yet unmistakably referred-to impotence. However that's a different matter.

I realised I was looking forward to the next semester. A distraction? A diversion?..

When it came to Registration I learnt that I was in for a class of 38. 38!

I had returned for Registration in order to get a pre-view of my pupils. Talking to people singly is the best way to get to know them. Talking to them in 38s rather less so.

Early in my queue – still in its first stages exiguous, since if you were on the ball you had to make sure first of getting into Shakespeare 1 and Advertising – there was a young man who gave his name as Steven Kalmay; Kalmay, he said, stressing the first syllable.

I couldn't resist showing-off. 'I hope,' I said, 'you don't have to endure fellow-Americans pronouncing it Kal-may?' I was thinking of such American horrors as "atta-shay" – in the face of all the rules about the syllables of French words being more or less evenly stressed. 'It is Hungarian, isn't it?'

'Yeah.'

I switched from showing-off to patronising. 'It's a relief to have a language in which proper names present no difficulties in pronunciation – stress invariably on the first syllable.'

He looked at me with a flicker of interest but not of impressedness. He didn't say anything. I didn't blame him.

While filling in the details about him required by the official form – required by the form but not by me – I managed to pass off other remarks expressing my Hungarophilia. Then he moved on. Quite tall, fair-haired, blue-eyed. Majoring in English!

Most of my registrands were women – 30 out of the 38. And most of them attractive. (If women aren't attractive at the age of 20, thought the hideous chauvinist whom you are now reading, when are they attractive? Well...) I was happy with this semester's collection.

I was particularly struck by one of them. She was pretty enough: what was striking was her unusual vivacity. She was of medium height, slender, nervously quick yet graceful in her movements – "body-language OK", as one might say. It was instantly clear that she was gifted with a humorous self-confidence: I liked that. In general the young women appeared to be more gifted with self-confidence – at this age, anyway – than the young men, who presumably had only just got away from their Moms. A few of them, the young men, assumed a spurious self-confidence in accord with some Hollywood fashion for machismo, but it wasn't difficult to see through it (as it is with film-stars' machismo). I could have wished they wouldn't do it: but fashion rules among the young – fashion often appears to be designed for the young: perhaps that's what makes it seem so flimsy.

The young woman – Petry, Anne-Marie.

Brunette... Sparkling hazel eyes, shapely red mouth. Alluring vivacity. French?..

I went through the prescribed questions about education etc. with unaccustomed interest. I was looking forward to the day when she might come to the pub with me after class.

She was followed by three comely young women such as were known at AULC as JAPs, (Jewish-American princesses). There were always a few in my class and I rather liked them. Some of the young men disliked them, and some of the young women were envious. They were usually quite intelligent – and often identifiable straight away in class because, being accustomed to The Best of Everything, they automatically disposed themselves along the front row. Sometimes they wore the latest thing in hats, (one year it was men's cloth caps,) sometimes carried Gucci handbags: one very hard-frozen winter they sent home for their fur-coats. (Rumour had it that one of the fur-coats, when it arrived, was seen to be mink dyed green: I didn't believe it.) But one could understand why some of the young women envied them and why some of the more lowly-born young men deplored them.

I rather like them because they were intelligent; and some of them, intent on getting Value For Money, worked quite hard at the course in order to get good grades. If they happened to be unlucky enough to get a D – a pretty rare occurrence – in the Final

Examination, their father wrote to the Chancellor of the University demanding that the D should be changed to a B, or C at the very least. The fee for their being taught the course was apparently taken to cover entitlement to the award of a certificate of success in it.

It occurs to me that although our Jewish American Princesses were immediately identifiable, there didn't appear to be any obvious category of Jewish American Princes. Our "Princes", (equally identifiable) were rich young men, sons of American upper-class families – just as readily identifiable as their English counterparts. Just like their English counterparts they seemed to recognise each other at the beginning of the course and to associate with each other throughout the rest of it, as if they had been raised to a personal habit of "keeping their distance" which they could shed when together. When the course was over they were liable to announce that they were going to spend the next year "travelling". I envied them myself.

So this Fall semester I was registered with a class of 38. I had turned down the idea of dividing the class in two, though the reason for doing that had diminished, since I was not writing another novel. In my present state I saw no prospect of writing another novel in the foreseeable future. The so-called foreseeable future was something I took no pleasure in foreseeing – anybody can have my foreseeable future, I thought. Empty. The thought of finding anyone to take Elspeth's place was out of the question. Not only could I never marry again, I was sure of that: I couldn't even see myself making love to some other woman. Nor could I see myself writing another novel. All that was over.

For the present I could find trifling consolations. Anne-Marie Petry chose to join an after-class pub party early in the semester. Good! When we settled ourselves round a table in the bar I happened to find her sitting next to me. (Surprise!) She had sitting next to her a quiet dark-eyed girl – it turned out they were flat-mates. The other girl was called Laura Zieman. She spoke rather little. Anne-Marie spoke rather a lot. I found it interesting. Today there was another young woman and a couple of young men – two out of the total of eight young men in the class, so succeeding parties were going to be grievously short of an equalising number of males.

185

When I realised that none of the party was going to drift away to find something to eat before the first class of the afternoon, I broke my habit of making off to the baths straight away. I had something to remain behind for: Anne-Marie showed no signs of leaving. She talked easily and modestly about herself and things that interested her. Laura listened. Anne-Marie was patrician and it was clear that her parents were not short of money. Without facts, since she so rarely spoke, I came instinctively to conclusions of a similar nature about Laura.

We talked about Anne-Marie's family and her education. Education at a moderately renowned school; her father the owner of a smallish, (pretty expensive, I gathered,) hotel at a classy resort, frequented by artists on the coast of Long Island.

'Did you see anything of Jackson Pollock?' I asked.

'Oh no... I don't live there – I don't live with my father. My mother divorced him.' Quietly conveying the necessary information.

I made sympathetic noises. The information was of the kind that was far from new to me from my pupils.

'Jackson Pollock was way back,' she went on, quietly correcting my knowledge of art history. (Way back by her measure, recent enough by mine.)

'Are you interested in art?' I asked.

She glanced with a smile at Laura, who said nothing.

'A little.' She put the matter straight. 'I wouldn't want to have a career in art.'

'Or English Literature?' I said playfully.

'Not English Literature either, Professor.' She glanced again at Laura who smiled and again said nothing. There was some shared knowledge between them – possibly Laura was hoping for a career in English Literature? I liked Laura.

It was my opportunity to ask the crucial question –

'What career are you thinking of, Anne-Marie, when you finish at Avalon?'

'You'll be surprised, Professor.'

'*Etonne-moi*, Anne-Marie!'

She gave me a serious, penetrating look –

'I'm hoping to join the AFSC.' She smiled. 'Do you know what that is?'

'I do.'

It stood for the American Friends' Service Committee – it sent young people abroad to help in Third World countries.

A blow below the belt for me – Viola, Viola...

'My elder daughter,' I said, 'is with Nursing Aid Overseas. So I do happen to know something about these things.'

'That's wonderful!'

'They've sent her to Ethiopia.'

'Is she in London right now? Can I meet her, Professor. Please...'

'Yes, of course.'

'Did your wife object to her going? It's dangerous, isn't it?'

'Yes. But Viola is a person who would keep that sort of thing to herself, so as not to upset her sister and me...'

'And your wife, Professor?..'

'I'm sad to say she died last May, and she was desperately ill when these decisions were in the air. So...'

There was a pause. I felt that a cloud had temporarily passed over Anne-Marie's vivacity. I was thinking what to say next: Anne-Marie was looking at her hands. The noise of the pub was going on around us. One of the young men got up and went to the bar to buy himself a dish of "meat and two veg".

I went on looking at Anne-Marie, and said in a gentle voice –

'You're taking something on, aren't you?'

'Why not?'

'I admire you for it.'

She blushed. 'I wasn't thinking about being admired, Professor...'

'I didn't mean that.'

'I want to do something! I want to help people... Maybe I won't be much use, but hopefully I'll be some...'

Viola, Viola again.

'You'll be going a long way away to be of some use to society, won't you?'

'That'll be good.'

I fell into thought for a moment. I was wondering why Anne-Marie was going so far away, if there was some connection between this separation and the fact of her parents being divorced.

'The Friends' Service,' I said. 'Are you a Quaker?'

'Oh no. My mother's a Catholic, lapsed Catholic. And I – I'm nothing. You don't have to be a Quaker to join the Friends' Service...'

I glanced down at our glasses. None of us had been drinking very much. The one boy already was deep in his meat and two veg, the other was waiting at the bar for whatever it was he'd ordered. The other girl was waiting for her turn with me. Anne-Marie picked up her glass suddenly –

'We appreciate you bringing us here, Professor...' She glanced at Laura and the other girl.

'I appreciate your coming.' I grinned.

Both girls saw my ironic fun. For a little while we drank small quantities of our drinks, then they prepared to leave – I had been very happy with them. I turned my attention to the remaining girl.

As she stood up, Anne-Marie said:

'My mother is probably coming over to see me later in the semester. I'd like her to meet you, Professor. Would that be possible?'

'Yes. Yes, of course.'

Anne-Marie turned to Laura. 'Laura's Mom's coming, too.'

Laura spoke. 'My mother and my father.'

'Shall I be invited to meet them?'

'Please, Professor...' Laura's oval face was pale as ever.

Anne-Marie said, 'I guess she was too shy to ask.'

'Anne-Marie, I was not!' Of a sudden her dark shadowed eyes were lit with dynamism. When Laura did speak, she could speak for herself.

'You see?' Anne-Marie was looking at me, laughing. She had established herself on friendly terms with me.

'I do see,' I said. 'And I like what I see.'

'Great!' (Virginia would have said "Brilliant!")

We were all three standing up. Then surprisingly the two girls, first Anne-Marie, then Laura, shook hands with me. Then they picked up their books and went out of the pub, leaving me to complete my social round. I sat down beside the remaining girl and drew her into conversation, then drew in the boy who was just finishing his meat and two veg. (The other boy had brought back to the table a huge helping of cottage pie.) I'd got to complete my social round – though it would probably be a pleasure. I checked that my swimming-kit was still safe on the floor; but it was going to be too late to go to the baths.

I realised that for a few minutes, it seemed, I had forgotten my woes.

Chapter XXV

The Art Show

The mid-semester quiz had taken place. The papers had been marked – without Paul Dugan to help! – and handed back to the persons quizzed: I had been asked not to read out the list of marks, because it was nowadays thought invidious for one person to be placed in order of merit above another. When I first heard of the idea I thought it was half-baked, but for peace and quiet had fallen in with it –

'I can see your point,' I said to Will Gower with minimal heat. 'Yet surely it isn't of great consequence? The quiz is merely a test of memory, not of intelligence.'

The open question was left open so far as I was concerned.

A published order of precedence in intelligence was apparently regarded as the ultimate in "divisiveness". Some of the more active pupils made it clear to me. An order of precedence was certainly not to be published after the end-of-term examination, which was a test of intelligence and literary ability – they had to write an essay. So I had obviously to keep the results of that to myself. I was not troubled by this, not at all – it made less work for me.

On the next class-trip to the pub I found the young man called Steven Kalmay falling into step with me. It was a chilly day and we were walking fast along a road lined with leafless trees. The young man modified his athletic pace to match my arthritic limp.

'Are you satisfied with your quiz results, Steven?'

'Yeah. I think so.'

'So you know you are somewhere round the top of the list?'

With amusement – 'That's right.' He was waiting for me to ask further questions. I obliged –

'How do you know you are at the top of the list, Steven? When I'm forbidden to publish it.'

'We compare papers when you give them back.'

I turned to look at him. 'Who did you compare yours with?'

'Just some friends.' He was clearly out to tease me.

'Who?'

We were turning into a fresh, narrower street without trees: at the bottom of it the pub sign was hanging out. The end of our walk was in view.

Kalmay's blue eyes glinted. 'I guess they're students you've taken to the pub already – Anne-Marie and Laura...' I could see that he thought he'd scored a point. I suppose Professors don't take enough account of what their pupils say between themselves.

'That's interesting... Then you must know they came out at the top end of the list as well?'

'Yeah, that's right.'

'Excellent results. I'm pleased with them.'

There was a momentary pause in the conversation. Then –

'We're planning a small party to celebrate. Will you come Professor?'

'Thank you, I'd love to. If it's a small party... I don't usually go to big parties, you know.'

He responded to the discouraging tone in my voice. 'I'll let you know when it's going to be.'

'And I'll consult my diary.'

Good-temperedly he went on teasing me. 'How small does a small party have to be, Professor?'

I laughed – admittedly with a touch of embarrassment. He didn't let me go –

'Just the five students from the top of your list, OK?'

'Well yes, Steven.' How would he know who else was top of my list if I was forbidden to publish it?

We were quite near the entrance to the pub. The rest of the present party crowded round, to go in.

I turned to Kalmay and said, 'I'm glad you're joining the party here, today, Steven.' There was an element of making amends in the speech. I could see that he accepted it. I went on, 'I hope I'll get a chance to talk to you about yourself.'

'I haven't got any more information about Hungary. I wrote my dad and asked where my grandad came from; but he hasn't replied.'

'Where is your dad?'

'On the West Coast.'

'What's he doing there?'

'Software design.'

'That can't leave him much time for writing letters.'

'Yeah.'

At this the conversation had to stop. We all surged into the pub.

I went through my usual professorial routine of taking orders for drinks. There were three young women and Steven Kalmay. He volunteered to help with the drinks, carried them across to our table, and sat down beside me – as if he liked me, whether or not I was going to quiz him still further about his family origins. Anyway he had already established that he had no more information to give. He chatted with one of the young women while I embarked on my friendly quizzing of the others.

I came round to Steven Kalmay again as the party was coming in sight of the end.

'How much longer have you got at Avalon, Steven?'

'This is my sophomore year.'

'You're Majoring in the Arts, in English?'

'That's right.'

'What do you want to do in life?'

'I don't know.'

'That's not unusual.'

He was silent.

'What does your father think about it?'

'He thinks Law School. He wants me to go to Yale.'

I smiled. 'Not another! Half the young men's fathers at AULC propose Law School – with Yale as first choice. The USA will become like Central Europe – packed with lawyers.'

'It is already,' said ironically.

I said nothing.

'You don't seem very happy with that, Professor?'

'I once worked for the Commission of the European Community in Brussels. It was packed with lawyers.'

'Oh really?'

'They were obsessed with the legal correctness of everything. Human consideration scarcely came into it. The law had nothing to do with human nature.'

'Not like the Realistic Novel, Professor.' He laughed with good-natured triumph.

I, too, laughed with good-natured triumph. 'My course has had some effect!' I was pleased.

I think he had something else to say, but it was too late. Everyone, including I, was going out. I guessed he wanted to talk about his future. It was too late. We parted.

Before he could give his small party for five, the Avalon London Centre, i.e. Will Gower, gave a very large party devoted to showing off – though he enjoyed parties for their own sake – the students' art-work, the said art-work consisting largely of painting and photography. All the faculty and all the students were invited. Two big rooms with huge paintings hanging on the walls, one smallish room divided by screens on which small photographs were displayed.

Will had arranged for glasses of wine to be handed round, also some particularly attractive bits to eat – no joints, no "snorts", and the like! I had no qualms about going and I persuaded Viola to go with me. (Virginia was too engrossed in her first days at the Evelyn – also she must have suspected, rightly, that there would be a good showing from the "slap it on! screw it in!" school.)

Will was standing rotundly just inside the first of the halls, alone, his wife not yet having arrived. When his intense brown eye lighted on Viola, it... lighted. They chatted for a few minutes, their glance meanwhile wandering round the pictures.

'What's your first impression?' he said to Viola.

'Very impressive.' There was still a fair bit of abstract expressionism around. 'Very American. I'm no judge.'

'Fair enough,' Will said. Many of the pictures were staggering in size and knock-you-down in colour, though not necessarily without talent.

Viola took this as a cue to begin wandering round the exhibition.

'Who,' she said to me, 'pays for the paint? Avalon or the students themselves?'

'I don't know.'

'They seem to have unlimited supplies of it. And no inhibitions about using it. It must cost a fortune for somebody. Slapping it on... As if they were painting a front-door.'

I didn't remind her of Virginia's simile because I was struck by a different, unexpected aspect of the phenomenon – at least three of the paintings had a "religious" motif: there was even one which looked like a sort of crucifixion. Very odd.

I introduced Viola to some of my pupils – I had already introduced her to Anne-Marie – with animated results, one of which, I was afraid, was a revival of her longing to get back to Ethiopia. Steven Kalmay appeared on the scene and I launched Viola into conversation with him – I went off to talk to some of the other young persons.

Viola rejoined me a little later.

She said, with a touch of irony: 'I think the blue-eyed man is very handsome.' She smiled ironically – 'He thinks you are wonderful.'

'He would say that, wouldn't he?'

'Not if he means it. I think he does.' She paused a moment. 'Have you been getting him enthusiastic about science?'

'I have no idea. Is that what he wants to go in for? Nothing about Law School at Yale?'

'He's wondering, if he stays on at Avalon for an extra year, whether he'll be able to switch from arts to biology.'

'Is that what he wants to do?'

'He wants to go in for genetics.'

'Good gracious!'

'I think he confided in me because Virginia and I are what he calls "medics".'

It seemed a pretty far-fetched excuse to me, but I didn't carp.

She said: 'I must go. I'm cooking the dinner tonight. We're expecting you at 7.30.'

I glanced round at the party. 'I shall be lucky if I make it.'

'Last night it was after 8.30 when Virginia and Alastair got home.'

I sighed, taken back to Elspeth's worries about the long hours worked by young doctors in public hospitals: it sounded as if it was going to turn out to be the same in private hospitals. Elspeth would have been worried but not surprised –

'All right. Expect me about 8.00.'

She gave me a hug and left. In the distance I had seen the Laura and Anne-Marie. I went over to join them.

'Have you got anything in the show?' I asked, knowing that neither of them were art students.

'I wish I had,' said Anne-Marie. 'I missed out on my opportunity. You remember, Professor, your speech about your courses on Registration Day? You recommended anyone who couldn't read novels to register for painting?'

Laura giggled. Anne-Marie looked modestly pleased with herself.

'With two of my brightest pupils in the Realistic Novel course, I simply don't remember anything about it. I think you must be mistaken.' Taking the war into the enemies' camp, I went on to Anne-Marie –

'Would you say you're strong enough to paint pictures as big as these?'

More giggles. But it gave me an excuse to look them up and down in their party attire. Anne-Marie had changed from her old jeans into some very slick trousers: Laura had changed into a beautiful dark dress. I was looking up and down some excellent material.

'I haven't got anything to show,' Anne-Marie repeated. 'Laura has. She wants to show it you.'

'Anne-Marie!..' Laura.

'It's a photograph,' Anne-Marie.

'Only one,' said Laura. 'I'm not in the photography class. I just turned it in as an outside submission. It isn't good, but Hugo' – that was the photography teacher – 'accepted it.'

'Then you must show it me.'

She remained still.

'Let's go.' I took gentle hold of her elbow and propelled her towards the room where the photographs were. As the two of us went through the doorway a waitress with a tray offered us glasses of white wine. We each took one.

'Now,' I said encouragingly.

'You shouldn't expect too much, Professor.' Laura led me between the screens and brought me up before the photograph she had taken. It was the study of a cat – a commonplace tabby – in the epitome of a feline pose, its back slightly arched, its tail up, its ears pricked and its eyes luminous...

'It's beautiful,' I said. 'I'm not surprised Hugo accepted it.'

Laura remained still beside me, with her perfect pale complexion and her dark shadowed eyes.

'How did you get it to pose for you like that?' I said.

'I just asked it.'

So simple, so easy, so natural. There was nothing I could say. I sipped my wine, Laura sipped hers.

This was my chance to talk to her. Compared with the painting hall the photography salon was underpopulated. I had spotted a couple of chairs in a sort of alcove between screens. 'Let's sit down!'

'Sure. It's quiet here.'

'Do you like quiet places?'

'Of course.'

'I've been standing up long enough.'

'Yes.' She gave me a sympathetic look. I had brought my walking-stick to support me.

'How much longer are you going to be at Avalon?'

'This is my final year.'

'Do you like Avalon?'

'Oh yes... I always wanted to come to Avalon.'

'Why?'

'You'll laugh at me, Professor. It's the name... I'm fascinated by the legend of King Arthur.'

I thought this was no time to air my conviction that there was a stupendous thesis to be written by some academic on *Legend and the Absurd*. I said:

'Alas, I'm not conversant with it. I seem to recall that Avalon was supposed to be The Isle of The Blest or The Isle of The Dead, I never knew which.'

Laura made a soft sound of laughter –

'It's both, of course!'

'What about its being The Island of Apples?'

'You have to understand the Celtic imagination.' She was quietly laughing at me. 'It was also The Island of Paradise in Water.'

I now laughed. I said, as I thought wittily, 'There you have me out of my depth.'

'They say you're a great swimmer, Professor.'

'Not in the depths of the Celtic imagination, I'm afraid.'

The wine was beginning to have an effect on me. (This was not my first glass.) A very slight effect, but appreciable. I said cosily:

'What are you going to do, Laura, when you graduate from Avalon? Have you thought what you want to do in life?'

'Oh yes.'

I looked at her. 'What?'

'I'm going to write novels.'

'Laura! What a fate you're marking out for yourself. Take an example from me!'

'Why not, Professor Lunn?'

'A life of suffering from beginning to end.'

'What about personal satisfaction?'

'I suppose I can't deny that.'

Laura sipped her wine again. 'No,' she said in agreement.

'So you mean to say you know?' I turned to look at her closely. 'Have you started writing already?'

'Yes.'

'What have you written?'

'About a third of a novel.'

'What's it about?'

'It's about a cat.'

Pause. I had a job not to exclaim Good Gracious!

'But,' Laura went on, 'she's a person as well.'

'I think you have got me out of my depth, Laura.'

'When you read it, you'll understand.' She paused. 'Hopefully.'

I was not sure I was flattered by the doubt cast (rightly) on my competence in metaphysics.

We were both quiet. I felt I was in the presence of something I'd rarely been in the presence of before. Laura was giving me a contained, tremulous smile...

I could only say tamely, 'I look forward to the day when I read it. If you'll let me read it.'

'I want to wait and see how it ends.'

'Well, don't forget, Laura!'

'OK, Professor.'

We both stood up, and looked again at the beautiful photograph of the cat.

Chapter XXVI

Parents

The semester rolled on – with a startling piece of news. I was called to Queen Anne's to be operated on for hip-revision – at a date which I was allowed to postpone till the end of the semester. (Will Gower was willing.)

Anne-Marie consulted me just after the great show of student "Art-Work". Her mother was due the following week, and she wanted to take Anne-Marie and her Professor out to lunch in a restaurant. In advance she had said she would like it to be a Thai restaurant.

'There are plenty of those around, nowadays,' I said.

'How about one in Soho?'

I smiled. 'You're getting to know your way around... Yes. There's one in Dean Street where we could go. It's quite small but not over-crowded.'

'Sounds great.'

So it was fixed – for a Tuesday morning, after my class, which Anne-Marie cut in order to be with her mother. I got to the restaurant ahead of time: I was sitting at a table in one of the two bay-windows which abutted on the pavement, giving a frontal view, on the opposite side of the street, of an Italian café, which appeared to be a busy independent centre of street-life – street-life of a dubious kind.

The physical resemblance between Anne-Marie and her mother was observable as soon as one looked. With age Mrs Petry had become scrawnier – possibly as a result of dieting to keep thin. She was wearing an unobtrusively dark red dress which showed off the same shapeliness and nice proportions as her daughter's; dieting had scarcely reduced the vivacity which her daughter inherited. Like Anne-Marie she had a patrician air. Her eyes had not quite the dazzling sparkle of Anne-Marie's: her hair had been assisted to a distinct touch redder... I took to her at sight and I thought she took to me. The one disappointment for me was her complexion: the explanation for this made itself apparent as soon as she sat down at the table – she lit a cigarette instantly. Her complexion, despite beautiful make-up, had the underlying faintly dirty, kippered look typical of a woman who smokes very heavily.

'This is a nice restaurant, Professor Lunn,' she said. 'I like your choice.'

Our table occupied the whole of one bay-window, and so, while being isolated, it picked up life from the pedestrians walking by, not to mention from the knots of dark-suited Italian-looking men engaged in their nefarious business opposite.

'I hope you're going to like the food,' I said.

'I'm sure I will.'

We spent some time over the menu and ordered a varied Thai meal.

'I hope you'll pardon my smoking, Professor Lunn.' She looked at me with smiling contrition. 'I've always said I'd conquer it but I just haven't got around to it.'

As I detested cigarette-smoke at the dining-table, I put on my best moo-ing tone of voice –

'Perhaps you've had a life of strain to put up with.'

'I sure have.'

Anne-Marie began to explain but her mother interrupted –

'I guess Anne-Marie will have told you – her father and I are divorced.'

It reminded me of the degree of intimacy with me that some of my pupils took in their stride. 'Yes,' I said. I added, somewhat irrelevantly:

'Anne-Marie is one of my best pupils... She's really very good, Mrs Petry.'

Looking at Anne-Marie, Mrs Petry's eyes took on a satisfied sparkle. She said:

'I hope she'll make something out of it.'

I glanced at her quickly. There was a faintly menacing tone underlying the remark. I glanced at Anne-Marie, who gave me a knowing smile. There must be a difference of opinion between mother and daughter – over Anne-Marie's plans for the future, no doubt.

At this moment the waitress brought us in our first course, steaming bowls of *tom-yum koong*, a deliciously hot and spicy transparent soup with prawns and mushrooms and bits of bright green leaf floating in it.

Mrs Petry stubbed out her cigarette.

'It's great of you, Professor Lunn, to take so much interest in Anne-Marie's studies. We certainly appreciate it.'

I made some self-deprecating sound, thinking my interest was a little wider than in Anne-Marie's studies.

'We do,' she repeated.

'She's rather a special pupil.' I smiled. 'One always hopes it will lead to special results.'

'Oh, I hope so, too!'

'I think she'll do very well.'

'Hopefully she will.' Mrs Petry looked at her daughter.

'Don't worry, Mom...'

'But I have to worry!' Mrs Petry spoke to me. 'You know she wants to join the Friends' Services Committee?'

'Yes. An admirable thing to do.'

'It's admirable, Professor.' With emphasis – 'But it isn't a career.'

'Mother, it could be.'

'Lost in a Third World country?'

'Not lost, Mom.'

'And in danger! In danger of being abducted, held for ransom, killed!' In the grip of great emotion – 'How many AFSC volunteers in the last five years have lost their lives?'

'I don't know, Mom. I've told you I don't know. And it doesn't matter to me. The AFSC is what I want to join.' Anne-Marie looked at me. I had not mentioned Viola, and for a moment I was afraid Anne-Marie might – to bear out her case. She didn't. Thank goodness for that!.. She said:

'Professor, can you make my mother see it's more important to me to do something I believe in than to have a career in Wall Street?'

'I wouldn't have suggested a career in Wall Street!'

'I couldn't!'

The discussion had run into the ground – obviously not for the first time in its history.

'Maybe you, Professor, can persuade her to think about her future before she makes a decision.' Mrs Petry paused an instant. 'I don't think she's considered the risk involved in being drafted to a Third World country – she might never come back!'

Viola, Viola... now I could think of nothing else. Viola was already hinting that she wanted to return to Ethiopia – all those babies dying...

I took a breath, and said:

'I see the point. But I don't think it's my place to interfere.'

Mrs Petry gave me a smile – it was not relaxed but it was warmer.

There was a pause. We had come to the end of the *tom-yum koong* and the waitress brought in our next course, a super-appetising assortment of dishes to share between us. We began to dole them out.

Mrs Petry leaned close to me. 'I hope you don't think I'm over-protective as a mother.' Then in a less agitated tone of voice, while looking me directly in the eyes from close quarters – 'She's all I have.'

I was caught by my own emotion. I had Virginia as well as Viola – as if anything could reconcile me to losing either of them! I felt sheer relief that Anne-Marie had not told her mother that Elspeth and I had let Viola go. (I resolved to thank her for her tact when we were alone.)

After that final, poignant, "She's all I have!" the meal resumed in calm. At the end of it Mrs Petry thanked me fulsomely "for everything". I felt she was taking me for an ally...

I had just about got over this encounter when Laura's mother and father arrived in London. They asked to entertain me to tea at their hotel.

A pleasing hotel-lounge typical of its kind: clean, airy, quiet; Scandinavian sofas and chairs of pale-coloured wood upholstered in flowery cretonne, walls painted a pale pink, a large coloured photograph of the Queen. One might have wondered how a couple from Minneapolis could have lighted upon it. Why not? It might be to their taste. (It transpired that it must be to their taste – this was the third time they'd stayed there.)

Laura was not tall: her mother and father were both shorter – and far from insubstantial. (Laura at the age of 20 was a substantial girl.) Both her parents were wearing suits, her mother's after Chanel, her father's after Armani; a modest amount of jewellery, in both cases made of gold. They looked to be more than comfortably affluent; and a little nervous of meeting their daughter's professor.

Laura introduced them and they shook hands informally yet diffidently. We all sat down to a low circular table for afternoon tea. We were almost the only people in the room. A middle-aged waitress, discreetly uniformed, brought in a large tray with a Devonshire tea ordered by Laura's mother.

'It's ages since I had a Devonshire tea,' I said.

'You like it, Professor?' Laura's mother.

'Love it! But rarely indulge myself in it – all that butter and cream and strawberry jam...'

'We have it every time we stay here.'

'That's right.' Laura's father.

Laura surveyed them with her quiet internal smile. I looked at her as if to say "You ought to say something to get things going." Laura did not say something to get things going: she said nothing.

Mrs Zieman took in hand the serving of the tea; I took in hand the initiation of the conversation – by favouring them with my high opinion of Laura, which went down well.

The upshot was that we all began to talk about Laura. As Laura didn't say anything, our conversation was much as it would have been had she not been there. She didn't look in the least put out by that. Just an occasional sensitive, meditative smile.

Once launched into discussion, Laura's parents on the other hand, had quite a lot to say, along lines which were admirable.

Laura's father – he had a round head and thinning combed-down hair, a well-fleshed face and slightly unseeing light eyes – declared himself; 'Laura must have told you, I'm a business man.'

As he said it he cocked his head a little in a confident smiling gesture – his photograph thus could well have appeared on a financial page in the *Times*.

'My career hasn't left me much time for literature,' he went on. 'But I'm going to give Laura all the support I can. I don't understand what she's doing, but I will try.' He smiled ironically at himself, and then gave Laura an affectionate look. 'Maybe something will get through to me. Hopefully.'

I couldn't help wondering how much would get through about a cat which was also a person, probably a girl. I made a sound approving of all Mr Zieman's intentions.

Laura's mother joined in. 'I'm not a literary person, but I do read.' She was dark-eyed like Laura, but lacking in the indrawn expression which was so characteristic of her daughter. 'I guess I've read everything written by Saul Bellow and John Updike...' She paused. 'Laura says she isn't going to work in their style.'

'That's true, Mother.' Laura was smiling.

'Bellow and Updike have their merits,' I said, holding what I meant to be a balance between the old and the new. 'I guess Laura's merits are going to be different.'

'Thanks, Professor.' Laura was laughing at that.

'I guess,' said Laura's father, 'that Laura's merits are going to be different from anything we've seen so far.'

Just as a novel about a cat, I thought, which was also a person, must be different from most novels he'd read so far.

'That's right,' said her father. He smiled at me. 'Sometimes we're amazed she's our daughter.'

'That's true,' said her mother with great feeling.

'That makes her all the more precious,' said her father with equal if not greater feeling.

I looked from one to the other of them. 'I think that's very good,' I said. 'It gives me great pleasure to hear you say it. I believe it's right.'

A feeling of amity moved us all.

There was a pause.

Laura's mother's tone of voice switched to that of a Minneapolis hostess.

'Professor Lunn, you aren't drinking your cup of tea.'

Nor was I eating the sumptuous combination of scones, butter, jam and cream. I dutifully fell to.

So the tea-party proceeded. I was sure that all four of us must be thinking Laura would become a novelist.

Chapter XXVII

A Revision

It was impossible for me not to see that Viola was pining to go back to Ethiopia.

For years I'd had a rule for myself in this kind of situation – if you have to go away, the sooner you go the better.

I came round to thinking Viola had to go back. She and Virginia had got my domestic arrangements into order; Viola was temporarily living in the flat "to look after me" marvellously well.

And Virginia had started a baby. It was clear that she and Alastair must have discussed it at great length – with some reason, since they had to worry about Elspeth's having in the first place had trouble over giving birth to Virginia herself and then having been warned afterwards against having any more children.

'My gynaecological prognosis is OK,' Virginia told me. 'Alastair agrees it is.'

It was not for me to counter that degree of decisiveness. Nevertheless... there's always danger in having a baby.

But you can't do anything about your children – especially about one of them who is decisively pregnant.

Viola was divided about going back to Ethiopia at this moment, as aware as any of us of the dangers of surgery and the dangers of parturition.

'You must go, my darling,' I said to her.

She talked about it constantly to Virginia and talked about it constantly to me. (It was the constant talking about it to me which wore me down.)

Viola had to go, ergo "a compromise" was arrived at. The moment there was any sign of untoward developments from my surgery, Virginia was to summon Viola back. (None of us had the nerve to remark on its being an exact repetition of an earlier compromise.)

By this some of Viola's dividedness was eased. She went.

For the farewell at Heathrow – only Viola and me, Virginia being chained to the Evelyn, just as her mother would have predicted – there were tears on both sides.

'I feel I have to go...'

'I understand...'

So back I went to a flat now empty, with the prospect ahead of surgery pronto, surgery that was likely to be "very bloody". I put in my last appearance at AULC, with final examination papers marked and grades reported to Headquarters, (the Department of English and Textual Studies). Admitted to Queen Anne's two days later. If it had to be done, then the sooner the better... I couldn't help recalling how I'd wanted to call that novel – a very good novel, don't you know? – *Old Age and Surgery*. Since the ur-replacement I'd had two hernias.

Safe in the maw of the ward, I gave myself up to doing what I was told to do. I gathered that it was likely to be the senior consultant who was going to do the bloody deed. (There's nothing like starting with the top man.)

So, as I'm required to tell the story, I report that the operation was said to be successful – so said by the senior consultant in person when he came round on his "morning after" tour of the ward with his train of nurses and baby doctors. I didn't ask how much blood I'd lost.

'You look a good colour,' he said with the appearance, I felt, of congratulating not so much me as himself.

I desisted from facetious rejoinder, not that I happened to be feeling anything but remarkably well after the deluge. He reminded me that in our first seance he'd promised me four weeks in hospital with the "revised" joint in traction – which turned out to mean my being kept on my back with a 5lb weight dangling from my left ankle for the first three of the weeks. Just to keep me additionally interested he told me the prosthesis was kept in position by means of a 9" spike thrust down the inside of the femur.

So there it was. Virginia and Alastair signified their professional belief that all was well: Virginia telephoned the good news to Viola in Addis Ababa. So there was I.

One afternoon. It was the time of day when visitors began to arrive at the hospital; the hour when I always seemed to feel an urgent need – whether physiological or neurotic, I could never decide – to perform one of the bodily functions. The more serious was too embarrassing to contemplate: that it involved the hospital's most grotesque instrument of torture was bad enough: think, then, of having to negotiate that instrument with a 5lb weight dangling from your left ankle! At this particular moment it was the less serious function. Against this eventuality I always kept a "bottle" on the floor at the right-hand side of the bed. (A "bottle" was a plastic flask, with a flat bottom permitting it to be stood up vertically, and a flat side permitting it to be laid down horizontally.) In lowering it back to the floor after using it, I was unable to reach any further than letting it down in its vertical position, where it was alarmingly vulnerable to being kicked over.

You will understand why it seemed to me important to keep visitors on the left-hand side of the bed.

E Ward was a light ward in any case: on this afternoon the light was brilliant December sunshine, which brought a springlike bounce to the low-toned green walls. I must have closed my eyes. I opened them at the sound of voices. American voices. Beside my bed. I opened my eyes to see with astonishment three of my pupils standing there, smiling at me. My three favourite pupils of the year!

'Anne-Marie!' I exclaimed with delight as she came towards me – sparkling as ever – to hand me a bunch of flowers, paper-white narcissus, yellow jonquils and dark blue iris.

'Oh, thank you!' Had I not been pinned down on my back by my 5lb weight, I should have upped and kissed her on both cheeks.

Then Laura. A bunch of freesias, large, white and powerfully scented. 'Laura – how sweet of you!' I should have kissed her on both cheeks, too.

And finally the third of my most favoured ones. 'Steve!' He handed me a Waterstone's envelope which contained a paperback. I quickly took it out. A volume of short stores by Raymond Carver – literate choice. 'Thank you!'

I tried to lift my head from the pillow so as to look at them better.

'How sweet of you all! I had no idea you were going to do this. I think it's terribly clever of you to find me.'

'We asked the Dean's office.' Steve.

I had been struck from my earliest days at AULC by the resourcefulness of my pupils; for instance by the speed with which in a completely strange city they found themselves apartments, having only a list of addresses given them by the Dean's office, a list the reverse of comprehensive.

'We took a bus. How 'bout that?' Anne-Marie. (They usually travelled by Underground, where it was easier to find their way.) 'Neat, huh?'

They were all standing beside the bed – thank goodness on the left-hand side!

'Do sit down!' There was only one chair supplied by the ward per bed; it was on their side.

Laura, the most retiring of the three, quietly sat down on it. Anne-Marie, standing beside her, gave Steven a glance so encouraging as to be commanding – he made off at once on a scavenging tour.

As they were the first visitors to the ward that afternoon it was a successful scavenging tour – he came back with two chairs. (Visitors to two other patients would have to sit on the patients' beds or stand up.) He put down one of the chairs beside Anne-Marie for her to sit on, and then – Horrors! – was about to put down the other for himself on the right-hand side of the bed.

'Put it beside Anne-Marie, Steve!' I cried. 'Then I can see you all at once.'

Pause.

'How are you Professor Lunn?' Laura in her soft, harmonious voice.

'I think I'm doing quite well. Within my limited range of movement, I feel quite well.'

Anne-Marie. 'You look great, Professor!' Her eyes were sparkling – as usual.

'That's what everyone says,' I replied. 'When the senior consultant surgeon came round with attendant train of supernumeraries, on his tour of inspection the morning after the operation, that's what he said. He told me I look "a good colour".'

'You do.'

'I liked that. It reassured me – while throwing a nice light of congratulation upon his performance as surgeon.'

Smiles all round.

'Why wouldn't you look a good colour, Professor?' Steven. 'You were looking great before the operation.'

'It's one thing to look great before an operation and another to look great afterwards, Steve. In my opinion a general anaesthetic does nobody any good – it takes ages to get over it, really. In this particular operation you lose a lot of blood into the bargain.'

Anne-Marie. 'Then I guess you must have a lotta blood, Professor Lunn.'

I suspected a neat blend of flattering me and taking the piss out of me.

'That's right,' said Steven. What he knew about it I couldn't say. I supposed he must be basing his view on my normal ruddy look.

I thought it was time for a change in topic of conversation.

'I know what may amuse you all,' I said. 'When they put in a new hip-joint – which a nurse once told me looks like a pork chop – it has a steel spike which goes down the bone of one's thigh, to strengthen it and hold it in place, the prosthesis I mean. This time in me it's a spike no less than nine inches long. The surgeon told me.' I paused. 'What's amusing is that when I have it X-rayed, the radiographer is liable to find she has to photograph me over again in order to get all the spike into the picture. The first radiographer was quite upset – a professional error!..'

'That's sad. I guess she was upset.' Laura.

'I guess she wanted to keep the professor lying on the table for a second deal.'

'Thank you, Steven – that's enough.'

There was a pause.

'How's your daughter?' Steven, undeterred. It was Viola he'd chatted with at the great AULC Art Show: having diagnosed her as a "medic", he'd confided an ambition to become a geneticist. (I'd raised it with him one day after class but made little headway. I suspected he was inspired by my changing – actually no more than into a tandem arrangement, between science and literature. However I didn't feel it was up to me to discourage him in an entirely radical change from literature to science, if he was prepared to begin studying for a degree all over again.)

'You're thinking of Viola?' I said. 'She's well – and she has just gone back to Ethiopia.'

'Still with Nursing Aid Overseas?'

'That's right. She knew what she wanted to do – she felt she had to do it.' I glanced at Anne-Marie, who was listening intently, while I went on to Steven. 'I gave in.'

'Another Lady Mary?..'

He was referring, half-playfully, to Lady Mary Palliser in the *Duke's Children.* Lady Mary Palliser was the daughter of the Duke of Omnium: she insisted on marrying the young man of her choice, a country Squire whom her father disapproved of on the grounds that he was not good enough for her. Her father, rather than risk making her unhappy possibly for the rest of her life, gave in.

'That's clever of you, Steve. A parallel I hadn't thought of myself.' I grinned at him. 'You may call me Duke. Or if you prefer it, Your Grace.'

'I guess I prefer Duke, Professor.' (He pronounced it Duke, not Dook.)

The two girls had been looking at me sympathetically. Now they laughed.

'So Viola's gone back to Ethiopia,' I said. And while they were all relaxed, I said to Anne-Marie half-privately, 'How do things stand with you?'

'A little more hopefully since my mom met you, Professor.'

'That's all to the good, then.'

'That's right.' Despite the seriousness of it, she smiled.

I was pleased – I hadn't given that lunch at the Thai restaurant in vain. I said to them all:

'My younger daughter, Virginia, married a man I thoroughly approve of. A doctor.' I paused. 'They're going to have a baby.'

'That's great news, Professor!'

Their congratulations were so heartfelt that I had to work hard to maintain a steady smile, since Virginia's pregnancy was temporarily running into trouble. I was perturbed. There's always danger in having a baby.

When further congratulations on the prospect of my becoming a grandfather had died down I turned to a topic less fraught for me –

'Are you all satisfied with your grades?'

(The grades in the end-of-semester examination – counting towards their final degrees.)

'We don't know what they are.' Anne-Marie.

Steven. 'They have to go through the University computers first.'

'Of course,' I said, with a touch of sarcasm.

'Hopefully we'll get out what you put in Professor?' Steven.

'Hopefully, Steven.'

'Did we all get A's?' Anne-Marie.

'A's of one sort or another,' I said.

'Can you tell us which sort, Professor Lunn?'

'Certainly not. I ought not to have told you this much.'

Smiles of pleasure were nevertheless lighting their faces. Steve and Anne-Marie shook hands. Laura spoke –

'Did any one of us get an A-plus?' Laura might be the most gentle and indrawn of them, but she didn't miss anything.

'I never give an A-plus,' I said. 'A-plusses are for the gods.'

'And we're Americans,' said Steven smartly.

'I'd noticed that. But I like you all the same.'

I liked all of them very much – Steven, who was bright and sexy and after a fashion fond of me; Anne-Marie more fond of me than I was prepared to see; Laura quietly devoted... Steven, now he knew me, didn't give a damn what he said to me; not that Anne-Marie gave all that much of a damn, either. Laura apparently did give a damn – though I couldn't help feeling that Laura's damn was constantly at risk of being thrown overboard: Laura, still waters...

On my side I have to admit, fair's fair, that my treatment of them all didn't exactly invite them to give a damn what they said to me.

'Tell me your immediate plans,' I said. 'What are you all going to do now?' I was interested. Before the present semester began and during the mid-semester break they had between them visited goodness knows how many countries with their Euro-Railcards. (Not short of money.) 'Are you going to do more travelling?'

'Flying back to New York tomorrow. ' Anne-Marie. 'That's why we came to see you today.'

'I'm touched,' I said. 'Giving up your last afternoon in London to come and see me... Thank you...'

'Leastways they are.' Not interrupted in her flow, Anne-Marie indicated Steven and Laura. 'Flying back tomorrow.' Then she spoke for herself. 'I haven't decided yet.' Pause. 'I don't have a reservation.'

'What! If you haven't got a reservation you can't fly back.'

'Maybe I can trade tickets with some guy who has a reservation.'

'Trade tickets!' In spite of astonishment that verged on disbelief, I thought they were capable of it. Resourcefulness... 'So that's the sort of thing you people do!'

'Spirit of the New Frontier.' Steven.

'Really!..'

'I love the way you British say "Really!.."' Anne-Marie mimicked me. 'Really!..' She mimicked me rather well. Several of my pupils had picked up English expressions – some of them, when they failed to hear something being said to them, came out with the awful, now-universal Englishism, "Sorry!"

I said, 'Are you all in a hurry to get home?' I looked at them in turn.

'I am.' Laura with an internal smile – 'My mother says my cat is pining for me.'

Anne-Marie, amused by Laura –

'My mom doesn't know I'm coming. I'm going to call her tonight. And she'll tell my boy-friend – if I'm coming – to pick me up at the airport.'

Steve. 'My dad's working on the West Coast till New Years.'

Anne-Marie's father was married to someone else; Steven's mother was married to someone else; only Laura was going home to both parents – and a beloved cat.

They were picking themselves up to leave.

'Well, *bon voyage*,' I said. 'Give my love to America! And when you're in London again, don't be too shy to call me if you feel like it. I'll take you out for a drink.'

'To a pub?' Anne-Marie with enthusiasm.

'If that's your pleasure.' I was returning the compliment of taking the piss by copying one of their less beautiful Americanisms.

Laura spoke, looking at me with her dark shadowed eyes –

'Will you read my manuscript, Professor Lunn?' She blushed. 'If I've finished it by then.'

'That would be my pleasure, Laura.'

They stood up to go. The scent of the spring flowers drifted across my bed – especially the freesias...

Impulsively Anne-Marie bent down and kissed me on the cheek.

Laura overcame her seeming distance from what was going on by following suit.

Steven gave me a rousing shake of the hand.

'Bye, Professor Lunn.' 'See you!' 'Get well!'

I watched them leave the ward – their final afternoon in London, spent with me...

At the door they turned back and waved. The three of them. If America could call up more young people like them, America's future was bright. I loved them.

'Bye!..' 'Bye!...' 'Bye!..' They waved again. On the threshold –

Anne-Marie Petry.

Laura Zieman.

Steven Kalmay.

Chapter XXVIII

Disaster

How to work what happened next into the pages of a novel, of this novel?

Not solely a step in my narrative, but a calamitous event which went into "history" – still not forgotten by the Western world.

The aeroplane in which the Avalon students were flying back to New York was blown up in mid-air as it was crossing the borders of Scotland. No one survived.

The news came to me through the back-of-the-bed set of headphones in the morning. I telephoned Will Gower as soon as a nurse could wheel the hospital instrument round to me.

'We can scarcely speak, here, Joe...'

'Will!..'

Silence.

'We have no more news yet beyond the radio bulletin which you heard,' he said.

'I didn't think you would have.' I hesitated, yet I had to say, 'What I beg of you, Will, is to let me know which members of my class were on the flight.'

'Will do... as soon as we know.'

I could only put down the receiver and reconcile myself to waiting.

So this...

I was overwhelmed by the feeling that I was pursued by Death.

Of course there was not the faintest evidence on which to personify Death, a metaphor which Virginia would seize on instantly; and what could I do but acquiesce? Death was not a person: one could only be pursued by a person or some living creature. I realised that more than half the world would not agree with me: I belonged irrevocably to the other less than half. Yet the disaster seemed to be exerting a pressure on me beyond itself. Lying there with the weight dangling from my ankle and the scent of freesias wafted by the draught from the window... I tried to think it out.

It seemed to me that my soul was as deeply bereaved as ever by the death of Elspeth. For some of the time I tried to tell myself that I was recovering, forgetting. But in my private moments I recognised that this was not so. The wound was still there, unhealed. Bereavement, it was beginning to dawn on me, stays with one for life... The present loss of my pupils, though so much less powerfully vital to me, touched upon the wound, creating a resonance of pain... It made me feel pursued.

Late that afternoon – I was still waiting – Virginia paid a flying visit to comfort me.

'Darling Daddy...' She embraced me.

There was a pause while we looked into each other's faces.

I said, knowing it was the wrong thing to say, 'I feel pursued by Death.'

'You mustn't think that. It's just imagination.'

'It's very hard not to think it.'

'You've always said you had no use for metaphor.'

I smiled. 'That's because metaphor tells you that something is something else which you know perfectly well it isn't.' My stock speech on the subject.

Virginia was amused, but that didn't stop me going on.

'Metaphor doesn't make the issue clearer to me. It makes it more confused, deliberately introduces ambiguity...'

She shook her head over my inflexibility.

'Oh dear! What can we do with you?'

'Nothing. Jim Yavner settled it – he proposed to call me Unambiguous Joe.'

'Well, that should convince you that you're not pursued by Death.' She took hold of my hand. 'But I know how you feel.' She paused. 'I still miss Mummy as much as you do.'

I was touched.

We chatted for the remaining moments about getting in touch with Viola. I said:

'If she hasn't heard about the crash already, she'll think the telephone call is going to be bad news about me. Actually the news about me remains good. I'm to lose the weight from my ankle tomorrow!'

'OK, then you'd better be the one to write. Actually we don't know yet if they've posted her back to the same hospital.'

I thought longingly, If only she were here! I said:

'She knew both Anne-Marie and Steven Kalmay. And Laura...'

'You don't know if they were all on board.'

I shook my head. 'There's some hope I suppose... Anne-Marie may have failed to "trade reservations".'

'That's right. Don't look on the black side, Mr Lunn!'

She kissed me and left. I returned to my waiting.

It was not until the next day but one that I got my letter from AULC.

"Of this semester's intake, 35 of our students were on the flight. Yours were:–

Banagher Lucy

Brown Tucker

Chu Elizabeth

Kalmay Steven

Korb Joshua

Lowenthal Debra

Poniatowski Robert

Zieman Laura

"At present the airline cannot vouch for the accuracy of its list. We are chasing them up with enquiries."

35! I was appalled. Eight of them my pupils whom I knew like friends... The list did not include the name of Anne-Marie Petry. I was haunted by her proposal to "trade reservations" Perhaps she had not found anyone willing. Perhaps there was hope. Perhaps.

Another four days and AULC had final news of the toll: the office telephoned me promptly.

'The list now includes the name of Anne-Marie Petry. Definitely.'

No more hope. Number lost by me, now nine. Among them all three of my brightest.

So far as her schedule permitted, Virginia was coming in to see me as often as possible. (By now I was free of my 5lb weight and learning to walk a few steps.) Virginia was taking her turn in writing to Viola. (I suspected that she didn't trust me to give a true account of my spirits.)

My first question always when she came in was of course about her pregnancy.

'OK again, now,' she said. 'Alastair agrees with the gynaecologist.'

I said nothing.

We turned to the disaster.

'Do they know why the plane crashed?' she asked.

'I haven't heard any more from AULC. I suppose it must have been a bomb. That's what all the press thinks.' The press was full of sensational headlines and photographs of the Scottish village strewn with debris.

'For once the press must be right.'

'I should think so.'

9 dead out of my class of 32.

'It's particularly hard,' Virginia said, 'that your brightest and best pupils are lost – those nice ones who came to see you here.'

'It's always the way.'

'No, it isn't always the way. This was chance. Chance isn't a way.'

'All right,' I paused. 'The news of Anne-Marie was the last straw, though.'

'I'm terribly sorry.'

I said; 'I shall have to write to her mother. You know her mother wanted me to dissuade her from joining the American Friends' Service Association. She thought it would be dangerous.'

I caught a glimpse in Virginia's face of the fear we both shared that Viola was in danger.

'Anne-Marie's mother said, "She's all I've got!"'

'That's hard...'

'And I shall have to write to the other parents I've met. The Ziemans, of course. They were going to do everything to help

Laura become a writer, even though they were un-literary people. They were good people. Laura told me she'd begun a novel.'

'Do you think she'd ever have finished it?'

'I'm absolutely sure she would.'

'Would it have been good?'

'It would certainly have been pretty strange. She had a very peculiar imagination – the sort of imagination that would have made her a very individual writer. It's too early for me to judge whether she had literary talent to match it. The standard cliché is "The book might have been nonsense: it might have been a masterpiece." I doubt if it would have been either, myself. But that's the situation. She was going to send me her manuscript.'

Another pause.

'Viola liked the young Hungarian.'

'Steve Kalmay – he was a good lad. One of the best.' I went on. 'I suppose I shall have to write to his father, whom I never met. I got the impression he was an only son. He never mentioned his mother. I shall have to get hold of his father's address, in Silicon Valley or whatever it's called.'

Virginia said; 'It would have been fascinating if he'd managed to become a geneticist in the end.'

'That's problematic. But he'd have become something.'

There was another pause – I thought it was probably time she was getting back to the Evelyn. She said:

'What about the others? The other six.'

'One can't bear to see them disappear. Some of the others were pretty bright. And they were all young...'

'I see what you mean.'

A silence.

'I shall really have to go.' She stood up. She looked at me firmly. 'And don't forget to put that metaphor about death out of your mind. No such thing as Death is pursuing you.'

'All right...'

We hugged each other fondly.

'And remember, Daddy' – she paused on the threshold – 'I'm carrying a new *Life*!'

Chapter XXIX

A Hospital Visit

A couple of days before I was hoping to be discharged from Queen Anne's I was unexpectedly visited by Will Gower. He came at the end of a stream of afternoon visitors – mainly women writers who had kept up an encouraging flow of visits throughout my incarceration.

I could see from his face that there was no ameliorating news from Avalon – there couldn't be.

We shook hands with a slightly uneasy formality.

'I thought I'd catch you here before you came out,' he said.

'Smart thinking, Will,' I said, facetiously with effort.

He sat down on the bedside chair.

'You did catch me. When I get out of here,' I said, 'I'm not going straight back to the flat.' Fending off conversation about the disaster, I rattled on. 'From here I'm going to the King Edward VII's Convalescent Home for Officers in the Isle of Wight. What do you think of that?'

'Very suitable.' A touch of irony matching my own. We were both sceptical about the presumed merits of "Officers and Gentlemen", or at least about thinking of ourselves as possessors of those merits – stuffy Tories!

'King Edward VII's is said to be super for physiotherapy, which is what I need after weeks on my back. They have an under-water physio-facility, as they call it.'

'Will suit you.'

'Not big enough to swim in, unfortunately.'

He shrugged his shoulder lightly. 'Provide you with immersion in your favourite element.'

'Let's hope it does me good.'

'I'm sure it will.'

There was a pause. Then he said:

'My original plan for the next time I saw you was to deliver what might have been good news for you...' There was a faint sign of the native twinkle in his brown eyes. 'It seems pretty trivial now.'

'What was it, all the same?'

'I've shamed Avalon into saying that if you'll do a second course on the Realistic Novel, they'll pay you an equal fee.'

'A triumph for you, Will.'

'I made them see sense, that's all.' Again the twinkle. 'In the end they were enthusiastic about it.'

He looked at me now with a slightly watchful glance. That told me what was in the wind, though it was obvious anyway. Will never missed an opening. He said, as if artlessly:

'By the way everyone hopes you'll go on teaching for Avalon at the earliest possible moment next semester.'

'I don't remember ever saying I would teach.' A false move on my part.

'You will, won't you? Now you're well again.' Said with fluid warmth and sincerity.

Ineptly I said, 'It's too late now, I suppose, to say No.'

'I've arranged a stand-in for you until you're ready.' He was amused. 'I think he's a good guy – of course he won't be able to replace your inimitable style, but I don't think you'll be dissatisfied.'

I didn't comment. My immediate fate was settled. I realised that there was a consolation. The desolating loss from my life of my last semester's pupils was going to make me feel a need all the more poignantly to be surrounded by the new pupils of another semester.

'You will be ready to rejoin AULC when you come up from under water?'

'I expect so – I see no reason why not.'

He gave me a suppressed triumphant glance. The nut-brown Welsh farmer.

I realised he was presuming I'd teach a course Number 2; but he couldn't expect me to run it up in a week or so – even for an equal fee.

I was not forgetting my desire to resign altogether. I let the moment pass.

But the moment could not be put off any longer when we must broach the major topic. After neither of us had spoken for some moments, I took it upon myself to say:

'What's the latest news from Avalon?'

The sparkle disappeared instantly from his eyes.

'They're devastated...' Then with a returning glint of humour. 'But not robbed of their powers of action.'

'I bet! What are they going to do?'

'That's building up. They're going to have a memorial service at Avalon and produce a memorial pamphlet of some kind. There's talk of a memorial wall, with all the victims' names incised in it. And I should guess it's inevitable they'll devise a memorial scholarship scheme.'

'That qualifies as action, all right. And a startling example of official action being good.'

His serious mood returned.

'Incidentally we're going to have a memorial service at AULC. The Chancellor of the University will be coming over for it, and various other worthies. But that won't be till towards mid-semester, when I hope you will be back in full form.'

'It will reduce me to tears.'

'The service at Avalon itself is going to be graced by some very big big-wigs of all kinds, beginning with a super-distinguished Senator.' Will paused and then went on again suddenly: 'Oh yes, I was forgetting for a moment – they're setting up an elaborate scheme of counselling services for the bereaved.'

'Very American, that! And a very good idea, too! A very good idea!' I was wondering if there were any counselling which might have helped me... I said;

'What else are the Americans going to do?'

'Move heaven and earth to have the cause of the explosion traced, and if it was terrorists – and everyone thinks it was – have them found, caught and punished.'

'Catching terrorists is next door to impossible. Look at our efforts in Northern Ireland!'

'Maybe the Americans will do better.'

'Maybe.'

There was a long pause.

'I feel it's pretty unfair on you, Joe, while you're still convalescing, to come here and give you all this stuff.'

'I wanted to know, Will. And I guess I'm strong enough.'

Will stood up to leave.

'Anyway, when you come out of King Edward VII's Convalescent Home for "Officers and Gentlemen", you'll be strong enough.'

'Strong enough and gentlemanly enough.'

'That's right.'

Will delivered greetings to me from the staff of his office; and took on, for delivery, greetings from me to them. After a final enquiry after Virginia's pregnancy, he left.

I found immediate occupation for myself of taking a tour on my new crutches round the ward. I hadn't bargained for its taking me past that open doorway at the end of the ward. The doorway where those three beautiful young creatures had waved their last goodbye to me.

But it was the doorway where Virginia had paused to say with great emotion, 'Remember, Daddy, I'm carrying a new Life!'

Chapter XXX

A Crisis And Life

It was early spring, the February pre-spring of 1989, when the view from the colonnade along the front of the building where AULC was housed was of grass still darkened through being sodden with rain, nevertheless airing a new underlying greenness which in a few weeks would be brilliant: it stretched from the white-columned walk to the road where automobiles flashed past all the time by day through all the seasons.

I had gone back to AULC a few days after finally coming up from King Edward VII's under-water physio-facility. I would not have boasted that I was as strong as an Officer should be, but I was at least able to walk in a Gentlemanly fashion with a stick – or "cane" as my pupils called it. (The function of the stick was not so much to prevent me from staggering as to get me offered a seat in the Underground.) I was glad to be back at AULC.

Having put off the day when I really must resign from teaching the young, I now realised that in my still-bereft state I was glad of something to do – my new novel being on the way to publication and my next novel invisible beyond the horizon. And still reduced by the bitter loss of my last semester's pupils, I found it restoring to be surrounded by this semester's.

One more academic year I had contracted for. No Course No. 2 – that had never been a serious proposition so far as I was concerned: merely a fleeting wicked fantasy of getting money out of AULC for work I hadn't done; and a confirmation alas! that with me such wickedness never really came off.

My title was changed to be "in closer accord with modern ideas": instead of being styled Adjunct Professor of English Literature I was styled Adjunct Professor of English and Textual Studies. (I never found out what Textual Studies meant.)

All was going well with Virginia. I was getting letters regularly from Viola. None of this hid from me that without

Elspeth my life was empty at the core – despite my love for the girls and their love for me. It was at this point that I realised how much of my imagination, my hopes and longings for the future, were invested in the birth of Virginia's baby.

Life moved quietly to August – the semester was over and I had agreed to teach just one more year – just one! I was unconcerned about it. I had enjoyed this last semester. Textual Studies had made no difference. Life was moving quietly when, out of the blue, the metaphorical Pursuer descended.

Virginia was suddenly taken ill. Alastair telephoned me from home – he hadn't gone to the Evelyn.

'What is it?' I asked.

'Headaches, abdominal pains... Joe, she's acutely unwell.'

'Oh.' A moment while the news sank in. 'Then it's serious...'

'I'm afraid it is.'

'Alastair, I hope you're not going to keep anything from me.'

'I've got to take account of what you've suffered already.'

'Look here, Alastair – I've never had a son, and I've come to look upon you as one. I trust you.'

'OK.'

'Virginia has told you about "Don't look on the black side, Mr Lunn!" There's something in it.' I paused. 'But I'm still here. You know...'

'That's right.'

I said, 'Is Virginia well enough to speak to me herself?'

'She may be, but I wouldn't advise it. She asked me to give you her love. She's in fair spirits, incapacitating symptoms notwithstanding.'

'Headaches, abdominal pains,' I repeated. 'God knows what!'

'That's right.'

'It's not signs of a premature birth?'

'No.'

'What is it?'

'We shall see in the next few hours.'

'As soon as that?'

'The sooner the better.'

'Alastair, will you promise to give me regular bulletins? Never mind about encouraging me to look on the black side. I've got to know.'

'I promise, Joe.'

'Every few hours.'

'Every few minutes if there's anything to report.'

'Bless you!'

This conversation was taking place early in the evening. Alastair called again in less than an hour later.

'Her feet and fingers are swelling with Oedema...'

'What does that mean?'

'I've measured her blood-pressure and it's through the roof. I'm just waiting for an ambulance to take her to hospital.'

'The Evelyn?'

'It's the best place I know.'

That was that. I had to wait an hour and a half for the next call.

'Alastair here. Speaking from the Evelyn. Everyone's agreed with the diagnosis, it's what we call P.E.T. – means Pre-eclamptic Toxaemia. They've put her on the Labour Ward immediately. She may have a convulsion at any time; and they're worried she may be developing renal failure.'

No details being kept from me. I said:

'Alastair, can this be fatal?'

'Yes, Joe. but it rarely is in these days.'

'Fatal just for Virginia or for Virginia and the baby?'

'Both.'

'Oh God!'

'I know.' I heard him take a sharp breath. 'It's my wife and my baby!'

'Is there anything the hospital can do?'

'They'll do a Caesarean as soon as possible. I'll stay here at the hospital. I'll keep in touch with you constantly.'

It was only a few minutes when I heard –

'Joe, they're going to do the Caesarean now.'

'How long will it be before we know?'

'Won't be able to say till it's over.'

'You'll let me know?..'

'Yes, yes, yes...'

At that I was left, left alone in the flat. I forced myself to go to bed, with the telephone beside me.

'It can't be, it can't be!' I kept saying to myself. 'I can't have Virginia taken away from me as well as Elspeth. I've had the past taken away – isn't that enough without taking away the future?'

There was no hope of my getting to sleep. I tried to read but my attention wandered from the book.

Hours passed.

Although there was no hope of my getting to sleep, I must have dozed.

The telephone rang terrifyingly. It was the middle of the night.

Alastair's voice.

'They're both safe!' Just that.

'Both?'

'Yes.'

'They'll both survive?'

'There's reason to believe they'll both be well.'

'Alastair!'

'Joe!' There was a catch in Alastair's voice, too.

Tears were running down my face as I lay with the receiver clapped to my ear.

'The surgeons are very pleased with the way she's come through it. They're both in the Recovery Room now. They let me go in and have a wee look at them.'

'You haven't told me whether it's a boy or a girl.'

'It's a girl. That's what we were hoping for.'

'She'll be as beautiful as her mother.'

'A braw Scottish lass...'

'Oh, Alastair, I'm so very, very glad!'

'I must go now, Joe, to see what's happening. You can look on the bright side, Mr Lunn. I'll ring you again in a little while with the next bulletin.'

'Thank you. Give Virginia and the little darling lots of love and kisses from me! And congratulations for yourself!'

'I will.'

The call ended. Virginia and the baby had both survived: there was reason to believe they would both be well.

A great burst of emotion filled my chest, so that I could scarcely breathe.

I was thinking, the future is safe, safe, safe!..

I picked up the telephone again to tell Viola – though Alastair might have got through to her already.

I got through to Addis surprisingly quickly, though it then took ages to find Viola at the Seventh Day Adventist Hospital in Maichuw. (A pleasing trick of fate, I thought – whenever Seventh Day Adventists had come to the door of our house asking for beds for the night, Viola turned them away very smartly.)

'That's marvellous! Oh Daddy, I'm so glad. So glad!' She drew in her breath sharply: I imagined her eyes glistening.

There was a pause. Then Viola said;

'I'm so pleased I've got a sister.'

'Now you've got a niece as well.'

'Just like Jane Austen.' – half in amusement, half in chagrin. In the family we had always looked on Jane Austen as the epitome of a maiden aunt. She went on. 'I'd love to see my new niece. I'll try and move the people here to let me come home again. For a flying trip.'

'That's good news for me.'

'And for me – I'm missing you and Virginia terribly.'

I said, 'I won't ask you about your work since we've had that comforting string of short letters.'

'Did you like them?'

'If one can like something that's so depressing.'

'I'm not depressed, even though I can see you may find my descriptions depressing. This is the best thing I've ever done.' She paused. 'Thank you for not trying to dissuade me.'

I laughed. 'There's nothing one can do about one's children.' She'd heard me say it dozens of times. I added, 'It's just as well. You know?..'

'This time it was,' she said earnestly. 'I shall always appreciate...' She broke off.

In the pause I thought How good my children are! Then she said:

'You know I shall come back? Because I shall. Before too long. I shall come home to you all.'

We rang off. I saw my consolation for years to come. Without Elspeth the past was carried away: yet in the vital being of two beloved daughters, and now a grand-child, the future was living.

SCENES FROM DEATH AND LIFE:

William Cooper's last novel in perspective.

Harry Hoff (William Cooper) talks to Graham Tayar.

In the nineteen forties and early fifties, Birmingham's New Street Kardomah Café was – together with a pub around the corner, the Troc – the city's focal meeting point for ambitious students and young aspirant writers, actors, musicians, painters, would-be intellectuals and the occasional criminal, budding or manqué. They were sure – most of them – that their time was yet to come and if Ken Tynan could do it, why couldn't they?

One afternoon, writer Bert Barton, unemployed and broke as most of us were, rushed into the basement café waving a library book (to buy hardbacks was beyond our reach). "Kid," he said to me, "It's us!"

The book was William Cooper's "Scenes From Provincial Life". It's actually set in Leicester, the author assures me, although he was secretive about it at the time, for reasons which will become clear. Anyway, the parallels with Birmingham and presumably many other non-Metropolitan towns were exact: in such matters as love, Art and friendship, Cooper spoke for all of us.

Published almost fifty years ago and later to be a Penguin best seller, it was the first of five "Scenes From…" scattered among the writer's twenty or so books, mostly novels. The latest and last, "Scenes From Death and Life", is about to appear. Does it look like being his final novel?

"It does. I've no intention of writing any more. When it came to this particular point I concluded that I'd said all that I'd got to say. Stop writing!"

Cooper's real name is Harry Hoff and his first four books were published as H.S. Hoff, three of them before the war. Together with Anthony Powell, Harry is Britain's only surviving pre-War novelist still producing work – and being published.

He adopted the pseudonym because of a legal threat from one of his friends who might have thought that a homosexual character in "Provincial Life" was based on him.

A later work, "Scenes From Metropolitan Life", was delayed for years because a young woman said she'd sue for libel if it came out. So it didn't come out! But finally she died rather early. Her husband rang me up to tell me and then I knew the book could appear.

It's quite a good book though that wouldn't have affected the lady in question. She didn't want to be identified; she said it made her seem as though she drank too much and slept around too much, which it didn't do!

She was after all only the alleged model for one of the dramatis personae. But Harry's novels run fairly close to reality, far more than most writers.

Alas, too close. This one nearly landed me in a libel suit; it never actually happened but I always felt it might. But I never wanted to do research; I always wrote out of the top of my head.

Friends, neighbours, colleagues and relations should now be grateful. This amiable, talented and utterly delightful man has only just stopped being dangerous to all in range.

After "Provincial", "Married", "Metropolitan", and "Later", "Scenes from Death and Life" completes a sequence which provides a fictionalized version of the life of H.S. Hoff.

I have to admit it's possible. (Even now, he's very cagey. Do writs still lurk around the corner?) *But there's a great deal more to my life than appears in these books.*

Harry was born in Crewe in 1910 and grew up there (– *a horrible place. I never want to go back).* His parents were teachers and the story of his childhood is vividly told in "From Early Life".

It's not a "Scenes From…" although my publishers wanted me to call it that. It's not a novel but a memoir of what I can remember from my early days.

He went up to Christ's College, Cambridge, to read Natural Sciences, the first from his school (student or teacher) to go to an older University. C.P. Snow, already a novelist, was Harry's supervisor.

After the supervision part of the deal was over, we indulged in conversation about novels. I don't know that he encouraged me to write, but there's an element of emulation about the beginning of my career. If he wrote, why shouldn't I?

I hear echoes of my own Birmingham youth. Many of us were looking for role models until we, unwittingly, were to discover whether or not we had any talents – and at what.

Harry began as a teacher in Leicester (at Snow's old school) but went on to follow a very distinguished career in various parts of the Civil Service. Would he rather have been a full-time novelist?

No, I wouldn't. I say that when I see what's happened to the other people who've become full-time writers. I think one ought to hang on to real life so to speak. And it does acquaint one with what's going on in the world, what people are like, things that interest me.

Not all Harry's novels are based directly on his own life. "Love on the Coast" was about flower children in San Fransisco trying to run a little theatre. Harry wasn't exactly part of that scene, but he observed it a close range. And although the "I" in the book is a character in fiction, the voice and attitudes considerably resemble his own.

"The Ever Interesting Topic" refers to Sex, especially gay sex. Why so?

It was probably at King's College, Cambridge, where there were quite a lot of homosexuals around. Somebody once said at High Table, "What did you talk about", and the reply came, "Oh, the ever interesting topic."

Sex?

Homosex in particular, that's what they were interested in at King's.

Once again, Harry is a listener and watcher, but he blends these skills with imagination, humour and gentle irony, as a master storyteller should.

However, Scenes from Death and Life" is in essence the final part of Harry's fictionalised autobiography. He ended the first novel in this sequence, Scenes From Provincial Life, with these prescient words: "I think of the string of delights and disasters that have come my way since 1939. And then I think of all the novels I can make out of them – ah, novels, novels, art, art, pounds sterling!

"My own life history. The past years suddenly spring up, delightful and disastrous, warm, painful and farcical. I reach for a clean note-book. I pick up my pen."

And until very recently, Harry was still at it, as he told me, writing, and at times recycling.

It (the new novel) includes something I wrote elsewhere, for a symposium on death in "Granta". I wrote this piece and a lot of people who knew me thought it was rather good; so I incorporated it in this book.

It's "Scenes From Death and Life" in that it begins with the death of my wife, and goes on to "Life". When a grandchild is born to one of my daughters, in fact. So it goes full circle. (Just to keep his public guessing a little more, it should be said that the birth is one of the completely invented scenes in the book.)

Harry Hoff was a key figure in the development of the post-war English novel. He preceded all the new novelists, Kingsley Amis, John Wain, John Braine and the other so-called Angry Young Men of the arts. But he wasn't one; nor indeed were they.

To see myself claimed as an Angry Young Man at the age of forty, as I was when William Cooper first emerged, is really quite futile. It was just a journalist's trick, a useful label to short-circuit thought!

Harry always was and still is a reasonably contented man. He wrote in "From Early Life": "My parents, intelligent and decent minded school teachers both…unfailingly did their best for me. I had a happy childhood, I think. I clearly remember days when my schoolfellows called me 'Happy Hoff'." How then would he sum up his temperament?

Part of it's in my nature which is relatively sunny, shall we say. And also there's the self-discipline of not feeling sorry for myself.

It's difficult to admit that I've been either happy or successful in anything, but nevertheless it could be true. I think that's probably a pretty good thing to be able to say that about one's life, that you've said all that's got to be said, and it's been published. That's not bad – it completes it.

And almost half a century after William Cooper's first book grabbed my attention so memorably, Harry Hoff – frailer than he was when I first met him ten years ago but still cheerful and articulate and on the edge of his nineties – poured me out another glass of wine.

Based on a conversation on 12th May 1999.

© *Graham Tayar 1999*